William Kirkpatrick Hill

William Henry Widgery, Schoolmaster

a descriptive and critical account of his life, work and character

William Kirkpatrick Hill

William Henry Widgery, Schoolmaster
a descriptive and critical account of his life, work and character

ISBN/EAN: 9783337095666

Printed in Europe, USA, Canada, Australia, Japan

Cover: Foto ©Raphael Reischuk / pixelio.de

More available books at **www.hansebooks.com**

WILLIAM HENRY WIDGERY

SCHOOLMASTER

The government of childhood is a duumvirate of teacher and parent. The teacher's duty is to study the child; the parent's, to study the teacher. For thoughtful teaching and parental support are the right and left hands of education, and weakness in either must defeat the aims of both.

From Photo. by Heath & Bradnee, Exeter.   Swan Electric Engraving Cᵒ

Yours faithfully

W H Widgery

WILLIAM HENRY WIDGERY

SCHOOLMASTER

A DESCRIPTIVE AND CRITICAL ACCOUNT OF
HIS LIFE, WORK AND CHARACTER

BY

WILLIAM K. HILL

LONDON
DAVID NUTT, 270-271, STRAND
1894

E. M. C.

CONTENTS

CONTENTS

APPENDICES

PREFATORY NOTE

THE following pages have been written in the hope of arousing some interest in the difficulties which surround scholastic effort by the presentment of a single remarkable scholastic career—remarkable for the lofty ideal which dominated it, the high promise which it unfolded and the sad and sudden interruption of its fulfilment. Something like a completion of the broken work has also been in my mind, if an exhaustive exposition of theories yet untried and a full-length portrait of a noble mind can ensure completion by arousing the interest, not to say the enthusiasm, which would bring those theories to the touch of practical experiment. My hope is that the scholastic world may be compelled to such experiment by the inspiration of a nobility so disinterested and so pure. Unhappily this work has been, of necessity, composed in odd moments of leisure and generally at the fag end of a day's teaching. Details of description, arranged at one sitting and worked up at another, threads of argument prepared at one time and woven together long afterwards, have inevitably become confused and twisted by the breach of continuity in mental effort, and redundancy and repetition have been the result. Whatsoever of this could be amended by careful revision has been amended. For what remains, because amendment would have involved destruction, I crave the leisured reader's considerate indulgence.

Many hands have brought their tribute of esteem and affection to the composition of these pages. My work has been to weave the opinions of other minds into one coherent expression, and so fill out a true picture of the man whom many loved in an intimate friendship and more esteemed from the remoter standpoint of acquaintance. Partly with the object of enabling some of these to feel that they have a real share in this tribute of affection, I have often embodied their opinions in the work without the distinction of quotation marks. They will recognise whatever belongs to them easily enough in the course of their reading, and the completeness of incorporation will, I hope, be a source of pleasure to most of them. But in such cases of complete absorption all responsibility rests with me, since I have first accepted what I incorporate. Elsewhere the usual inverted commas inform the reader that another than myself is speaking and the responsibility lies with him, or her. Among those I have to thank for invaluable help, either by word of mouth or by written statement, are Messrs. Morgan, Rose, Bowden, Hutchinson, Elfstrand, Lattimer, Thomas, Bowen, and Foster Watson, Dr. Klinghardt, Professor Haddon, and

Mr. H. B. Garrod, the Secretary of the Teachers' Guild. Mr. Henry Bradley's kindness in sending me a written expression of his opinion on Widgery's capacity as a philologist is acknowledged in the body of the work. Such a statement, under the circumstances, is as valuable as it is generous. To Mrs. Bryant I am indebted for most valuable advice that has modified in a material way the most delicate and difficult part of my task. Without the records and papers zealously collected and freely entrusted to me by Widgery's sister, Mrs. Tozer, and by Miss E. M. Childs the work would have been impossible. Indeed the help supplied by Mrs. Tozer, both in the way of collecting materials and carefully reading and criticising Parts I. and III., has been so great as to amount almost to collaboration and, if any credit should be attached to the work, a large portion of it must be allotted to her. An equal share belongs to my friend and colleague Mr. John Russell, who has given no less valuable and extensive help in this difficult task of criticism and revision. Lastly I have to acknowledge my indebtedness to Mr. Payne's translation of Compayré's "History of Pedagogy," a most useful work, which has supplied me with a large fund of illustration and confirmation of the theories held by the subject of this monograph.

Having thus acknowledged my indebtedness, it is a great pleasure to me to look back upon the names I have mentioned and reflect that these were the nearest and dearest friends of him whose life and work have inspired my task, to feel that they have done me the honour to accept me as the mouthpiece of their affection for him and the recorder of their esteem, and to know that I have thus helped them in the effort to preserve the memory and continue the work of a zealous and able teacher and a noble man. May the verdict of the scholastic world endorse their effort, even if it should not be able to approve their choice of a spokesman.

W. K. H.

Holly Hill, Hampstead,

1894.

CHRONOLOGICAL TABLE

1856: March 11.—William Henry Widgery born at Exeter.

1863.—To Hele's School.

1869.—Passes Junior Oxford Local Examination. To Exeter Grammar School with Scholarship.

1872—3.—Passes Science and Art Examinations.

1873 : MAY.—Tucker Prize at Exeter School of Art.

1874 : OCTOBER.—Leaves Exeter Grammar School with Stephens Exhibition and enters St. John's College, Cambridge, with Vidal Exhibition. Elected a Proper Sizar.

1876.—First illness. Retires to Exeter. Tour through Cornwall and Devon (?).

1877 : OCTOBER.—Returns to College.

1878 : MAY.—Elected Foundation Scholar. NOVEMBER.—Religious difficulties.

1879 : JANUARY.—Tripos Examination. Illness between the two Parts of the examination. Graduates Seventh Senior Optime. Assistant Master at Dover College.

1880.—Harness Essay and Prize. *First Quarto of Hamlet.*

1880—3.—Second Master at Brewers' Company's School, Tower Hill. Attends English Literature Classes at University College. Joins Stepney Committee of Charity Organisation Society.

1881 : DECEMBER.—Studies Flemish.

1881—9.—Frequent trips to Continent.

1882 : APRIL.—M.A. Cambridge. NOVEMBER.—*Beówulf* (Lecture).

1883 : JANUARY.—Assistant Master at University College School.

1883—7.—Secretary of the Education Society.

1884.—Studies Sanskrit. Appointed Hon. Librarian of the Teachers' Guild.

1885 : MAY.—Elected Member of Council of Teachers' Guild.

1886.—*Ethics of Aristotle* (Review). APRIL.—*Anglo-Saxon Dictionary* (Review). JUNE.—*Public School German Grammar* (Review). AUGUST.—Five months leave. Visits Continent. Matriculates at Berlin, attends lectures on Pedagogy and Teutonic Philology and examines working of German schools. Takes part in Educational Congress at Berlin. *Outline History of German Language* (Review).

1887 : JANUARY.—Returns to England. *Gothic of Ulfilas* (Review). JUNE.—*The New English* (Review). SEPTEMBER.— First engagement. DECEMBER.—*Principles of English Etymology* (Review).

1888 : JANUARY.—*Teaching of Modern Languages* (Speech). *Class v. Form System* (Speech). MARCH.—*Teaching of Languages* (Two Papers). APRIL.—*Teaching of Languages* (Series of Articles begun in " Journal of Education "). JULY.— *Comparative Grammar of Indo-European Languages* (Review). NOVEMBER.—*Principles of English Etymology* (Review). DECEMBER.—*William Shakespeare* (Review). *Teaching of Languages in Schools* (Pamphlet).

1889.—Persistent attacks of illness. JANUARY.—*Grundriss der Romanischen Philologie* (Review). MARCH.—*Bacon-Shakspere Question* (Review). APRIL.—Sheffield Conference of Teachers' Guild. *Teaching of Modern Languages* (Letter). *Recent Advances in Science of Language* (Lecture). MAY.— *Teaching Tripos* (Paper). *Present Classical Régime* (Speech). JUNE.—*Lectures on Pedagogy* (Review). JULY.—*Grundriss der Germanischen Philologie* (Review). AUGUST.—*Educational Congress at Paris* (Report). *Public Instruction at Paris Exhibition* (Report). SEPTEMBER.—*Secondary Education at Paris Congress* (Report). NOVEMBER.—*Early English Pronunciation* (Review). *Paris Congress* (Report to Education Bureau, Washington).

1890 : JANUARY.—*Cradle of the Aryans* (Review.) *Class Teaching of Phonetics* (Pamphlet). APRIL.—Cheltenham Conference of Teachers' Guild. MAY.—*Educational Museum* (Speech.) *Teaching of English* (Speech). *Teaching of Algebra* (Paper). JUNE.—*Educational Museums* (Article). *Pestalozzi* (Review). *Classical Philology* (Review). *Aryan Reader* (Review). SEPTEMBER.—Second engagement. *Notes on Modern Philology* (Series of Articles begun in "Modern Language Monthly" and continued till his death). NOVEMBER.—*American Journal of Philology* (Review). *Educational Reformers* (Review).

1891 : FEBRUARY.—*Aryan Antiquities* (Review). *Der Französische Klassenunterricht* (Review). *Outlines of English Literature* (Review). MAY.—*Language of Mediaeval Writers* (Speech). JULY.—*Principles of English Etymology* (Review). AUGUST 26.—Dies at Exeter.

PART I—LIFE

A.

WILLIAM HENRY WIDGERY

LIFE

" I OFTEN think of the grand Devon scenery with passion." The wild freedom of its upland moors, the poetic witchery of its romantic valleys cleft by streams of surpassing beauty, and the soft purity of its southern clime, were a constant source of pleasure and inspiration to William Henry Widgery.

Here in North Molton, one of those quiet little villages that nestle among the lovely lanes and sequestered valleys of Devonshire, John Widgery, labourer, married Urah Bawdon. The husband's name seems to have been common in the neighbourhood. Several tombstones in the sister parish of South Molton bear it. We are concerned only with the child, born of this marriage in April, 1826, William Widgery, who adopted, when he grew up, the calling of a builder. But the spirit of beauty that dwelt in his native haunts had entered into him with power. One day he threw aside his workman's clothes and took up the artist's brush. He kept those clothes, lest he should have misunderstood the promptings of his destiny, but was never called to resume them. Success attended him from the first,

and his pictures are now a constant pleasure in many a
home throughout the kingdom.   Several years before
this he had married and settled in Exeter.   Some of the
intellectual power and original energy, which had drawn
him from the little mining village into the larger
activities of the county town, he transmitted to his
eldest son, William, the subject of this memoir, who
also inherited a large stock of sturdy independence
and a Puritan nature from his mother, the daughter
of a family of farmers who had lived in Devonshire
for generations back.   It is interesting to note that
his mother is the sister and daughter of a school-
mistress.

Childhood.—William Henry Widgery was born at
Exeter on the 11th of March, 1856.   His childhood
was not unlike that of all children who have the good
fortune to be watched throughout their tender years
by the joint solicitude of father and mother, full of
influences that leave their traces in the work and
character of the full-grown man, but are themselves
lost for ever in the unwritten records of domestic history.
We first get into touch with his life at Hele's School in
Exeter.

Like most boys, he gave his whole mind to play and
boyish tricks, though even here his characteristic earnestness was manifested.   His preparations for the 5th of
November began seven or eight months before.   The
embryo chemistry-master of course made his own fire-
works, regardless of the safety of his father's house.
Judicious financing of his pocket-money led to the
purchase of cheap and coarse gunpowder, which he
reduced to the requisite fineness by grinding in a
coffee-mill!   Yet he never had an accident.   At this

time he gave little thought to earnest work at school. Not till, by process of time rather than anything else, he had gradually risen to the First Class did he wake up to the reality of work. Then he suddenly formed the resolution to go in and win a prize. In the result he won all the four that were awarded to his class. Thenceforward his school career was one continual success. All the prizes obtainable fell to him. Whatever he put his hand to he carried to success. Some botanical specimens he found and prepared for a special prize, though now twenty years old, still bear evidence of the neatness and care with which he did everything even as a boy.

In 1869 he passed the Junior Oxford Local Examination in the Third Division, and then with a scholarship entered the Exeter Grammar School. Such meagre records as remain of this period of his life show him to have excelled in classics and mathematics with some preference for botany. Specimens of his efforts in this direction, eloquent of the pleasures of long rambling in country lanes and leafy woodlands, are still treasured by his family; but it is doubtful whether this work ever passed beyond the limits of a summer hobby. As he moved gradually up the school many prizes fell to his share. In the Lower Fifth Form he obtained these coveted distinctions for his excellence in English Composition and French and for botany; in the Sixth Form for Classics, Mathematics, and Recitation, and also the Senior Mathematical Prize. Twice he got prizes for Latin and Greek and once for Divinity. The list is closed by the Senior Prize for English Subjects and a First Prize for Mathematics. Outside the school itself, in the examinations held by the Science and Art Department, between

the years of sixteen and seventeen, he obtained first
classes in the Elementary Stage of Mathematics and
Theoretical Mechanics, certificates for Freehand and
Model Drawing (first grade), and a prize for Geometry
(first grade). His position in Mathematics and Mechanics
won him the Tucker Prize at the Exeter School of Art,
which was connected with the Department. So far his
abilities appeared to be of an "all-round" nature—the
reputation they retained to the end of his life—but a
penchant for Mathematics was already evident. Some
of the school registers of this period are extant, dating
from Michaelmas, 1870, to Midsummer, 1874. They
show him to have been nearly always at the top of the
classes in Classics, Mathematics, and French, often with
the maximum marks attainable. Generally he seems
to have won a leading position in the school. An
extant newspaper account of one of the prize days
represents him as filling in brilliant style, with great
intelligence and a fine elocution, the rôles of Antigone,
Allantopoles (the sausage-seller), Bottom, and Wolsey,
and delivering with the same spirit a passage from the
"Pro Murenâ." Duly discounting the enthusiasm of
the provincial penny-a-liner, we have still in this the
proof of early distinction among his boyish fellows
destined to be fully endorsed by the future successes of
the man.

Despite the fact that, as a boy, he was thin and
delicate-looking, or certainly not robust, he played in the
School Eleven and excelled in gymnastics. Like all
boys in their teens he had his troubles about atheism,
wherein he was much helped and comforted by some
passages in the works of Ruskin—what passages his
diary, desultory and abortive as all boyish self-registers,

omits to state. This was in 1873, though the trouble
had begun years before when he was at Hele's School.
June of the same year contains an entry of his affection
for a new friend, the works of Samuel Smiles, again
without any specification of the particular work whence
he drew wisdom and inspiration. One entry in this
connection is remarkable, as pointing to the early vigour
of the indomitable will, a family heritage from the
builder-artist, which afterwards became so marked a
characteristic of his nature. "Smiles says all great men
have become so through their will (underlined) and
perseverance: and Hagarty (a phrenologist friend) tells
me that my organ of will is large and therefore I ought
to be a great man: AND SO I WILL." (The last
words are written large and black.) Here too we have
the record of the first beginnings of the general popularity
and affection he afterwards attained in the naïve entry,
"A little better success in the art of pleasing." And
here also we learn of the fires of an early passion, that
burnt into his sleep and doubtless shook the very
foundations of his boy world, and yet existed only to
prove that he, even thus early, felt what he himself
calls "the *besoin d'aimer*," the need which afterwards
found its vent in the passion of cosmopolitan altruism,
deep and lasting friendships and a companionship of
nobler worth.

In these days of boyish turmoil his passion for the
repose of Nature, his kinship with her, so persistently
attested in later life, led him frequently to the wild
beauties of Dartmoor. His favourite haunt seems to
have been the romantic spot called Fingal Bridge, near
Drewsteignton, which his father painted and he describes
in eloquent language. "Drewsteignton is intertwined

with my earliest and dearest memories. For several years when I was a lad father went there every summer on a sketching visit, and now whenever I am ill or sad the holy hills, closing in the valley with its brown waters and dappled sunshine, spring up in the memory unbidden and bring peace. Once just before sunset the purple earth was covered with a golden haze and lay all Danaë to the sky. As we neared the well-remembered valley thrill after thrill of deep emotion ran over me. The hills remained: all the old friends save the miller sleep well. To the music of falling waters we walked through the sunlit woods. Over all was a beauty as indescribable as the light of good deeds done in a woman's face."

One charming trait of his childhood, the earnest and loving help he gave to a favourite schoolfellow, to whose grateful memory we owe the above account of Widgery's youthful habits, we note with pleasurable reminiscences of the same helpfulness on a larger scale in later life. This was a real friendship that lasted into manhood, though it began as usual with a mutual swearing of eternal devotion and an agreement to be brothers "all our time." The two friends played and worked and walked in the country together. Even when Widgery had plenty of his own work to do, his schoolfellow might command him at a moment's notice. And there was no grudging in the help. It was loving, earnest and complete. When Fate called away one of the friends into the rougher paths of life, many letters passed between them, laden with the exchange of confidences, hopes, aspirations, fears, though the latter were few on Widgery's part in those days, save as regards his health, which troubled him even then with vague forebodings. So the friendship lasted through college life and further, till death brought it to a premature end.

College.—Leaving Exeter Grammar School, as head boy, with the Stephen's Exhibition, Widgery passed with the Vidal Exhibition into St. John's College, Cambridge, which he entered in the autumn of 1874. He was elected a Proper Sizar,* and afterwards, in 1878, Foundation Scholar of his college, won several prizes and developed considerable mathematical ability. In 1876, at the end of his second year at college and again during his Tripos examination, his constant foreboding of a breakdown in health took definite shape in serious illness that first betrayed the presence of a mortal disease in his constitution. It must always be cause for regret that his buoyant spirit led him to revolt from any realisation of the terrible nature of the disease that had taken hold of him. Had he thoroughly recognised the malignant enemy that had entered into his life, one cannot help thinking that he might have baffled him with the aid of the innumerable resources of modern medical science. His was one of those cases where the loss of a day, an hour, may decide an issue many years ahead. Unhappily he did not know this. He failed to consult the most advanced specialist skill of the metropolis and contented himself with degrading for a year, retiring to his beloved moors and trusting to the restorative of a year's holiday in the country with such aid as he might obtain from the best local knowledge of his complaint. In the autumn of 1877 he returned to college and during the winter of 1878-9 graduated 7th

---

* The "nine Sizars on the foundation of Dr. Dowman were usually termed Proper Sizars. Apparently peculiar to St. John's College, the term did not express, it would seem, any University distinction."

Senior Optime.   He never quite got over the disappointment of finding himself outside the list of Wranglers.
Often in later life, when he was seeking coveted appointments, the iron of this disaster (for so he regarded it)
entered into his soul and made him cry out against the
fatuous blindness of the public opinion which judges the
communicative power required of a good teacher by the
purely acquisitive test of an academic degree.   A born
teacher, he saw himself thrust aside by men more or less
devoid of the teaching faculty simply because at a critical
juncture, when he was handicapped by ill-health, their
acquisitive power had surpassed his.   The injustice of
this embittered him and the folly of it, from the point
of view of the progress of education, filled him with
contempt for the examination system.

Though he continually suffered in health throughout
his college career, he always took good places in the
annual college examinations.   His vigorous, enthusiastic
way of working reacted on a physique never too strong.
Ignorance of the importance of proper food seems to
have led him to constant neglect of dietary precautions.
But even apart from the weakness generated by such
neglect, his brilliancy was always far ahead of his
physical power of producing work.   While his head
worked it produced better results than those of most of
his class-fellows, but their sounder bodies produced more
work of a lower order.   He would often pin himself
down to a period of hard work, do it thoroughly and
then break down.   "I heard," says a contemporary,
"the safest judge we had place him among the first
fifteen Wranglers.   His strength placed him about a
class lower."   Nevertheless his vigorous spirit led him
to join the 3rd Cambridgeshire (University) Rifle

Volunteer Corps, in which he served from October
1874 to November 1876, being classed as "efficient" in
the return made in 1874. But his combative activity
was not confined to the "tented field." "I frequently
recall," says another college-fellow, "our pleasant intercourse at Cambridge and discussions, often heated but
never angry, which we sometimes continued far towards
morning"—after the shortsighted manner of students
unacquainted as yet with the great principle of self-
economy, which subsequent life brought home to him so
keenly when the consequence of these late hours became
apparent in the swift approach of fatal exhaustion. But
the pleasures of argument were judiciously diluted with
the recreative pleasures of social intercourse, and he
seems to have thoroughly enjoyed occasional festivities
in the rooms of his fellow-students, but always with the
mental and moral sobriety of a character naturally pure
and guileless. The most striking proof of this perhaps
is to be found in the fact of his trembling once at the
bare suspicion that he could not hold himself altogether
unsullied by the influences through which he passed.
"I should like," he writes in his diary, "to show myself
fully to myself in black and white, but I'm afraid that I
haven't the courage yet. I fancy the feeling for, and a
desire for, a greater communion with God is growing on
me, but He does not at all supply the mainspring of my
actions. I can't exactly analyse what is the real mainspring, but I fancy it is pride as much as anything.
Matthew Arnold's 'Culture and Anarchy' has sent me to
Bishop Wilson's 'Maxims.' I pray I may get some good
out of them. I have never failed, thank God, in my
virtue, but I do not feel so strong in it as I used. I do
not seem to keep my health for any continuous time. I

am much better than I was six months ago, but still there
is something wanting before I begin life's battle, and I
fear whether I shall go through it without a scar or two."
Thus he wrote in November of 1878.

While at college, as afterwards, " his mind and tastes
were essentially literary and artistic. He received more
influences from these sources than from Nature. He
seems not really to have had," at this time, "the mental
attitude of a scientific man or observer." Yet, apart
from his college work, as might be expected of a man of
broad sympathies and intellectual aspirations, he took a
keen interest in all intellectual matters and pursuits. The
friendships of his boyhood were continued through his
college life.

Teacher.—So far we have watched him amid the
aspirations of boyhood and their partial realisation in a
college career of mixed success. Already he had learned
something of the futility of those boyish aspirations. We
follow him now into the final arena of public life, where,
in addition to the academic disappointments whose
savour he had learned in the esoteric and close artificial
atmosphere of the University, he was to experience the
shock of contact with the tragic elements that dominate
life in the great world. As he passed out of the Factory
of Learning, his mind, with the instinct of original genius,
turned, not to thoughts of intellectual rumination in the
cloistral associations of some great public school nor to
cultivated repose amid the social amenities of a country
curacy, but to schemes of reproduction in altruistic
channels. Two professions lay nearest to his heart—
teaching and the dissenting ministry. He inclined to
the latter, because, as he wrote to a friend, "a minister
is better able than a layman to influence people for their

good." But he did not hold to the idea. His views would have allowed him to enter none but the Unitarian body. The strong dissuasion of one of his college friends reinforced the uncertainty of his own theology. He abandoned all thoughts of the ministry and sought the last refuge of the cultivated mind that dwells in a body unadorned by wealth and unaided by social influence—teaching.

Dover College.—He had obtained temporary work for a term at Dover College directly after his Tripos in January 1879. He now devoted nearly a year to the study of English literature and modern languages. Some portion of this time he gave to the composition of an elaborate essay on the "First Quarto of *Hamlet*," which divided with another the Harness Prize for 1880 and attracted attention in Germany as well as in scholastic circles at home. He was living at this time in No. 27 East Southernhay, a quiet house in a retired square of Exeter, much like the West End squares familiar to the Londoner, but differing from them in its greater wealth of rural associations. In front lay a thickly-wooded public garden that cast a poetic gloom over the low-pitched front parlour in which he composed most of the essay. At the back, the windows of his favourite room near the top of the house, which he shared as a study with his sister, looked out across the open country to the far-off heights of the Haldon Range, behind which lies Dartmoor, the range itself being a sort of preliminary suggestion of that favourite haunt of his youth and manhood. Fingal Bridge had been his favourite spot in boyhood; now in his manhood he wandered again and again to even lovelier scenes, up the magnificent gorge from Lydford waterfall, along the narrow footpath that

glides beneath the lofty arch of Lydford Bridge and on
to Tavy Cleve. In the immediate neighbourhood of
Exeter the slopes of Hoopern Fields knew well his
leisurely tread, as he sauntered book in hand or rested
on the fresh grass to dream and scheme for a future that
was never to be his. But his passion for the beauties of
Nature, especially in his native county, led him yet
further afield. Probably at this period, perhaps during
the year he was rusticating for his attack of illness at
Cambridge, he made a tour through Devonshire and
Cornwall. A desultory "log" of this walk records his
course and some of his experiences. Starting from Comb
Martin, he passed through Trentishoe to Lynton, where
he visited Watersmeet and the Valley of Rocks, and then
entered the Doone Valley, doubtless to worship at the
shrine of Lorna. Hence he turned to South Molton,
where he devoted some time to raking up family records
in the churchyard and neighbourhood. He also sought,
but in vain, to discover some foundation for a traditional
connection between the Widgerys and Turner. At
Clovelly he climbed to Gallantry Bower, and he was
much struck by the "wonderfully contorted strata" on
the opposite side of Mill Hook Mouth. After that he
visited Pentargan Cave and Waterfall, Boscastle Harbour,
Black Pits, and Bossiney Cove. At the last place he had
the good fortune to encounter a "very fine sea." The
log ends abruptly at Tintagel Castle with a note of the
"wonderful view from the end of the island" and a
comical lament that he "could not see the famous
Trebarwith Sands."

This was a happy year, full of the fun and frolic of
youth, health and good spirits. Indeed good spirits
characterised Widgery throughout his life whenever he

was not a prey to illness. When he left school and went home for the holidays, he threw off the schoolmaster on his vacation tour and became the schoolboy in his holiday. He would turn windmills, as he called them, dance about, take his sisters up in his arms and swing them about pendulum-wise, and loud and hearty was the laughter when his father vented the dry wit for which he was noted in the family. Always amid the sparkle of the fun and frolic of a high-spirited family the brightest eye was Widgery's and the merriest laugh. First his sister and in after years her musician husband were in constant requisition to play to him joyous airs of Music's brightest mood.

Brewers' School.—During 1880–1881 Widgery was second master at the Brewers' Company's School on Tower Hill. Of his work here, apart from written testimonials, we have but one record, the remark in a letter to his sister that his classes had on a recent occasion done splendidly, beating even those above them. Such leisure as he had at this time was divided between Professor Morley's English Literature classes at University College and the Stepney Committee of the Charity Organisation Society. Of his work in the latter direction no record appears to exist, but at University College he won a First Prize in the Icelandic class, a Second Certificate and marks qualifying for the prize in Anglo-Saxon, and in 1881–2 the First Certificate and Prize for Moeso-Gothic and Icelandic. In a letter referring to this period he remarks "I did not know I was considered a shining light in Morley's classes."

M.A. 1882.—In 1882 he took his M.A. degree in the ordinary course at Cambridge, not, we may be sure, without some qualms as to the manner of its receipt in accordance with the custom of the elder universities.

University College School.—In the same year he was introduced to the present headmaster of University College School and had some conversation from which he went away under the impression that it would lead to nothing. But some months after he was surprised by the offer of an assistant mastership in that school. Entering upon indefinite tenure in January 1883, he was soon permanently appointed and retained the post till his death eight years afterwards. Here he had from time to time classes in Mathematics, Chemistry, French and German. But latterly his increasing tendency to specialise in English led him to gather around himself all the senior work in that branch, so that at his death he was practically the senior English Master, though the custom of the school did not attach any such title to the position. During these years his personal popularity among the boys was augmented by his hearty share in the school games, so long as his gradually failing health permitted violent exercise and the growing demands on his time left him leisure for recreation. Nor did he avoid the worrying and responsible but unpaid labours of helping in the preparation and performance of those end-of-term entertainments that concentrate and illustrate the æsthetic capacities of school-life, of which prizes and examinations take little account. His success in such work, attested by the hearty applause of grateful pupils, completed his claim to the character of a true schoolmaster. During the years 1881 to 1889 he made frequent trips to the continent.

So far Widgery's life had been not more unfortunate than that of most men who do not leave the Universities with a halo of first classes about their brows, though his efforts to advance in the scholastic profession had been chequered by numerous disappointments at the hands of electing committees. More than once he stood second and not far from first, but there his hopes ended. Now, however, he was to taste for the first time the irremediable bitterness of disappointments that last through life. On the 16th of March 1883 a friend of his later youth and the confidante and comforter of his manhood passed out of his life for ever. Her husband had become an intimate friend of Widgery's and her house was always a city of refuge for him, when he wished to fly from the worries and disappointments of life into the soothing atmosphere of generous and unshakable friendship. The blow was a hard one, but his passionate lament closes in manly resignation—"Let us weep no more, but guard her memory serene." Yet the recurring anniversaries of her death forced from him the pathetic cry " In London now I have no one to whom I can lay myself bare with easy carelessness." The last words point to the characteristic longing of a passionate nature for sympathy that might be absolutely trusted, a confidante that could never be suspected of covert contempt. The limitation to London betrays the constant affection which could not forget, even in the moment of grief, the faithful sister who still lived to minister a sympathy no less reliable in his native home. But he never forgot his friend, and his feet constantly tended towards her resting place in Highgate Cemetery, which was often brightened by flowers that his hands had gathered. The entry in his diary is touching in its simplicity—a dark oblong under the date and in it " Mary."

On the Continent.—He used to say that but for the

ability to plunge into work, his reason would have failed him on more than one occasion of dire distress. He turned now and flung his whole soul into his profession. In 1886 his enthusiasm for it led him to ask for five months' leave of absence, in order that he might visit Germany and study there the latest science and the history of educational methods. He successfully matriculated in Berlin, attended lectures on Pedagogy and Teutonic Philology, liking those of Paulsen best, and examined the working of German schools by personal investigation. He also took part in the Educational Congress in that city. He had already prepared himself for the study of Philology by taking lessons in Flemish (in December 1881) and Sanskrit (in 1884).

His letters from Berlin, lively, humorous, affectionate, are full of descriptive power and shrewd remarks on men and things. But ever and anon breaks forth a ceaseless craving for his beloved England. " Here," he writes from Berlin, " my own natural bent is making itself felt. In London I fancy M—— pulled me somewhat out of my own orbit into the realm of minute investigations of the changes of sounds and meaning of the words in various languages, but now all that seems as dry and interesting (*sic*) to me as dead leaves. There must be somewhere some quickening breath of spirit in my subject or it cannot detain me long." So he wrote to his sister and no doubt meant what he said, though it is doubtful whether his mind was not after all best fitted for the work which he seems to decry here for the moment. An eloquent passage in a pocket-book in use while he was in Berlin throws a faint ray of light on his life at this period. " Soon after nine the sun came out so beautifully that it was a case of *hodie non legitur.* . . . . The forest quietude is broken only by its own noises: the busy tapping of the woodpecker, the caw of some distant crow and the booming sounds that the forest makes for its own sake. The sun is strong and the sky clear, blue and cloudless. The heat makes the mist rise from the ground, bringing the fragrant odours from the soil. The few late flowers are heavy with drops of dew. Butterflies white and brown flit in the sunshine and the busy grasshoppers jump with shrill noise from blade to blade of grass. The firs suffer no undergrowth, not even on themselves. Like man, if one shoots up, the rest must follow if they would share the sun and life. Below the broken branches show the traces of earlier life. Man too in his upward striving bears the scars of past struggles. Before me the Havel runs into a narrow bay with the mirror-like water broken only by the trail of a solitary swan. The extreme edge of the water blinks in the sunshine. A thick bed of reeds absolutely motionless cuts off the lake. Boats with white sails move, but that hardly, along the water throwing long shadows free from any tremor. The faint sound of a man cracking stones is borne on the air and ever and anon comes the rumble of a cart in the woods. My coat has many spiders' webs floating around me. Ever and anon the sun shines upon them and a beam of light seems to sway up and down in the air. So perhaps in the spiritual world we carry away unnoticing the faint webs of thought and know not whence they come." Another jotting made in a sketchbook while sitting in the library at Weimar throws a strong light on the state of his mind at this time.

" At last I am in the land of Goethe and Schiller, but alas ! no wave of enthusiasm passes over me. I think the custodian in the library must have unhinged me, and

I am so easily put out of a dreaming mood. Goethe somehow I do not like half so much as Schiller, and in looking at the various busts and portraits I feel somehow that I have nowhere yet seen the real men. The artists have idealised too much. Why should they fear to give them as they really were? This intense feeling for reality is increasing in me. Even the gods and goddesses of Greece are beginning to fade in interest, and I see more clearly than ever that a writer can write whether for good or evil of his own time only. All my life up I have been fancying that something will "turn up": society or money or love or some magic influence that will put me on a pedestal. There is no help outside a man's own soul. What I really want I really cannot say. A vague, undefined air, not alas! of noble discontent but of small jealousy, seems to puff me out. The sight of the various places at which Schiller lived has aroused a wonder which has not yet as fully leavened me as I hope it will. Personally I have always had better physical conditions, but they have helped nothing. Let the desire for ' position' go utterly *if* you desire with all your heart to be a writer. Again, remember that Schiller spent two or three years over one piece, or that a single song was the solitary fruit of one summer. But above all this lies the fact that I haven't a first-rate brain, a fact I fear not yet sufficiently realised by me. Even if I had, I think I should be paralysed by the immensity of things and the keen perception of the smallness of the circle from which a man wins recognition of his gifts. A fatal habit of procrastination and a weak digestion: there are my chief faults! Some unimaginable felicity must be mine; I do not care to seize the middling pleasure that lies in my path. When shall I cease from these

vain desires ?—not I fear until I read less and live more.
Do biographies of great men give us a false impression
of the totality of their lives? The glancing periods of
brightness are lively portrayed, but are there not the
weary barren roads connecting the lovely scenery? It
would be something to get a human soul really laid bare ;
nothing extenuated, too highly praised, nothing set down
in malice. Such a biography would help the inner
chambers of the mind more than the ones usual among
us : many really only a kind of Baedeker through a
man's life. Now for work and one attempt against procrastination ! "

But, lest this should create the impression that
Widgery's thoughts were wholly given up to introspective
moralising and gloomy repining that his brain was not of
first-rate quality, I give another extract which shows
him in quite a different mood—in a complete abandon
of exuberant animal spirits. " I've been a-sledging to-day,
Juche ! and the tip of my nose is red, you'll say. It was
fine. I had just come out of the School Museum and I
saw a noble cabbie clad in an enormous blue overcoat
with the flap artistically thrown back to show the har-
mony of the two blues. On his head he had a fur cap,
the top of a brilliant red. I inquired of his driverness
what honorarium he would deign to accept for taking me
to the Circulating Library. ' A bob,' said he in German.
' All right,' says I and in I jumps to the admiration of
one small boy and his smaller sister. Away we went
smoothly over the shiny road or through the small heaps
of snow. Smack went the whip, jingle-jingle went the
bells, and the farthing dip shone bravely in the lantern.
Had the horse been an Arab—which he wasn't—he
would have snorted and pawed the ground—which he

didn't.   However, at the end of the journey a lieutenant
honoured me so far as to stick his eye in his ocular to
see me dismount.   'You do me proud,' I thought.   So
I filled my chest with cold air (without coughing) and
stalked like a bold Briton into the shop.   Berlin is
looking very pretty.   Imagine an innocent Easter Fair
bubbling all over ;the town. . . . . One shop has a
colossal Noah's Ark where the animals are all so alike
that they could mistake themselves for one another.
. . . . Next door is a fancy dog with the most pathetic
tail I have ever seen.   Some of the better people
apparently are about making purchases and one can lose
a little the feeling that the mass of Germans look uncommonly common."

First Engagement.—No sane mind can accept the
bilious pessimist's gospel that life is all sorrow and disappointment, but there are certainly points and periods
in life when the strokes of fate seem to accumulate and
the heart is lacerated with wounds that never really heal,
however long Death may tarry in his coming.   Such a
period in Widgery's life now lies before us, a period of
passionate hope, followed by the bitterest disappointment,
difficult to estimate from the inevitable secrecy of its
operations and hazardous of judgment from the peculiar
readiness with which such operations lend themselves to
prejudice and partisanship.   If the memory of pain
were alone in question, we might, like him, forget it
utterly.   But, though the mind may forget the instrument
of suffering, the scar of its wound can never be obli-
terated and some day must be accounted for.   He did
forget the shock, but its traces endured till his death,
and we cannot understand those traces unless we know
their cause.

Some little time before he went to Berlin, the vague and half-conscious workings of the craving he had noted with boyish naïveté in his diary—the *besoin d'aimer*—had begun to take definite shape and cluster about a single personality. The novelty of his new departure in continental study for a time distracted his mind. Once or twice he pulled himself up sharply and wondered why he had thought so little of her since he left England. Even in those days stray doubts flitted through his mind concerning compatibility and kindred difficulties. However, it wanted only the æsthetic and emotional atmosphere of an autumn walk beside the sea to open the flood-gates of passionate worship, and, whether for good or ill, the deed was done. Somewhere in September of 1887 the engagement was made public. It lasted till March of 1888 when, by a strange fatality, his letters and presents were returned on the anniversary of his friend " Mary's " death.

Amid the many uncertainties of this miserable affair but one thing is certain, that he never recovered the effects of the blow—at any rate fully. That is all that concerns us in this story of his life; for new hopes and a perfect realisation of love's ideals were waiting for him till their appointed time.

Teaching of Languages, 1888.—As after the death of his dearest friend, so now upon the destruction of his glowing hopes of ideal companionship in an even dearer relation, he sought and found relief in copious and determined work. He gathered together the fruit of his recent studies on the continent and his own experience in a small book: " The Teaching of Languages in Schools." On this work, which appeared in 1888, rests the reputation so prematurely limited by

the hand of death. Here we see the promise of great
and good work that he was never allowed to undertake.
These last years of his life were full of activity. Besides
teaching at University College School, he had some
private pupils, did much in the way of examining schools,
expended a large amount of energy, that he would have
done well to store up against the attacks of his mortal
disease, on gratuitous lecturing—sometimes to audiences
that sought only amusement where he lavished the best
effort of a conscientious mind and enthusiastic heart.
He was Honorary Librarian of the Teachers' Guild
and one of its most active and unselfish members. And
he had for several years been a contributor to the
Journal of Education, the *Athenæum,* the *Educational
Times* and other periodicals, writing reviews of works
connected more or less intimately with Philology and
Pedagogy and a few special articles. He attended
many important educational meetings and delivered
speeches always well received and applauded for their
bold originality and trenchant expression of the views
they advocated. An extant letter gives a graphic account
of one of these speeches. The occasion was a Conference of the Teachers' Guild and a debate on the
Teaching of Modern Languages, a subject in which he
was peculiarly at home. " I got on my legs and blazed
away, the words tumbling out in what I felt was a deep
silence. There was a debate rule of ten minutes for
each speaker, but I didn't know of it and just when I
was about a third through the chairman rang his bell.
On looking round, I saw him holding up two fingers to
intimate that I had two more minutes to speak. I said
I hadn't anything like done, at which the audience
laughed and began to applaud. 'May I trespass on

your kindness, as I have spent a good deal of time on the subject?' I sailed away again and, as it seemed to me, in less than no time he pulled me up again. Then I laughingly said I would stop and sat down with no end of applause. There was a pause for a minute or two, but no one seemed inclined to continue the discussion and, as there seemed to be a general inclination to hear me go on, the chairman said 'I think it is the general wish of the meeting to hear Mr. Widgery further.' So I got on my legs again and had another blaze and finished. I was a good deal congratulated afterwards and, when one gentleman said 'It was very good of you to go on after so many interruptions,' I was suddenly and gladly aware how unconscious I had been all the time."

Among Widgery's papers is one of special importance, on the Class Teaching of Phonetics, delivered at the College of Preceptors, reproduced in the *Educational Times* and afterwards published in pamphlet form.

Paris Exhibition.—Even his holidays were not sacred. He worked himself into an illness at the Cheltenham Conference of the Teachers' Guild in 1890. The year before he had done his utmost for the Sheffield Conference and foregone a much needed holiday in order to visit the Educational Section of the Paris Exhibition. Here he met Dr. Harris, the United States Minister of Education, and accepted from him a commission to make a report to the American Government on the Educational Section. He was unable to complete the report before his death and it was finished, as a tribute of old and close friendship, by Mr. Foster Watson. Two minor notices were, however, printed at the time in the *Athenæum.*

Widgery's devotion to his profession was manifested in many indirect ways, among them the representation in London of the Girls' Collegiate School at Pietermaritzburg in Natal. To this school he rendered valuable assistance in the selection of teachers, every one of the appointments he made proving satisfactory, and he managed in a difficult and delicate position to earn the gratitude of his nominees by the kindness and courtesy of his inquiry into their qualifications. He was moreover Honorary Secretary of the Goethe and Shakespeare Societies and a member of the Council of the Art for Schools Association.

Second Engagement.—Despite the ravages of a mortal disease, these last two years of his life were probably the happiest of all. While his mind was constantly occupied in congenial work, rewarded with ever increasing success and the gradual but sure growth of a reputation reaching beyond his native land, even as far as Moscow, where the question of translating his book on " The Teaching of Languages in Schools " into Russian had been mooted, his life was illuminated by the realisation of an ideal companionship. In the last months of 1889 he began a friendship which slowly deepened into the closest and tenderest relation of life. Unlike his first experience, this happiness came imperceptibly upon him, and it had struck its roots deep into his soul before he realised and gladly, passionately, acknowledged this compensation for all the disappointments of the past and the worries of the present, which had been sent him in the evening of his short life. Perfect sympathy of mind and heart and unshakable mutual devotion, weighed and proved in a year of friendship drawing ever closer, found their logical acknowledgment on the 5th of September, 1890,

when he became engaged for the second time. The
happiness that now filled and softened his life was never
for a moment, after its complete recognition, shadowed
by the pain of a single doubt, a single regret. The
perfect constancy of the new devotion blotted out the
memory of the old disillusion. The sense of this constancy
sweetened the bitterness of the old humiliation, softened
and ennobled his whole character, checked the aggres-
siveness of a strong nature thwarted in its dearest hopes
and, growing ever stronger and closer, as his hold on life
grew weaker and the prospects of enjoying its full
fruition faded from before his eyes, it clung about him
in passionate devotion as he lay breathing heavily in the
arms of Death, and his last cry was for the devoted
companion whom he must now leave behind him—
alone.

Last Illness.—His illness, as we have seen, began as
far back as 1876. Congestion of the kidneys was evident
in 1879. He suffered on and off for years, always by
some strange delusion associating his symptoms with
disease of the liver instead of the organ actually
attacked. The symptoms generally followed on a period
of unusual mental stress. In 1881–82 he worked ten
hours a day and said, alas, that he "enjoyed it." He
little knew what the enjoyment was to cost him. There
is abundant evidence in his letters of the habit of working late into the night and even far into the following
morning. His life in chambers, where he spent the
last eight years, lent itself with fatal ease to utter
irresponsibility in the matter of keeping reasonable
hours and cut him off from the watchful care and
nursing he needed during these attacks, which often
came upon him in the night after a hard day's work.

Sometimes he would rise from his table so exhausted
that he had barely strength to stagger into the next room
on to his bed and none to undress or in any way help
himself with restoratives.   His friends and relations
repeatedly urged him to move into rooms where he
could have the help and comfort of a woman's nursing.
But his passionate and independent nature loved the
irresponsible freedom of chambers and he would not
listen to his friends till his landlord at length, for his
own convenience, turned him out, but unfortunately too
late.   Widgery warehoused his furniture and went home
for the summer holidays, intending to go into lodgings
next term—the term that never came for him.   It is
probable that his death was hastened by his strange
disinclination to submit to the restraint of medical advice.
He would rush into a chemist's shop, when distracted
by violent pains in the head which he connected with
anything but the complaint that was eating into his life,
and beg the man to give him anything, no matter what,
so long as it would remove the pain he was immediately
suffering from.   In this way, probably, he often absorbed
what was actually rank poison, considering the real nature
of his complaint.   He sought relief in vigorous exercise,
tricycling and gymnastics, and with his usual enthusiasm
overtired himself and got no real good.   He would hurry
from a hasty meal to snatch a game of fives before afternoon
school, as boys with their boyish digestion love to do, little
guessing that to him it was a refined method of suicide.
People—some people—thought he "looked so strong
and sturdy."   He himself, in a letter to his sister dated
June 1887, exclaimed "There is nothing wrong with
me, save that I am tired, tired!—tired in the morning,
tired at night!"

Two years before his death the attacks became more persistent. But he never treated them seriously till the term before his death. Constantly urged by his friends, he at length consulted Sir Andrew Clark. The physician sent him home to his native air to rest. His friends, or rather one of them, a friend of the doctor's, received a different message—the intimation that Widgery had left his presence a doomed man. Never really strong—constitutionally strong—Widgery had of late years taken no rest. He had worn himself out in the work of education. Whether this overwork actually caused his death it is impossible to decide; that it hastened the inevitable end none who knew him can doubt. "The ill effects of this overwork were aggravated by the constant fret and chafe of the 'bitter injustice' (to use his own words) of the assistant-master's position. Had he lived, he might some day have won a lucrative head or housemastership; but of the two qualifications for this, a high degree and a safe orthodoxy, he had by a mischance just failed in obtaining the one and the other he scorned to feign." But his eminent natural qualifications for both positions, as apart from those which a shallow and short-sighted public opinion postulates, were implicitly acknowledged in the Memorial raised by his numerous friends in connection with his last labour of love—the extension of the position and influence of the Teachers' Guild. The subscriptions to this fund, varying from half-a-crown to five guineas and amounting altogether to close on £170, were contributed by 133 friends. Out of this sum 142 volumes, more or less intimately connected with Pedagogy, were bought and added to the Guild Library under a separate grouping styled the "Widgery Memorial Library," and a grant was made sufficient to print the first of the two

parts in which the Guild Library Catalogue was issued—
the Pedagogic Section. The rest was devoted to defray-
ing the cost of raising and administering the memorial
fund and the purchase of two platinotype enlargements
of a recent photograph of Widgery, one copy of which
was placed in the room where he so often worked as
Honorary Librarian of the Guild and the other presented
to University College School, where he taught for the
last eight years of his life.

"*Rest.*"—And so at the end of the summer term in
1891 William Widgery went home to rest—to rest for ever.
For awhile he kept about the house and garden. Then
he took to his bed. An old friend, who had once forcibly
carried him off to be nursed through a violent attack of
illness in his own home, passed with his wife through
Exeter on a summer tour, and Widgery must needs rise
from his bed to conduct his friends to the Cathedral,
though he was too weak to do more than sit in the
carriage while they hurriedly glanced in at the door of
the minster. No remonstrance could hold him back. His
one cry was "Do not thwart me!"—He had been so
often thwarted in life—and he had a great longing to get
out into the open air. He returned home with the hand
of Death upon him. He was out in the garden the next
day but in the evening took to his bed for the last time.
Even then he did not realise how near the end was. On
Sunday, the 23rd of August, he was at last obliged to
face his fate, and his repeated calls for the dearest companion of his last days led to her being summoned by
telegraph. She reached him next day. He ceased to
wander, recognised her and thenceforward seemed to
be at peace. So he lay dying with all his dearest
on earth around him. They kept him company

and tenderly nursed him through all the days of his illness till the Angel of Death at length entered the chamber. The last agony of physical suffering passed away. Gradually he fell asleep. At twenty minutes past five on Wednesday morning the eternal calm settled on his wasted features and the watchers knew that he was at last indeed at rest. Far away in the east the sun was gilding the horizon with his bright warm rays. So the spirit of William Henry Widgery passed "in a perfect dawn to a yet more glorious day."

His body lies in the cemetery at St. David's in view of the room in which he died and next to the last resting-place of the headmaster of his first school, which also looks down upon his sleep. So the end and the beginning of life are one.* Over his head stands a block of Dartmoor granite and a mantle of Dartmoor turf (graceful token of his mother's thought) covers his heart. On that block of granite the affection of his friends has written that "He was an ardent worker and able writer for education; a lover of men, truth, justice, and beauty; a friend to many who deeply mourn his loss. 'His virtue survives all mortal change in lasting loveliness.' 'He worketh still.'" Those who more closely knew, more intimately loved him, still strive to cover his grave with the bloom and beauty he loved so passionately in life. His friends cherish the memory of his pure and noble nature in their hearts. So he is once more united with the great earth of which he believed himself to be an integral part and, standing beside his grave in the quiet churchyard, one seems to hear the

* Since these lines were penned Widgery's artist father, of whom he was so justly proud and to whom he was himself a cause of equal pride, has gone to rest close beside him.

echo of his own poetical conception : "Some sense of an
ancient brotherhood seems to link me to the hills and
river, the trees, the birds, nay the very reptiles and the
stocks and stones. I am a part of all that I have seen and
heard. Through them as through me courses the same
divine breath of life. They too are glad to have lived
and seen the sun." To that echo our hearts make
answer "We also are glad that he lived, and saw and
loved the sun—and glad that in that great and generous
love which could embrace even the unfeeling stocks and
stones in its brotherhood we too had a place and part."

PART II—WORK

" Thy leaf has perished in the green."

CHAPTER I

CRITIQUE OF HARNESS ESSAY, REVIEWS, SPEECHES,
LECTURES AND PAPERS, "TEACHING OF LAN-
GUAGES IN SCHOOLS," AND GENERAL CRITIQUE.

I. Harness Essay.*

With regard to this Essay very divergent opinions have
been expressed,† but there is a consensus about certain
points. Widgery's theory that the First Quarto is an
early and naturally inferior sketch of the work which
appears in undoubtedly nobler shape in the Second
Quarto seems to be generally accepted as correct. He
seems also to be successful in establishing the existence
of an Urhamlet or early version of the subject afterwards immortalised by Shakespeare, but unsuccessful in
fathering it upon Kyd or proving it to be the base
of the Brudermord. He fails also to show that the
Brudermord is wholly independent of Shakespeare's
First Quarto.

Whether his arguments for the date 1596–8 be accepted
as conclusive or not, his attack upon the conclusion

---

* The first Quarto Edition of *Hamlet*.
† See Appendix II.

drawn from the absence of *Hamlet* from Mere's list appears to me to be entirely successful. While the mention of a play in such a list is proof positive of its existence at the time, provided its existence at some time be an established fact, the omission of any play means practically nothing. There is no warrant for assuming that the list was meant to be a comprehensive one, nor have we any right to assume that a play of the highest importance in our judgment now would hold the same rank in that of a provincial pedagogue three centuries ago.

I think the *Athenæum* critic is right in saying that Widgery's destructive work is successful and his attempts at construction, comparatively speaking, a failure. Little else could be expected where the data are so scanty and such as do exist so contradictory. The whole essay conveys to my mind the impression of an airy web of brilliant and ingenious hypotheses, whose texture nowhere assumes that closeness and consistency which compels the mind to exclaim "This is palpably true!" The impression of brilliancy, penetration, sagacity, ingenuity, is very great. One feels here the pervading presence of a mind that is not merely furnished with the dogged perseverance of the antiquarian word-miner, who digs and digs till mere digging results inevitably in the unearthing of treasure, but gifted with the intuition, the clairvoyance of original inspiration. This essay is not the work of a dusty book-worm, feeding on verbal variations and corrupt scripture, but of an artist full-armed with æsthetic insight and saturated to his fingertips with æsthetic sensibility. *Pace* the *Academy* critic, the æsthetic reflections are the finest part of the book, even though they may not all be indisputably correct. Dealing, as needs must, with opinion, they may well convey differing degrees of conviction to different minds. But their originality, beauty and force remain unimpaired by any sarcasms the unimaginative brain of the mere literary verbalist can level against them.

Nevertheless it must be admitted that the language of the essay, at least in places, savours both of the undisciplined imagination of youth and the artificial exotic colouring fostered by an academic atmosphere. Indeed, if we would rightly estimate the work, this last fact—its academic rearing—must always be borne in mind. Brilliant and original, the essay has all the mixed characteristics of an academic exercise. The writer is a learned man appealing to learned judges. He has saturated his mind with all that bears even in the remotest way upon the dispute in hand and he knows that his judges have, or may safely be assumed to have, an equal familiarity with the subject. Consequently he revels in ellipses of argument, merely hints at facts which he assumes to be thoroughly familiar to his reader and so weaves a brilliant web, which is not incoherent to him or his judges, because they possess the links he knows but does not show. Yet for the lay reader it is wrapped in a cloud of academic argument that nothing can enlighten but a study of all the material dealing with the subject in hand as deep and as prolonged as that which the writer gave to it. In short, the author of this work has not yet emerged from the intensely technical atmosphere of the academic life, nor been called upon to carry conviction of the wisdom of his argument to minds utterly unacquainted with the data on which he bases it, nor required to observe the fundamental canon of successful teaching—the need of bearing ever in mind the

ignorance of his audience. Widgery did learn to obey
that canon and no one obeyed it more successfully than
he—afterwards. But in this work it seldom appears.
He writes as a god conversing with gods far above the
heads of astonished mortals. As a work of pure criticism
the essay is admirable, but as a specimen of argumentative style it is not, I think, to be judged with his later
controversial efforts.

II. Reviews.

One would hardly look to unsigned reviews* for light
on a man's educational opinions under ordinary circumstances. Reviews are so often mere cut and dried
analyses of new books, laying special stress on inaccuracies of scholarship and printing with a few hints
for improvement and perhaps a smart witticism or two
at the expense of some one or other (not seldom the
author), to make the thing palatable to the jaded reader
who looks in reviews for guidance in his reading.
Usually cramped for space, they seldom launch out
into general observations. In Widgery's case it was
otherwise. To him a review was not merely an analysis
of a book, an exposition of its faults accompanied by
suggestions for its improvement. It was an opportunity
for expounding original theories of education to which
the contents of the book discharged the office of a text.
Without neglecting the technical and academic inaccuracies of the work, the faults he sought most keenly
after and laid greatest stress upon were its shortcomings
as an agent of education in its highest aspects. He
always looked upon the book from a large and liberal
point of view. He had in his mind a new and almost

* See Appendix IV.

revolutionary scheme of public education, and almost every review—certainly the best of those—he wrote served as the text for the development of some portion of this scheme. A good example is his review of Skeat's " English Etymology " (First Series).

He brought to this task a wonderful amount of penetration, sense and breadth of criticism and no little of the element which adds so much to the convincing force of mere ratiocination—wit and humour. The exceptional ability of his reviews on Teutonic philology was remarked before their authorship was known. The review of Elze's " Biography of Shakespeare " is interesting. That on the " Bacon-Shakespeare Question " by Stopes is a good specimen of trenchant and sarcastic treatment. The one on Max Walter's " Franzoesische Klassenunterricht " gives some useful hints about Widgery's methods of teaching. His intellectual ability and breadth of view are particularly apparent in those on Paul's "Grundriss der Germanischen Philologie," Rendall's " Cradle of the Aryans " and Skeat's " Principles of English Etymology " (Second Series). The two on De Guimp's " Pestalozzi " and Quick's " Educational Reformers " display the most notable characteristic of Widgery's educational attitude—nobility of sentiment and broad humanitarian interest. The service these reviews have done to the cause of higher education, though perhaps never to be recognised, still less estimated and valued, must have been very great. A casual thought picked up in a review, read in some moment of leisure and then tossed away, often sinks deep and bears fruit in unlooked-for directions. It is therefore to Widgery's credit that he put his whole heart and some of his best work into mere reviews of other men's thoughts and theories.

III. Speeches.

Widgery's speeches* were always well received. The originality and daring of the views expressed and the trenchant language in which they were couched formed the chief attraction. He carried his audience with him, but rather by the force of personal emotion than by rhetorical brilliancy. His earnestness was very palpable and it was at once seen that he believed and meant all he said. Hardly anything has a greater hold upon an audience of specialists than a sense of the speaker's earnestness, and no one was long in doubt that Widgery had convinced himself before he stood up to convince other people. These speeches, like his reviews, were all opportunities for expounding his general scheme of educational reform and he made as much use of them as of his reviews. They were characterised too by the same breadth of view and nobility of conception, but greater vehemence of expression, as might be expected from the fact that they were spoken and therefore under the influence of the animation and emotion of public delivery. It cannot be doubted that their influence was as far-reaching and deep as that of his reviews and, unfortunately, even more elusory in estimation.

IV. Lectures and Papers.

All the remarks I have made concerning characteristics of Widgery's reviews apply equally well to such fragments as exist of his lectures and papers,† whether read or contributed to periodicals. The difference is merely in the greater scope offered by a lecture or paper for a more elaborate and comprehensive statement of

* See Appendix IV.   † *Ibid.*

his general educational scheme, or some considerable section of it. One paper, however, which afterwards appeared in pamphlet form, requires more particular notice.

Class Teaching of Phonetics as a Preparation for the Pronunciation of Foreign Languages.

This was originally a paper read before the College of Preceptors. It was afterwards published in the *Educational Times* and finally brought out in pamphlet form.

It is an able and singularly lucid digest of the fundamental principles of phonetics, divested of all excrescences and brought within the grasp of an ordinary school class. With the aid of it, almost any teacher possessed of common sense and determination can lay a sound foundation of scientific principle that will prove invaluable in the elucidation of many of the so-called "irregularities" of declension and conjugation in modern languages. The theories advanced are all more or less directly based on the great principle that "the unit in language is the spoken sentence." Starting from this base by an admirable process of thoroughly scientific analysis Widgery explains the distinction between "sonant" and "consonant," the phenomenon of "voicing," the nature and functions of the "organs of speech," the long-ignored difference between "sign" (letter) and "sound," the varying "positions of the tongue" during the utterance of the various sounds represented by the letters of the English alphabet, the location of the "sonants" (vowels) in the mouth, the interesting phenomenon of "rounding," "glides," the "fronting" which justifies, or at least explains, such a vulgarism as "dontcherknow," and lastly the phenomenon of the "liaison," which has been hurled at the heads of schoolboys for centuries but never explained to them, doubtless because the simple explanation was unknown before phonetic analysis attacked that great "bogie" of language teaching, the Exception. The pamphlet is written in a clear direct style, excellently adapted to school use, and the various phenomena are described and explained with masterly simplicity.

V. "Teaching of Languages in Schools."

A summary statement of criticisms of a wide nature, dealing with the character, aims and value of this work as a whole, culled from various reviews which appeared in literary periodicals, will be found in Appendix III. Criticisms bearing on individual sections of the work will be quoted when I examine the theories enunciated in the book and the methods it suggests. A fit opportunity for this will occur when I proceed to consider in detail Widgery's methods of education in general. This work may be considered as an exhaustive exposition of those methods.

VI. General Critique.

Having thus briefly considered Widgery's writings individually, let us glance at the products of his intellectual activity regarded as a coherent whole.

Widgery "thought his own mind was not creative but analytical. Yet he teemed with ideas too much to be classed entirely with analytical minds. His criticisms seemed more intuitive than analytical, especially in the Hamlet Essay." Here Widgery shows more power in historico-literary analysis than in comparative analysis of textual variations. These were too material — not

spiritual enough to interest him sufficiently. "There
must be somewhere," he once wrote, "some quickening †
breath of spirit in my subject, or it cannot detain me
long."

Widgery was a born poet of Nature. He seems to
become electrified directly an opportunity arises for
establishing a link with Nature. Note the passage beginning "The warm love-languorous air of Verona,"
&c., on p. 184 of the Harness Essay, and again
"Sweet and holy is that Persian custom," &c., on
p. 175. We have already observed this trait in the
quotations I made while recounting the facts and events
of his personal life. It will become still more apparent
when I treat of his character in the Third Part of this
memoir.

All his works show wide preparatory reading. Before
he attempted to write on any subject he knew it well.
This is most apparent in the Harness Essay, but is
patent everywhere in his works. Not less marked here
is the acuteness of his intuition in theorising. But perhaps the feature most prominent is the sincerity of the
writer. It is obvious that he thoroughly believes in his
theory about the First Quarto. The management of
the arguments does not create any suspicion in the mind
of the reader that Widgery is speaking from his brief in
favour of a case he does not believe in. However un-
stable his theories may seem to us, we perceive that to
his enthusiastic absorption they appear reasonable and
well-founded.

Another characteristic strikes us in his "vigorous"
reviews—width and loftiness of view. This appears in
his elevation of the "review" by transforming it from a
trade advertisement-board to an educational pulpit.

I have already remarked that personal emotion seems to have been a more powerful factor of Widgery's influence than intellectual brilliancy, though he certainly possessed the latter also in a high degree. This quality of emotional influence may reasonably be assumed to have shown itself most markedly in his speeches. The scanty accounts we have of their reception appear to justify the hypothesis.

The power of lucid simplicity of exposition, which is yet eminently scientific in its rational development and artistic coherence, is most evident in his " Class Teaching of Phonetics."

Passing to his chief work, " The Teaching of Languages in Schools," we have two excellent examples of laborious devotion to truth in the sketch of the history of grammar and the exhaustive bibliography that closes the work. A man who considered it necessary to consult so many authorities before he ventured to formulate his own opinion was made of the right stuff to be a missionary of truth for the spread of knowledge. All Widgery's work bears the stamp of this spirit—a strong impersonal desire for the truth, combined with real insight and original thought.

Widgery's intellectual and moral stride was never shortened by prejudice or meanness. There was in him —well-known to his intimates and proved by his works— a rare combination of philosophical originality with cool practicalness, daring with reasonableness, broad conception and great power of generalisation with concentrated insight into detail. But again the most prominent thing in all he said and did is the moral altitude of his standpoint. Look round the scholastic horizon—all who know anything of the strange scenes and motley activities it encloses—and try to imagine for a moment what a " moral sanctification," so to speak, would come over education, if all teachers were to approach their teaching with motives so noble, so disinterested, as those which permeate Widgery's plea for a more rational method of "Teaching Languages in Schools." So looking with an enlarged imagination and an impartial spirit, one cannot but perceive that with the death of the author of that book a great educational promise was nipped just as the bud had begun to show signs of unfolding, a bright light of original thought quenched just as it had begun to mount into brilliant flame.

CHAPTER II

METHODS OF TEACHING

1. IN the great and thick forest—for such it is at present —of scholastic method there are certain broad beaten tracks which all men tread who are teachers. But though these may be the safest and surest ways to the El Dorado of headmastership, they are not always the shortest cuts to the successful inculcation of true know-ledge or the successful manufacture of fine brain. Not seldom they have all the dreary and ignoble character of the common highway, where the wealthy and " good easy " merchant of wisdom ambles comfortably on to a vicarage or housemastership, careless and too often ignorant of the beauty, the grandeur, the nobility of the paths that branch off here and there from the smooth highway and travel through the mysteries of infant psychology and the fascinations of infant ethics into those regions of conscious or unconscious mental evolu-tion where Dantes and Shakespeares, Raffaels and Mozarts, Pitts and Demosthenes, Newtons, Columbuses and Luthers, Alexanders and Napoleons are born and bred. In these by-ways of experimental scholastics the subject of this memoir loved to wander and it was there he acquired the " divine discontent " with the antiquated conservatism of modern scholastic methods. Millions of good easy parents, having themselves been inoculated

with misconception in their own youth, continue to misconceive these methods to be fit preparation of their offspring for the battle of life. But their misplaced confidence is not altogether without occasional misgivings and even final disillusion and despair, when their well-beloved stands on the threshold of public life with sixteen years of grammar weighing heavily upon his brain and not a sentence of language familiar to his tongue! It is to this despair that Widgery has a word to say of comfort and advice. Let those who, not yet face to face with the last act of disillusion, already feel some misgivings as to whether their dear Tom, Dick or Harry, will be able to utter a single sentence of French or German, or even compose half a page of decent English, when he emerges from the goal of his scholastic ambition, the Sixth Form, consider "while it is yet to-day" and take counsel and make united protest against the fetish of Grammar and the Exercise Book.

Before we pass to Widgery's systematic attack upon the unscientific science of modern teaching, it will be well to consider briefly some of his own methods. In these we must not look for original and unknown ways of operation, for in the scholastic world too there is "no new thing under the sun." We shall see rather a different degree of insistance on certain well-known points and a proportionate depression of others at present unduly emphasised. In the result, out of old materials we shall see created a new system by mere rearrangement of ancient elements. This is the essence of reform.

2. *Chastity.*—The dominant motive of Widgery's scholastic activity was an earnest seeking after what he termed "chastity." One element of this appears to have been absolute intellectual honesty in dealing with

the subject in hand, no matter to what branch of knowledge it belonged. Cram, unscientific abstracting or excision, all effort to eliminate thought and pander to a facile memory for the mere sake of temporary retention he regarded intellectually with the loathing a pure mind has for personal defilement. Equally strong was his detestation of all truckling to conventional notions of education in order to obtain a better footing financially in the scholastic world or curry favour with a scholastic superior by insincere expressions of agreement. He hated the interested suppleness which openly accords a papal infallibility to the headmaster or—to use his own expression—"cottons to the chief" in the hope of a "rise." Slothful burking of difficulties under the knowledge that the boys "will not know any better" and the headmaster "will not find out," snobbish airing of a superior specialist knowledge to the detriment of the reputation of a colleague in the eyes of his pupils, narrow emphasising of non-essentials to win an artifical dignity in the eyes of small boys or weave a chain of red-tape about the mechanical operations of class-work, and above all any physical slackening or intellectual indifference which allows the supreme aim of education, perfect mental and moral culture, to be for a moment obscured —all this he regarded as "unchaste." No milder term could describe his transcendental attitude towards unworthy education.

3. *Readiness to allow Observation.*—Side by side with this high estimate of the teacher's moral attitude stood an absolute frankness about his own doings in the class-room. Sincerely striving to do his best, he courted any criticism that would enable him to better that best. Having nothing to hide, he cared not a whit who stood

and watched him. He had striven hard to qualify himself for good teaching and the knowledge that he had so striven gave him confidence in himself and his methods. Hence he was never ashamed to be seen and heard teaching. His eagerness to tell of his own experiments and submit their results to public judgment was only equalled by his eagerness to hear of the experiments of other teachers and learn what they too had to communicate.

"Gladly wolde he lerne, and gladly teche."

He was one of the few men at the school whose class-room door was always open to the enthusiastic foreigners who came to investigate the teaching of English in England. He appeared to feel no reluctance in admitting them and no embarrassment in their presence for hours at a time. Whatever opinions they may have formed of his methods, they never failed to carry away the impression of having witnessed a frank exposition of sincere convictions, in which nothing that was to be learnt had been in any way spoiled by a suspicion of artificial or interested colouring.

4. *Desire for Identity of Method.*—Widgery's eagerness to discuss method was not the result of mere dilletante curiosity. "I never knew," says his last headmaster, "any one who set himself more systematically to study method in teaching." The fruit of this study was invariably brought to the test of practical working, so far as the limited opportunity and indifferent means at his disposal allowed of any practical application. He was constantly longing for the establishment of some great institution where this lack of opportunity and means would be remedied—some great experimental college

D

devoted entirely to the practical testing of the theories of
educational reformers.   He would have made an ideal
head of such an institution.   It must come some day
and there are men who could do grand work in that
direction, if they were called off from the worry and
anxiety of earning a precarious living by teaching in
small schools under the depressing and cramping influence of unenlightened chiefs, who shrink in terror
from any radical experiment for fear of that *bête noire* of
education, the "fussy" parent.

Widgery had too a great desire for "identity" of
method, even on minute points.   He grieved ceaselessly
over that fruitful source of ineffective teaching, the liberty
of the individual master.   When four classes of the same
rank are taught by four different masters in the same
subject and each is allowed to fix his own pace, not to
mention his own method of communication, it is inevitable that the end of the term should find each of the
four at very different points in the development of the
subject.   Then follows of necessity much heartburning
and discussion ending usually in a compromised programme of examination, which takes no account of much
of the labours of the most advanced class and unduly
strains the limited knowledge of the most backward.
Add to this a lax and unscientific graduation of the
subject through the various forms in which it is taken,
and we may imagine the intellectual anguish of a man
like Widgery with his strong belief in the necessity of
rigidity in method and rational graduation of effort on an
enlightened psychologic basis.   Unhappily headmasters
are more often chosen nowadays for their scholarship
than for organising power, and too many of those who
happen to have also the latter capacity waste much

precious time in teaching which it would, in the long run, pay them to have done by assistants. If all head-masters would do, as one of them said he intended to when an electing committee questioned him as to his ideas of his own functions in the school—" walk about," we should get a well-organised, well-graduated and well-supervised school. There all the assistants would be rigidly carrying out the headmaster's central conceptions of education, all the boys would be in their right classes at their right age, every assistant would feel that the headmaster was helping and encouraging him and that he was helping the headmaster to build up an enlight-ened and coherent system of education, and there the sloven, the shirker and the "tradesman" (to use Widgery's own expression) would have no tolerance and no place.

Widgery was always trying to refer even the details of scholastic work to general principles. In other words his methods were dominated by a great moral purpose, a great psychological concept, that was built up of wheel within wheel, every individual cog of which required to be of perfect workmanship and deserved the honour of individual care and cleaning. From the same high ideal he believed education to be no easy profession, no mere convenient "last refuge of the unsuccessful literary man," but an elaborate and complex science, worthy of long study and purposeful preparation under the influence of enlightened training. In training he believed most firmly and never ceased to regret that he himself had had to enter upon the practice of teaching without that equip-ment. He did not forget, as too many believers in "salvation by training" do, that the great teacher, like the great poet, is born, not made; that the faculty of psychologic diagnosis of the pupil's difficulties, which is the crown of scholastic ability, is a gift of the gods not to be bought or fashioned in any training college; but he saw that half the bad teaching in schools is due to a combination of inexperience and ignorance. This he felt, and felt rightly, might be benefited, if not wholly cured, by a systematic course in the history of educational methods and a careful study of the experience of teachers in the past scientifically arranged and exhaustively codified. It was with the object of contributing to such a codex that he constantly made notes of the difficulties boys encounter and of the various ways of treating them suggested by his own experience and experiments. Of this particular form of his ceaseless industry I shall have something more to say later on.

5. *Readiness to Take Trouble.*—Widgery was distinguished by a most untiring perseverance in digging for "origins" for his boys, in finding reasons for everything, as, for instance, for the form and order of the letters of the alphabet or the symbols used in algebra. For a geography class he would work out some simple explanation of the way in which maps are made. He went specially to the Mint in order to make a set of standard English weights, because, as he wrote, "I do believe in making boys able to guess fairly well the leading weights and measures." In his English class he gave ingenious illustrations of the mechanism of the organs of speech, using for this purpose a real throat preserved in spirits of wine, which a medical friend presented to him, and a false palate which he had had made specially for his teaching of phonetics. On hearing of Widgery's death, an old pupil wrote "I never had a more pains-

taking or patient master." As Widgery spared no pains in improving his own teaching and in making thoughtful use of his own experience, so he shrank from no effort that would enable him to add to that experience in every way, both at home and in Germany. Whatsoever he gleaned in this way from the vast fields of educational experience he strove to store up with the unselfish object of advancing knowledge in the subject he had most at heart. "Keep a record," he writes, "of all these little difficulties" (of boys). "They will soon swell up and may form some day a solid basis for papers." In teaching phonetics to a German class "I write down what I actually say, noting at the same time wrong answers. This will soon give me workable material." "I let the boys see me thinking hard sometimes, and they are always highly amused when my little note-book is whipped out and they know from experience that the point will soon be cleared up." But perhaps the unselfishness of his devotion to educational science is most strikingly apparent in the cadence of the following quotation from one of his letters. The light of subsequent events adds a touch of pathos to it, showing what "tiredness" meant to him. "I gave my boys plenty of rope to-day and let them ask me as many questions as they liked. And wasn't I tired after!" Let us consider more in detail some of the experiments he made with a view to arriving at a better understanding of the difficulties that beset the youthful mind.

6. *Experiment.*—Once he made every boy in the class write down individually (1) what had been his chief difficulty in learning Euclid's Geometry and (2) how he would like to be taught the propositions it contains. The answers of the boys are unfortunately lost. I

cannot find more than the merest fragments of them. But the collection of such suffrages would be an easy and an important function of the Institute I have shadowed forth above. When, upon one occasion, a change was proposed in the syllabus of work for English classes, Widgery made his boys write down what works of literature they would like to read in class, how much of them should be read and in what manner, and further what subjects they would like included under English— Political Economy and Philology for example—and so forth. As he collected typical mistakes, so he was in the habit of jotting down "happy ideas" for illustrating and explaining difficulties on slips of paper, which he afterwards classified and preserved. Hundreds of these exist; but, unhappily, when his effects were removed after his death, these slips were taken out of the pigeon-holes in his study and thrown into hopeless disorder. They contained, besides typical mistakes, also typical faulty ways of learning (for example, the not uncommon blunder of learning geometrical theorems by heart) and examples (or traces) of typical faulty instruction he detected in boys when they came to him for the first time. On one slip is the memorandum—"Suggest. Society to send circulars to collect information as to boys' methods of learning and their difficulties. Classify evidence and publish." That is another clear definition of one of the duties of a possible Institute of Experimental Pedagogy. In the pursuit of such information Widgery naturally encountered many humorous and startling pieces of school-boy intelligence and opinion. These unconscious witticisms also were jotted down on slips of paper, to be afterwards used in pointing the moral of some ludicrous failure in instruction through incapacity on the part of the teacher to assimilate his mental stand-point with that of the boy—the commonest trouble, be it noted, in all instruction and the one most vividly prominent in the instruction of the very young.

Widgery believed the historical method superior to the schematic—if used judiciously. "The schematic method," he said, "towers up above the boy. He is bound to assent—not consent—but cannot imagine how on earth it got there. We should rather restate the problem as it appeared to the discoverer, giving his answer, not hiding that he perhaps went wrong several times before he hit upon the right method. The personal element in a book does humanise it and brighten up boys." There is great depth in this dogma. I It amounts to saying that a boy should be taught, not to absorb knowledge as the earth absorbs rain by process of soaking, but to think it out for himself by being trained to watch the thinking process in others, who have thought before him, and to rediscover the knowledge for himself. The examination crammer will of course object that life is too short for this slow process. It is—because so much of the available portion of life has been and is wasted in writing Greek exercises and Latin verse by rules-of-thumb that starve the imagination and sterilise thought under the pretence of developing the logical faculty. Were this precious time devoted to teaching boys to acquire the rational processes of science, and training them to appreciate the æsthetic treasures of French, German, and English by giving them early in life a colloquial and reading acquaintance with these tongues, they would be vastly better able at thirteen or fourteen to tackle the difficulties of original composition in any language living or dead, and far better fitted at eighteen or nineteen to appreciate the immortal treasures of Greek and Latin verse. It is not with the Classics that an enlightened pedagogy has a quarrel, but with the abominable prostitution of them to the fetish of Grammar and Exercises. But of course there has never been any successful teaching which has not more or less consciously rested on a basis of thinking for oneself.

The following quotation shows Widgery again striving after that humanising of the dry bones of knowledge which was one of his constant aims—which must be a constant aim in teaching the "young," who seldom learn because they love to, who have not the stimulus of the competition of a struggle for existence in the battle of life, who must therefore be enticed by the establishment of some palpable connection with the strongest factor in their entity—their human animalism. "I managed to get some algebra into the class this morning by making boys do a large number of examples in books, saving the answers, and then making them get the factors backwards. They seemed to feel under a moral obligation to do what they knew had only just passed through their hands." And again we see him experimenting in the statement—"A point of capital importance, neglected by the text-books, is the recognition of *form* as distinct from value. On this side algebra touches literature and art. That it may be useful for a certain purpose to put say $2 \times \frac{1}{2}$ for 1 is a revelation to most boys. I am invariably asked 'Please, sir, why don't you cancel?' To which I invariably reply 'Because I don't want to go out.' To reduce a large number of special cases under a few typical forms is useful training. And the gradual swallowing up of typical forms in more and more general expressions without any limitations whatever on the symbols is science of the first water."

The method of repetition in chorus was a favourite practice of Widgery's, especially in teaching phonetics. "The tendency to imitation is so strong in children that in phonetic work it is advisable to have the answers given at first in chorus. Let your best boy repeat alone, and then pitch on your worst. If he fails, you can bring down on him a deluge of sound by simply saying, 'Tell him, the class!'" Another hint for teaching phonetics may be noted here. "I have found it useful to make boys hold up the hand when a given sound occurs in a piece recited by the master, the phonetic symbol for it being pointed out at the same time on a large table containing all the French sounds, those common to English being painted black, and the others red." He strongly recommended the use of coloured chalks for emphasising differences, such for example as that between stem and inflection. Colour distinction will always draw a dull boy's attention to the importance of considering and allowing for every part of a word instead of carelessly thinking only of its most striking element—the root syllable. Many other opportunities for utilising the distinction produced by variety of colour on the blackboard will readily occur to the experienced teacher.

7. *Interest.*—Very closely allied with this desire to humanise learning is the last feature I shall notice in Widgery's scholastic method—the ceaseless effort to interest his pupils. "Oh, sir," said the boys of a class he had once taught to his successor, "why don't you tell us some stories" (*i.e.*, life-like stories about men in history) "as Mr. Widgery used to do?" "Another hobby of mine," writes Widgery, "the attempt to render the schoolroom as pleasant

as a drawing-room, was officially taken up by Mr. Eve at
a masters' meeting yesterday. I have a good number of
illustrious men framed and shall set them up as a fair
example." The historic attitude, his invariable endeavour
to trace and bring out the historic development of the
subject he happened to be teaching, made for the same
object—the awakening of interest in the mind of the
pupil. "Of course these interesting little facts—*e.g.* that
x for the unknown quantity in Algebra is an abbreviation
for "xei" (schai), the Arabic for "cosa," thing—are only
introduced by the way as they turn up in teaching, but
they have, I think, a distinct moral value. We ought to
be grateful to those who have worked before us. Besides
we can hardly overrate the value of showing the gradual
and painful progression of learning, as it compels the
belief of more to come, and an occasional hint that there
is plenty to be done will sometimes produce a burst of
extra work on the part of the cleverer boys."

8. *Summary.*—Widgery's scholastic activity, then, was
based on "chastity" of motive and directed to a high
aim, moral and intellectual. This aim was double. It
was on the one hand subjective in so far as it consisted in
the imparting of knowledge that would fit a boy for the
battle of life. It was objective in so far as it embraced
the study of the methods of imparting knowledge and the
results of the application of those methods with a view to
improved success in future efforts to impart. His activity
was characterised by a frank readiness to submit his own
efforts to observation and an eager desire to benefit by
the efforts of other workers. He was possessed by an
overmastering conviction of the need of method for the
economy of effort—the conservation of scholastic energy
—and of uniformity in method to prevent the waste and

neutralisation of the results of effort. He believed that analytical experiment should be relegated to an Institute of Experimental Pedagogy and that general scholastic effort should busy itself only with synthetic experiment, and herein he justified a claim for practical sense. He believed in training as a remedy for inexperience,* but did not suppose that it could supply the place of native educational gift. He strove constantly to collect materials for an Educational Case-Book, that should record pedagogic difficulties and their remedies, and a Codex Scholasticus, that should formulate and classify canons of scholastic method. The mainspring of his own method was the awakening of moral interest in the pupil by humanising knowledge, by making it pleasant to the eye and heart, by forging a link between the soul of the inventor of knowledge and the soul of the learner, between the psychology of discovery and the psychology of reception. He believed the historic method, judiciously applied, to be the most natural, scientific and, in the long run, the most speedily effective. He strove by experiment to assimilate the intellectual standpoint of the teacher and the pupil, seeking from boys frank written statements of their difficulties from their own point of view. He experimented also for the collection of evidence from which to generalise rules for the guidance of future diagnosis. And he neglected to consider but one thing in education—the cost of labour. He was too noble to put a price upon knowledge. He gave his heart—his life, and gave it gladly, sorrowing only that opportunity was denied him to give more.

* Hence he actively supported the movement for the registration of teachers.

CHAPTER III

THEORIES

Papers II. and III. and Speech I. (Appendix IV.) should be read in connection with the theories enunciated in the following pages and the remarks made upon them. The extracts from the speech and papers just mentioned deal in a general manner with the points now to be treated in detail. As I have already remarked, Widgery made his speeches and papers opportunities for ventilating those theories of education which he afterwards put together and embodied in the booklet on " The Teaching of Languages in Schools." Some amount of repetition must therefore be expected in what follows. I must also crave indulgence for repetition due to the plan of making extracts from the text, adding quotations from various writers and then appending by way of commentary my own opinions and criticisms. My object was to obtain the juxtaposition of diverse opinions without destroying their individuality by any attempt to blend them in a single review.

In dealing with this booklet, I propose to quote first several passages from one section of the work as nearly as possible verbatim, selecting those which embody or expound the fundamental principles of Widgery's new scholastic scheme. I shall then review these principles, quoting criticisms made upon them by other writers, and add my own opinions where Widgery's theories seem to me to be open to misapprehension. In this way, section by section, I shall deal with the whole work. My general aim is the eradication of errors, the strengthening of weak points whenever possible and the construction of a coherent and sound scheme of educational reform. It is a pleasure to know at the outset that but little correction will be necessary, nor, I think, will it be easy to point out anything seriously unsound in the scheme as it now stands. But it is, I think, capable of some little amplification here and there.

I. DIRECTION OF REFORM.

We learn foreign languages for two reasons—a lower and simply utilitarian one—to hold our own in the world—a higher one—to free ourselves from insular onesidedness and acquire a new soul by penetrating into a new realm of thought.

Nowadays the educated man is saddled with at least five languages, and we try, but try in vain, to carry in our schools the same heavy weight. Something must be cut out.

Our great reformers, Rousseau, Pestalozzi, Froebel, have been the sources of mighty inspirations, but they failed in system. We need now rather some powerful organiser, well trained in philosophy, in logic, in psychology, one who will do actual school work for some years and then clear for us the jungle of educational literature.

Our new educational reformer must combine the desire of Comenius for widening the realm of positive knowledge with Pestalozzi's enthusiasm for heightening the intellectual powers. He must wed the formal education of the Middle Ages to the spreading science of the moderns.*—Pp. 5, 6 of " The Teaching of Languages in Schools."

* Compare Section XIII. of Theories.

The second paragraph above touches a very serious fault in our modern system of education in schools. 'A boy of eight or nine comes to school for the first time and at once begins to learn English, French and Latin. Within two or three years, not seldom, he begins to dabble in Greek or German. And then we have, quite naturally, ludicrous muddles in vocabulary, and a boy puts down "canis" for "chien" in his French exercise or gives "mère" for "Mutter" in his German lesson. We laugh—and forget the blunder. But do we ever sit down and consider what it means? Does it ever strike us that we are making an unreasonable demand on the boy's mind? We ask him to retain at the same time, and at a period when his faculties are less than half-grown, three, or even four, different vocables for the idea represented by "dog" or "mother." The demand is unreasonable enough and the consequence regretable enough, were they limited to the vocabulary. But this blunder in vocabulary betrays a mental confusion which has far more serious results in a far more important direction—in idiom. If a boy finds it hard to keep clear in his mind the formal difference between four vocables for the same idea, what hope is there of his retaining any clear conception of the variation in the collocation of a set of vocables constituting an "idiom" in four, or even three, different languages? Is not this the reason why the average boy writes Latin sentences in his English Composition and English sentences in his German Exercise and, oftener still, sentences that are neither French, German, Latin, Greek nor English even? Surely it is this multiplicity and confusion of linguistic forms which makes the attainment of any extensive notion of "idiom" impossible in school life even to a

Sixth Form boy. If we could reform our system so far as to confine a boy's attention to English till he is twelve, adding then French and German till he is sixteen and leaving Latin and Greek for the age when he enters College, we should attain very much more satisfactory results. The vast quantity of time saved would render possible a far more intensive and comprehensive study of each of the five languages. That intensity and comprehensiveness would enable the teacher to saturate a boy's mind with one language at a time. Only such saturation can create a sensitiveness for idiom. That inexplicable part of language cannot be taught by little emasculated scraps of the language, doctored out of sound and sense and collected in exercise books, or acquired by committing pages of paradigms to memory. It can only be absorbed *through the pores of the mind*, so to speak, by constant reading of connected and idiomatic prose and constant listening to the real language itself, unsimplified by the excision of grammatical irregularities, unadulterated by the insertion of unrythmical and incoherent substitutes for the natural idiom, such as we find in the very best of exercise books. It is not that we learn too many languages, but that we learn too many of them at the same time. Instead of running four languages side by side for ten years, we should give the first five years to the most important and most fundamental one (for an Englishman)—to English. In the remaining five years English should have just enough time to keep it up and add gradually to the knowledge of it already acquired, and the rest of the time should be divided between, say, French and German. Working in this way, a boy of sixteen would get such a firm hold of the "spirit of language," would know so much French

German and English, that he would plunge into Greek, Latin, or any other language he might require, with a confidence and intelligence, born of experience, that would remove a good half of the difficulties of learning a new tongue. The result would be that at five-and-twenty, instead of having the most superficial of superficial smatterings of five languages, he would know three at least of them thoroughly and be able to make a very fair show in several others. A curious comment on this fact is the remark of a headmaster who is one of the staunchest defenders of the present ineffective system. " I would guarantee," said he to me, "that if I were to take up, say, Japanese now, I should know vastly more of it in a year than if I had taken it up as a boy, because [Note his reason !] I have learnt how to learn languages." Precisely so ; and yet he makes his boys learn four languages together at the age of twelve or thirteen. Shall we ever realise in full force the appalling failure of a boy who spends nine years in learning French and then emerges from the Sixth Form utterly incapable of holding five minutes conversation with a Frenchman ? We have too long laid the blame on the stupidity of the average boy. Let us have the candour to acknowledge, though so late, that the failure is due to the psychologic stupidity of our present system and the pusillanimous conservatism which makes us bear any amount of disappointment with our children and waste any amount of money on a sham education rather than try a new system and boldly face its risks. But in " bearing those ills we have, rather than fly to others that we know not of" we too often turn our backs upon many a blessing that beckons us to better things. A fussy nervousness is at the bottom of our present system. We cannot learn a few things at a time and trust that we shall live long enough to learn others. We must be learning English, French, German, Greek and Latin at the same time, so that we may feel that we are actually learning them. We cannot learn only English, French and German, and have faith that we shall live till we are sixteen to take up Greek and Latin. At least this is the state of mind of the average parent, who, moreover, is the slave of that arbitrary modern institution—the competitive examination. There is little hope of reform till the Examination Boards determine to require only three languages up to the age of, say, sixteen, and offer no inducements to learn—I should say, to pretend to learn—any more before that age. Want of courage to rearrange our scholastic scheme, want of faith to postpone a part of our learning in order that we may first get a better knowledge of another portion of it, are at the bottom of our failure to learn any language effectively in these days. *

With regard to Widgery's demand for a powerful organiser to clear the jungle of educational literature, the translator of Gouin's "Art of Teaching and Studying Languages" claims that M. Gouin has in great part accomplished the labour and organised the work. As a matter of fact the trouble lies deeper. The jungle would soon be cleared, there would be no lack of pioneers to clear it, if the educational public would only wake up to the *necessity* of a general clearance. We want rather some benignant despot, who could gather into his heart all the disappointment of all the unhappy parents that pay heavy school fees for years and then discover that they must further pinch themselves to get special "coaching" for their poor Tom, Dick or Harry, or to send him abroad for a year or two, nominally to finish

F.

his knowledge of French and German, but really to make a beginning of teaching him those languages (for all he got of them in school was mere intellectual leather and prunella) before he can enter the counting-house or the pedagogue's chair. We want some despot who shall feel all this, and give it voice and issue a decree that this waste of time is no more to be tolerated, and that we must begin to do in school what we do out of school when we send our boy abroad—*i.e.*, immerse him over head and ears in the sounds and idioms of the foreign tongue *ab initio*, so that from the very beginning he may learn, not such banausic nonsense as " My sister is tall, but yours is short," not " parler," not " finir," nor any such grammatical pedantries, but French — French sounds, French rhythm and French idiom. Given such a despot—who need not have any carnal shape, but may well be a consensus of public indignation finding voice in a public conference of parents—to rouse up head-masters from the lethargy of nineteen centuries of grammatical pedantry, we should soon have the jungle clear and the bright rays of the sun and the warm airs of a free heaven bringing forth ripe crops of boys who could read and write and speak, not French and German only, but their own English, of which so many of them know such a marvellous little.

The last paragraph I have quoted above supplies food for much unhappy reflection—unhappy because the difficulties it reminds us of are so vast and the means for overcoming them so scarce. There has never been any lack of desire to widen the realm of positive know-ledge since mediæval scholasticism was exploded by the renascence of modern science; but "enthusiasm for heightening the intellectual powers ! " Where shall we look for this enthusiasm ?—in the housemaster, who sooner or later is almost compelled to look upon boys as so many pounds, shillings and pence more or less towards the maintenance of a wife and family in decent comfort ?—in the private coach, who is paid to show his pupil how to avoid everything that does not " pay " in examinations ?—in the assistant-master, who must believe, or at least profess, that everything his chief does *must* be right under penalty of not being recommended for his five or ten pounds rise at the end of the year, if indeed he be so fortunate as to have a rise at all ?—in the head-master, who must think twice before he sanctions the introduction of a new and improved class-book, lest he should have a visit from " Mother " or " Father " to know the reason of another half-crown in the terminal bill ?—in the principal, who dare not keep a backward boy down in the class best suited to his slowly develop-ing mind, lest he should hear the ominous remark " Oh, Tom doesn't get on at this school ! Let's send him to Mr. So-and-so's " ? And supposing all these difficulties absent—supposing we may count on a courageous chief with enlightened views and the determination necessary to give effect to them, and supposing we have to deal with an intelligent and trustful parent, who will allow the chief a free hand in the education of the child, how many assistant teachers can a chief count on in a staff of, say, twenty to get up an enthusiasm for the psycho-logic development of the boys in his school apart from their success in that acquisitive faculty which will be tested at the terminal examination ? And yet surely this " heightening of the intellectual powers " is the *summum bonum* of education. The greatest achievement of educational activity is surely the moulding of a mind,

not the creation of a good writer of exercises in Latin prose
composition, nor a faultless reciter of τύπτω. But if we
are to expect enthusiasm for psychologic development of
the pupil in the teacher, we must make that species of
development the goal of the teacher's efforts, the crown
of his activity. This cannot be till we give the prize at
the end of the term to the boy who displays the greatest
intelligence and originality in his answers and the most
supple thinking faculty, not to the one who gives the
most faultless translation of an artificial phrase that
belongs to no language known outside the exercise book,
or writes down the most complete list of "exceptional"
forms that are never heard in real life or met with in
ordinary standard writers.

Among reforms not specially indicated in "The Teaching of Languages" the secularisation of education was a
strong point with Widgery. He returned from his visit
to Berlin with a firmer disbelief than ever in the
"spiritual bigamist," as he used to call the man whose
right hand is given to the church, his left only to the
school. It is an irritating subject, but one that has been
already well thrashed out in the educational world. To
many minds it is a mere truism to say that instruction in
religious dogma, as distinct from the ethical education of
the mind and character, if a duty at all, is the duty of
the parent and not of the schoolmaster. Belief in the
truth of this fact seems to be growing and must certainly
lead sooner or later to the complete secularisation of
education. It is hardly necessary to discuss the matter
here. But I believe that considerable light would be
thrown on the subject from the parent's point of view, if
some parents would bestir themselves and inquire what
this much-lauded "religious instruction" in schools

really amounts to. Speaking from behind the scenes, I can assure parents that they would be astonished to discover how much mere secular fact and how little real religion is taught in a Scripture class. In some schools any and every master is considered competent to take a Scripture class without any question as to his own convictions, or absence of convictions, regarding Holy Writ. As for the religious influence of the Rev. Headmaster's daily ministrations, do not we assistant-masters know that Morning Prayers afford a most convenient opportunity for a boy to finish a belated exercise—to say nothing of a game of Noughts and Crosses or Spelicans under the desk! Alas for religious instruction at the hands of the schoolmaster!

I have already noted Widgery's strong opinions on the advisability, the necessity, of training† for the teacher and need not dilate again on a matter of such obvious importance. There are, however, some teachers who openly profess the appalling belief that, to make a great teacher, a man needs no more than to know a great deal! But such teachers, being obviously deficient in the elementary faculty of distinguishing between acquisitive and communicative power, may be considered past praying for and not worth powder and shot. I shall leave them to the certain reprehension of the reader's better sense. Not all men who have eyes can see, nor all who see consider and take heed.

II. CLASSICS *v.* MODERN LANGUAGES.

For new inspiration and hope we must turn ever and again to Greece, the bright home of our literature and art.* Latin has had its day. In the intellectual world Rome is but the

* See reference on p. 70.   † See p. 51.

pale reflex of Athens. Latin has died twice—once as the language of ancient Rome, a second time as the *lingua franca* of Europe.

We shall be told we cannot understand modern Europe without a knowledge of antiquity. Well, the study of origins is not everybody's business, and our religion, our politics, our painting* do not spring from Greece or Rome. The first small beginnings of our science only are found in Greece.

The Classics are said to be superior to modern languages as a means of culture.† Who has a right to affirm that this is so? The latter have never been seriously tried in schools.

"Men keenly seeking reasons for the study of the language of Greece and Rome have been able to find none better than that of the so-called 'mental training.' As far as my experi-

* These two statements seem contradictory.

† "Diderot is not able to discern what, in pedaggoy, is the true title of the classics to nobility—that they are an admirable instrument of intellectual gymnastics, and the surest and also the most convenient means of acquiring those qualities of justness, of precision, and of clearness, which are needed by all conditions of men, and are applicable to all the special employments of life"—COMPAYRÉ. M. Compayré here departs from his usual good sense and penetration to make a series of unwarrantable assumptions. Doubtless the classics are an admirable instrument of intellectual gymnastics, but there is no warrant for asserting that they are the surest and also the most convenient means of acquiring qualities of justness, of precision and clearness. The study of the modern languages affords an equally sure means and, in virtue of the facilities offered for their more complete study by the fact of their living state, they also afford a far more convenient means than the dead languages. The loose incorrectness and partiality of M. Compayré's dictum furnish a fine satire on the justness, precision and clearness which he claims as a monopoly of classical studies. The shallow arrogance of the average classicist has only been equalled by the presumptuous scorn of the militant scientist. The classics are excellent for adding grace to culture, but they have no monopoly of those more solid qualities which are the natural fruit of all honest mental effort in any direction.

ence goes men who devote themselves to the study of Greek and Latin grammar are not markedly superior to other mortals in the possession of well-balanced minds. Unless some more powerful reason can be brought forward, the classics should be banished from our schools."—BOECKH.

Another great advantage of the modern languages over the ancient as a school subject is the effective criticism to which our work can be subjected. If a Frenchman or a German comes into our class-rooms, he detects instantly the slightest mistakes in our pronunciation, in our language, in our explanations. Can the classical student obtain such efficient supervision?

Again, as we are nearer in time to our modern classics, not only do we understand them, we feel them. Boeckh once finished a lecture on Pindar thus—"You have heard the commentaries and the various readings of one of the finest odes of Pindar. If you ask me to point out the passages that moved Greece to a transport of admiration, I must answer, *I do not know.*"

In school we must be content to understand* the ancients. The modern languages we must learn to speak, to feel, to write.—Pp. 6-8.

The following detached statements, culled from letters, &c., seem to bear more or less directly on this section.

The meagre results of our Latin teaching are mainly due to our asking from the child more than we give him.

Ask the apple tree to produce pears by pricking in a few drops of pear juice every day and then ask the English boy to do Latin prose.

Modern Latin prose is as like real Latin as Wagner's homunculus is like a man.

Sentence must always precede grammar and vocabulary. Therefore at first in Latin and Greek the scholar has no

* In Greek, Rollin censures the study of themes, and reduces the study of this language to the understanding of authors.—COMPAYRÉ.

preparation to do but merely to repeat what the teacher says.

French ought to precede Latin. The psychologic spring from English to Latin is too great for an ordinary school boy.

A grave objection to classics from a psychologic point of view is that the child has nothing to couple his knowledge on to.

The teachers of classics have ceased to be the high priests of humanity. They have become collectors of specimens for their Museum of Philology.

Latin is the sere and yellow leaf on the tree of knowledge that is now shooting out new and mightier branches than the world has yet seen.

For those who can read the signs of the times " This block coming down " has been written for a long while over the classical building. But the men who dwell in it are so rich that they have shored it up on every side. When will the ground be cleared for English hands to rear English homes for English hearts?

After these extracts I need scarcely draw attention to Widgery's utter disbelief in the classicist and his firm faith in the supreme educational value of the vernacular. But we need not enter very deeply into the question of classical teaching. That its importance has been much overrated in past times is generally granted now among enlightened teachers, and the remarks extracted from Widgery's work fairly cover the indictment against the classical *régime*. One or two points must, however, be touched on here.

A reviewer in the Tacoma *Morning Globe* says : " Mr. Widgery is probably right in saying that Latin could be dispensed with for mental training and replaced by modern languages. He is right, too, in saying that the study of the ancient classics as conducted in our high schools and second-class institutions is far less profitable than would be the same time devoted to the study of modern languages. But when that has been said, all is said. To men who seek the very highest culture, who desire to become familiar with the greatest intellects of all time, a knowledge of Greek is absolutely necessary." But this last point has never been in contention. No one was more ready to acknowledge the surpassing excellence of the Greek literature than Widgery, nor did he ever deny that the highest culture would be incomplete without a knowledge of that literature. He merely contended that our present method of obtaining that knowledge is an ineffective one, and that we should acquire a more perfect knowledge of Greek and Latin by postponing our study of them till a later period in our mental development. He contended for two things —first, that the early years of a boy's education should be devoted to training his mind in the art of learning and thinking ; and secondly, that for this purpose Greek and Latin could claim no superiority over the vernacular combined with French and German. In another direction he asserted, and with reason, that not all boys have the capacity, or the desire, to "seek the very highest culture," and that for them the study of Greek and Latin is a waste of energy. This waste is emphasised by the two striking advantages of the vernacular over Greek and Latin—the advantage of a vast quantity of ready-made raw material, picked up in the ordinary intercourse of daily life, at the disposal of the teacher for practice and illustration, and that other and greater advantage that every word committed to memory, every idiom absorbed, every sentence constructed, will be of practical use in the future life and mental development of the boy. To nine boys out of ten all the raw material absorbed in the Greek or Latin class is utterly lost five years after leaving school. But the same amount of material acquired in an English class remains by him all his life, and any material acquired in French or German can be worked up into a highly valuable form by a few visits to the Continent. This difference in the relative " future utility " of the classics and the modern languages is so obvious, that the classicists soon abandoned the contrary assertion and took refuge in saying that the classics are superior, not for future use, but as a " means of culture," an " instrument of mental training." " French and German," says the *School Guardian*, " are acquired for exceedingly different purposes than (*sic*) those of Greek and Latin. The former are for practical use and they can never be used practically so long as the student consciously thinks of his conjugations, declensions, and genders, and is haunted by lists of irregularities. Why, however, should not the two processes go hand in hand ? Because French is recognised as being alive, there is no reason for leaving the schoolboy altogether ignorant of the logical processes which are absorbed so well from Latin grammar." No reason whatever why the " two processes " should not " go hand in hand " *after* a certain point ; for life is very short and the practical must always come before the ornamental and theoretical. The languages a boy will most immediately need when he leaves school are English, French and German. Now these can be thoroughly and expeditiously acquired only by an intensive and constant study (The *Guardian* concedes this by its remarks about "conscious thinking ") requiring a very large portion of school time. Therefore let the major part of school time be given to them and afterwards let him who seeks the "highest culture,' or shows any inclination to become a linguist pure and simple, study the dead languages, which are no longer wanted in real life. As things are at present a grave injustice and injury is done to the boy who wants to enter into practical life directly he leaves school. A vast part of his school life is wasted in studying what he will throw away directly he passes out of the school gates for the last time and, in consequence, he has not time enough to learn the languages he will want, when he leaves, in anything more than the most superficial manner. For the making of one classical scholar, who, to speak candidly and without academic prejudice, will never be anything more than an ornament to society, injury, perhaps lifelong, is done to nine practical men who intend to devote their lives, more or less consciously, to strengthening the foundations and amplifying the super-structure of that society from whose strength the orna-mental classical scholar draws his physical and intellectual nourishment.* How long will society tolerate this enormity? How long will parents remain blind to the wasting of their money and the defeating of their desires in regard to their children? Then again the last clause of the *Guardian's* criticism begs the whole question. *Does* Latin grammar enable a boy "to absorb so well the logical processes," or is this a mere delusion of the classical mind? This is the very question in dispute. Here comes in Widgery's pithy remark that the modern languages have "never been seriously tried in schools" as a means of mental training in logical processes. And

---

* I am not decrying ornamental studies *per se*. I am merely objecting to their undue predomination.

then we have Boeckh's confession that, so far as his experience goes, "men who devote themselves to the study of Greek and Latin grammar are not markedly superior to other mortals in the possession of well-balanced minds." Alas, no! On the contrary they are no better than other specialists in the narrowness that prevents them from seeing the soulless littleness of the gigantic fabric of artificial "learned lumber," which the misdirected energy of centuries has reared up in the irresponsible atmosphere and wealthy leisure of the great academies. Indeed the study of grammar, which concerns itself merely with the classification of existing material and makes ceaseless attempts to stereotype language and choke with arbitrary rules the avenues of its growth, most directly and inevitably fosters mental sterility and encourages a lordly intellectual insolence, which sets up its own fancies for standards of right and refuses to allow language the free growth and unlimited modification of form and meaning that constitute the supreme charm of poetry and the master-nerve of prose. Logical processes are common to all languages, and the synthesis of modern German is as good a training in logical synthesis as the most formal grammarian's most formal Latin.

Widgery's remarks about the possibility of effective criticism of teaching in modern languages and the facilities for æsthetic appreciation offered by them are too true, too weighty, to admit of dispute. Such facilities belong to any living language as compared with the most perfect of the dead—Greek. It is said that classical scholars acquire a keen sensitiveness for the æsthetic subtleties of the dead languages. They may or they may not. But it is open to question whether the appreciation is not almost entirely illusive and artificial. Can a sound which has never been heard be recreated by the imagination? Can the charm of an æsthetic beauty, which has never been absorbed through the pores of the mind by a sojourn in the very atmosphere and amid the very surroundings of its nativity, be recreated and re-imbibed by force of the imagination of a different race in a later and most distant age? It is doubtful—it is improbable—it is impossible! But grant its possibility for the sake of argument. If it be possible to do all this for a dead language, what can be impossible with a language that may still be heard in all its latest perfection of beauty and development and still studied in the land of its birth among the surroundings of its most perfect exposition? What then but the assurance of academic prejudice could dare to deny the superiority of the tongues of Goethe, Dante, Hugo, and Shakespeare over those of Homer and Virgil as instruments of linguistic education in these latter days? Truly the insolence of learning has waxed fat in the groves of Academe!

III. REARRANGEMENT.

For the future our school time must be saved by limiting the teaching of the classics strictly to the acquirement of the power to read them, except for the classical student.—P. 6.

Another important task for the future reformer is the effective grouping of our school subjects. At present they run in unconnected straight lines—they ought to spread in concentric circles.

The beginning of our language-teaching must of necessity be English. Around English alone can our teaching be properly concentrated. In English alone can we make any attempt at a proper study of grammar as such, for in the mother tongue alone have we enough preliminary knowledge to arrange into a scientific scheme.

"English is of all existing languages perhaps the best for explaining the development of language in general."— TYLOR. From the Teutonic words that passed into currency among the Finns and Lapps in the first century, we can follow the course of our language for close on two thousand years. We can see it pass from an inflexional stage, nearly as full as that of Greek and Latin, to the most analytic in the world. And yet, with all this incessant change, with this unceasing incorporation of new elements, we have retained much of the old. Our consonantal system is nearer than any other allied modern language to the Primitive Teutonic.

English may be roughly classed " as an isolating language which is passing into the agglutinative stage with a few traditional inflexions. Hence the value of English as a preparation for the study of language generally, when studied rationally. It enables us to watch many linguistic phenomena in the very process of formation."—SWEET.

By a good preliminary training then in our own tongue we ought to acquire a general framework into which we can place afterwards as many languages as we please. " The richness of our sound-system, both consonants and vowels, the delicacy of our intonation and stress distinctions, and the comparatively rational nature of our grammar ought to give us great advantages " as linguists.—SWEET. Pp. 8–10 of T. of L.

Very little need be added to the above remarks. Few practical teachers will fail to see that the postponement of Latin and Greek would immediately make a great many hours in the week available for a more intensive study of English, French and German. Other subjects too might benefit by the gain. At present we have from twenty to twenty-five hours in the week for actual teaching. Into this short time we endeavour to cram a large quantity of Latin, a fair amount of French, a little German, far too little English, just a taste of History and Geography, as much Mathematics as we can manage, and an apology for Science. Not content with this absurdity, we struggle hard to stow away in odd corners Music, Drawing and Constructive Geometry, Shorthand, Book-keeping, Drill, Gymnastics and Carpentering! Here are sixteen subjects, and I have known a poor boy of twelve attempt to do a little at thirteen of them in the course of his twenty-five hours every week! No wonder the average boy is so "stupid." The strange thing is that he is not grey at sixteen and in a lunatic asylum at twenty-one. Of course every one knows how he avoids this fate. He does not learn all these things—he only pretends to! He merely dabbles in them and never gets any real knowledge of any one of them. It would be impossible for him to study one-third that number of subjects with the intensity and concentration he will apply to French, or German, or Latin, when he leaves school and goes to a "coach" to be prepared for a scholarship or the counting-house. But then, we shall hear, a boy doesn't go to school to learn any particular thing; he goes to have his mind trained—in fact to be educated. Let the parent who looks to have his son taught to speak French and German and write English take note of this sagacious objection. As a matter of fact the present system does not educate a boy's mind. It merely stupefies it with the infusion of a plethora of incoherent and too often utterly useless information. Were he confined to a thorough mastery of some few choice subjects, he would undergo the same amount of mental training without any tendency to confusion and stupefaction, and at the end of his training he would have at his disposal a thorough knowledge of a certain few subjects—a knowledge com-

prehensive enough to admit of practical application,
instead of a superficial smattering of twelve or fifteen
subjects, no one of which he knows well enough to put
into actual use. It is a wonderful delusion, this theory
that unlimited variety of mental diet produces a higher
development than a choice and limited dietary. We
feed the mind of a boy now as if we were to compound
his dinner of every article in the shops of the butcher,
baker, grocer and greengrocer. Unhappily, while in
such case Death would speedily enlighten our folly, the
tenacity of the mind enables it to defy for years the
destructive influence of this appalling diet of hetero-
geneous knowledge, or rather, while any one can
understand the language of physical death, it takes a
shrewd intellect and much intimate observation to
detect the necrosis of brain tissue and the murder of
mind. It is high time parents looked into the number
of subjects taught to boys—I should say, shovelled into
their craniums, there to lie unused till the boy grows old
enough to escape from the tyranny of the pedagogue
and fling the rubbish out of his mind.

The effective grouping of school subjects is a hard
matter, which can only be simplified and rendered scientific when we agree to have fewer subjects taught to
individual boys. Till that point is granted, discussion is
useless.

The remark that "by a good preliminary training in
our own tongue we ought to acquire a general framework
into which we can place afterwards as many languages
as we please" is a notable one. Many minds will be
struck at once by the truth of the theory. Such a framework, made of English, would render the subsequent
acquirement of other languages, by fitting them into it,

far easier than learning them by our present method of contemporaneous study. But there are others who, saturated with the customs of the old system, will view the theory with doubt and even utter disbelief. Nothing but actual experiment can finally settle the question. Why should we not try? Almost everybody, when the point is pushed home, is obliged to acknowledge that the present system does not produce satisfactory results. Since, then, the new system suggested is based on sound psychologic considerations, why not try it? It can but fail, as the present system, which does not rest on sound psychologic considerations, has failed, and it may succeed. As usual a timid conservatism stands in the way of progress. But some day despair will give us courage and we shall at last advance to better things.

IV. STUDY OF ENGLISH.

With regard to the study of English I venture to propose the following :—

Increase the reading-lessons in it. Let them be mainly in modern prose.

Teach the very first elements of phonetics and grammar purely inductively.

Pay special attention to the vocabulary, grouping the words which children meet in their reader under psychologic and grammatical categories.

At ten, or earlier, begin to work backwards, say to the age of Anne.

With Shakespeare, the child's attention should be directed to variations from modern usage, and the beginnings of a sense of the development of language made.

At eleven, we might start French, reading at the same time a little Chaucer

Between twelve and thirteen, we might just touch Old

F

English by means of a short Reader with the text on one
side and the necessary grammar on the other. Some slight
knowledge of the laws of language should be introduced,
analogy and the regular changes of sound at least being
fully illustrated.

The child of twelve and a half is now fit to begin German.
After a year's study, bifurcation must come in.

The future classical student could begin Latin at fourteen*
and gradually drop French, begin Greek at sixteen and
devote his time to the classics.

The student of the modern languages could now begin a
scientific study of his three, keeping English always in the
centre.—Pp. 10, 11.

The above scheme may be considered the heart and
centre of Widgery's proposed reform in the educational
curriculum.   Wonderfully bold, it is at the same time
thoroughly scientific and rests on intelligent psychologic
considerations.   I fear, however, we shall not see in our
day a headmaster bold enough to put it into practice.
Let us consider it seriatim.

"Increase the reading lessons."

This means several things, the most important being—
soak the adolescent mind in the sounds and idioms of its
native tongue. Do not give it scraps of sentences and
phrases, doctored out of idiom and emasculated by simplification. Do not give it an incoherent mass of
irregularities and anomalies to learn by heart. Let it
absorb irregularities and anomalies, as well as regularities
and normals, *through the pores of the mind*. Let the
child feel the language, not analyse it. In short, let him

---

* Comenius fixed twelve as the age for beginning Latin. Diderot
postpones classical studies to the pupil's nineteenth or twentieth
year.

learn it by Nature's method, as he would if he did
nothing but run about the world trying to express his
own ideas of men and things to other children and trying
to understand the communications they make to him.
Let him learn genders and numbers, conjugations and
declensions and all the concords, not by logical analysis,
but by practical experience, in the same way as a literary
artist like Stevenson learns to make sweet-sounding
phrases and as Swinburne learns to mould the rolling
assonance of

> " The wrathful woful marge of earth and sea,"

or Vergil to compass the magic of

> " Quadrupedante putrem sonitu quatit ungula campum."

These suggestions apply to the teaching of grammar and
phonetics inductively.

" Group the words according to psychologic categories."

Here again Widgery strikes a high note and pleads for
attention to psychologic development of the child's mind
apart from the mere acquisition of mental material. The
adolescent mind naturally and instinctively forms these
psychologic categories for itself. The tendency is to be
encouraged and nourished. It is easier to remember a
word, a meaning, in association with others that convey
an associated idea. It is easier in dealing with lists of
words to remember "mare" in connection with "horse"
than in connection with "bitch," though a list of feminine
nouns would contain "mare," and "bitch" but not
"horse." Similarly, it is easier to remember "mare" in
connection with "bitch," both falling into the grammatical category of "nouns," than to remember either of

them in connection with "drive," which belongs to the different category of "verbs." In every case help out the memory with the reason. Never lay the whole burden upon the memory. Do not discourage memory, but be most tender and considerate of reason, the nobler faculty of the two.

"Back to Anne at ten."

This is a stumbling-block. The late Mr. Quick, in a private communication to Widgery, thought this "a large dose by ten." It is an insignificant matter. The age was fixed by Widgery quite arbitrarily and must of necessity be a matter of opinion to be settled by experiment and observation. The important point is that we *should* go back in this manner. The exact hour and age of retrogression experience will decide.

Note the scientific development introduced with Shakespeare. Observation is now to be invited and encouraged and the comparative faculty called into play.

"Chaucer at eleven."

Here again Mr. Quick interposes, from excess of timidity, I think. "Stories of Chaucer, yes—language, no, say I." (Quick.) Experiment only can decide whether this is asking too much of the eleven-year-old mind. But a child of that age is not troubled by the rigidities of spelling, and I doubt if he would be much inconvenienced by the orthographic peculiarities of the "well of English undefyled." Chaucer, except for the meaning of unknown words (which the child would have to learn in the same manner as he does his French and Latin vocabulary), would probably be just as easy to him to read as his own curious efforts in English composition. Let us try the experiment—that is all Widgery asks, and he is willing to abide the consequences. We should be equally brave.

These remarks apply also to Old English at twelve or thirteen and perhaps with greater force, since the confusion and foreign appearance introduced by the French element in Chaucer is here absent. Surely no boy of twelve would be much alarmed by, for example, such language as this drawn at random from the "Old English Chronicle": "Her gefor Aelfred Aþulfing. syx nihtum aer ealra haligra maessan. Se waes cyning ofer eall Ongelcyn. butan ðaem daele þe under Dena onwalde waes." Certainly it would be no harder than the German and Latin sentences he is expected to tackle about this time of life.

The juxtaposition of text and grammar on opposite pages of the Reader was a great point with Widgery. It is part and parcel of his principle that the grammar should be drawn out of the text and viewed in close proximity with the living language of which it forms the bony framework, or skeleton, as it were. The help which such a contemporaneous view of grammar and language, logical concord and literary cohesion, gives the memory in retaining the classified facts of grammar has never been thoroughly recognised and sufficiently valued. It is far easier to remember a gender, number, or person inflexion when one sees it actually embodied in a living sentence than when one learns it out of all thought-connection in a grammatical paradigm. The grammar of the text on the left page should therefore be on the right (opposite) page, close at hand and ready for reference and comparison with the language of which it is the analytical abstract. This again is Nature's method./ A child at first talks about "foots" till it has heard sentences in which the plural is given as "feet." This it soon grasps and retains, while one might lecture to it for a week about "sonants" and "mutation" and yet fail to teach it the right plural of "foot." Very often when a small boy cannot give the plural of "foot" straight off, it may be got from him at once by asking him to complete some such sentence as this—"I have been for a very long walk. The soles of both my . . . . are quite sore." The fact is the boy knows the plural well enough as an integral part of the unit of speech—the spoken sentence —but not as an isolated element in a grammatical list. The little experiment I have suggested will speak volumes to the intelligent teacher.

"Laws of language."   "Changes of sound."

The child's mind is now ripe enough to justify us in adding to his practice in linguistic synthesis some little analytic knowledge of the various components of speech and of the manner in which they—not, are put, but— grow together. That which he has imbibed uncon- sciously, much as he drinks in ozone, he must now begin to analyse consciously. Our present system makes a mistake in introducing this conscious attitude too early, in fact at the beginning of the process of unconscious absorption. The conscious attitude should not be assumed till the unconscious absorption is so far advanced that a considerable quantity of raw material has been acquired and is ready for conscious investigation. Now is the time to draw an intelligent attention to those linguistic laws which have long been obeyed instinctively and unconsciously. They will now be a help to the memory without danger of being a confusion to the immature infancy, so to speak, of the ratiocinative faculty. They will now enlarge the mind by playing upon the capacity for reasoning, by this time grown to some strength through the accumulation of a number of small occasional and voluntary efforts, instead of stupefying and stunting its development by overtaxing it when half-formed and weak.

A knowledge of sound-change will now be very useful in helping the memory by assigning a reason for such anomalies as "thief—thieves," "dogs" pronounced "dogz," and so forth. It is a cardinal mistake in teaching to point out the phonetic law underlying such a phenomenon as "dogs—dogz" when the first example of it occurs, for the simple reason that a single example of a law is not sufficient to create upon the mind the impression that the phenomenon is the outcome of a general law. Only when a great number of examples have become familiar to the mind through frequent meeting and absorption as mere raw material of grammar should they be drawn together and their natural falling into a single category be pointed out. Then the obvious frequency of the phenomenon creates a strong impression that the frequency is due to a general law, and the law, being discovered * as a striking peculiarity, interests the mind, and interest, as all teachers know, is the mainstay of memory. "Who," says Widgery elsewhere, "has failed to see the pleasure in a child's face when a rule is confirmed by the rise in his mind of examples that had

---

* The theory that learning should be a process of re-discovery, invented by Bacon, was elaborated by Condillac in his *Grammaire*. Spencer makes it a fundamental law. Bain asserts that it can only be applied occasionally. But a judicious teacher will find many occasions.

lain unnoticed till then in his mind?" So the law is remembered and its illustrations, tied, as it were, into a bouquet by the law, are not forgotten as if they were isolated flowers of speech.

"Bifurcation."

Little need be said under this head, as bifurcation is one of the recognised customs of modern education. The only thing to be insisted on is the fact that it is introduced too early in school life. Latin is begun at ten and Greek at twelve. I have already given reasons against this, the chief being the necessity of gaining time for a more intensive study of the three most important languages, English, French and German, and for a more thorough training of the child-mind in the methods and principles of language as exemplified in living languages before attacking the more difficult and less appreciable dead tongues. Another point of importance is that Latin and Greek—which may, not unjustly, be called the ornamental languages—should be taught only to those whose future work in life requires that higher culture which a knowledge of the dead languages completes, or to those who mean to make a study of these dead tongues their life-work. For others they are a waste of energy and a most pernicious infliction when, as often happens, the brain is not of the quality that can take with benefit this higher culture. Injudicious culture is a common fault and many brains are stunted in growth, if not utterly destroyed, by the attempt to force them into effort of which they are incapable or colour them with a pigment which to them is poison.

The necessity (for Englishmen) of keeping English always in the centre of the modern languages has also been pointed out. It is difficult to understand how any sane mind could give it any other position, and yet our native tongue is the most neglected of all the languages we study. We are too apt to think that, because the fact of its being our mother-tongue enables us to acquire a working knowledge of it without special effort, there is no need to acquire a knowledge of its theoretical structure and literary capacities. This is a lamentable mistake, which we have begun, though only in late years, to remedy, but still in a very half-hearted fashion. Patriotism, so foolishly developed in many mean directions, would do well to busy itself with the glories of English literature and the possibilities of the English tongue.

V. Language.

We may now pass to a discussion of the principles set up by modern philology, and their application to school teaching. We must first endeavour to get some sort of clear idea of the nature of language.

One of the main hindrances to a just view of language has been the use of similes. Still worse, terms proper to morals were intruded into science, and we hear of phonetic decay, loss, degradation, corruption, as if languages had in them something inherently wrong. The new recuperative force, replacing and improving the old, was conveniently left out of sight.

The science of language has now definitely taken its place as a mental science. Speech is not a thing that can be handled or seen. It is mental activity manifesting itself through physiological means.

When we speak we are quite unconscious of all the complicated movements in our mind and body. The proof of unconscious activity is one of the greatest triumphs of modern psychology. The neglect of this capacity of the mind is the chief defect of our language teaching. By exercise power consciously acquired can be translated into power manifested unconsciously.

With the acquirement of what we consciously teach runs the unconscious formation of certain beliefs and prejudices. By beginning Latin too early, we encourage the theory that languages are to be learnt by the eye, that the letter is more important than the sound, that there is no need to express one's own thoughts in a foreign tongue, that languages are built up mosaic-like out of paradigms and syntax rules, and many other views diametrically opposed to the truth.

The whole process of speech consists in the reproduction by memory of forms already heard, and in the shaping by analogy of new ones on their model. When a set of these groups has been made in the mind unconsciously, forms lying outside them constitute the "exceptions." These are the remnants of earlier normal groups which occurred in every-day speech so often that they became fixed in the mind firmly enough to resist change. Now, as these forms can be retained only by a pure act of the memory, the child is more likely to make mistakes in them than elsewhere, and a fair length of time must be allowed before we can expect them to be accurately reproduced. It is hard to imagine anything more unsound psychologically than the method in our grammars of putting a list of "exceptions" immediately after the rule, often without a single example obeying the latter. These exceptions will probably not be met with in the school-life of a boy, and they ought to be felt as "exceptions" when they are first met with.

Not only must our rule be invariably derived from the language, but enough examples must be given at a time to make the rule spring up as it were by itself. The master must know how by skilful questioning to entice out of the child what lies dormant in his mind. Then, when the unconscious knowledge rises into the light of the conscious, the mind comes down with a snap on the example and the rule, and it is no burden to retain them both.—Pp. 19-22.

Extract.—That delightful intercourse, the charm of teaching, when eye meets eye with a half questioning look, while the boys learn French and the master learns his boys.

The intrusion of morals into science is due, of course, to the innate tendency of the human mind to put life and action into the inanimate dry bones of fact. It is apparently easier to remember abstractions, if we can associate them with the active and palpable processes of life and nature by an imaginary personification. Unfortunately there is much danger of carrying this to an extreme and mistaking the symbol for the abstraction it represents, the idol for the god whom it makes visible to the eye. This is a danger to be strenuously guarded against in teaching, especially in mathematical formulæ representing geometrical figures. The process in language which we struggle to vivify and render graphic by such terms as " degradation " is rather to be described as a process of "detrition," as regards words, and "rearrangement," as regards idioms. Inflexions do not decay, but they are worn or rubbed away by constant and more or less careless use, and difficult symbols are chipped and cut in the effort after greater speed and facility of utterance for the sounds they represent. Idioms are modified by alteration of the relative position and importance of the words of which they are composed. "Change," but not "decay, in all around we see " is a good motto for treatises on the growth of language.

It is hardly necessary to remind the reader that our whole modern system of "grammar and exercise " teaching is in direct opposition to the theory of "unconscious activity " enunciated above. Imagine a Sixth Form boy going over to Calais or Boulogne for the day on a Channel steamer and trying to make himself understood

in a French shop. Think of him proceeding to con-
struct a sentence conveying his desire for sweets or
refreshments in the same way as he made up the sentences in his last French exercise, *i.e.*, by considering
all the concords, numbers, genders and what not and
then stringing them together with one or two inevitable
blanks in vocabulary, ill-supplied by English words
mouthed in a fanciful imitation of French sounds. Five
minutes over this sort of truly unscientific scientific
synthesis might or might not result in some dim idea of
the boy's wants, upon which the shopkeeper would proceed to act, perhaps with the most ludicrous results. As
a matter of fact the boy ought to have his mind primed,
by much reading and more practice in sound utterance,
with one or other of the numerous idiomatic formulæ of
request in French, so that he could slip it off his tongue
without a moment's thought. Any blunder in vocabulary or lack of a particular vocable is of course pardon-
able, since a boy cannot be expected to carry a dictionary
in his head. There is no time to think out a sentence
by one's memory of grammar. The skeleton of idiom
must be ready in the memory, and the only thing that it
is lawful to hunt for on an emergency is—words, not
concords and inflexions.

The "formation of certain beliefs and prejudices,"
mentioned above, is all the more pernicious because it
is unconscious. "Use doth breed a habit in a man,"
and still more so in a boy, whose unformed nature is
very much more plastic than a man's and many times
more receptive of impressions, good and bad. The
constructive effort of the boy at Boulogne is an illustration of what one might call the "prejudice of
paradigm"—the effort to make up a sentence by reference

to the verb-tables, declensions and exception-lists in the grammar, instead of drawing at least its skeleton ready-made from the memory.

The question of exceptions is a most important one, and yet it is difficult to say anything more comprehensive, more trenchant or more profound than the simple statement "Exceptions ought to be *felt* as exceptions when they are *first* met with." Will any man capable of thought and reasoning deny that an abnormal fact can only be felt to be abnormal when some other fact, with which it is compared, has been met so great a number of times as to create a sense that this is the common, the normal fact, and that no such sense of abnormality is created when both the asserted normal and the asserted abnormal are met together for the first time? It is vain to tell a boy that a certain gender, number or person inflexion is normal and certain others abnormal. He believes you—because he does not know enough to deny your assertion—but the *difference* which you ask him to note and remember does not produce a deep and lasting impression on his mind. Why?—because he was not forced to see the difference by his own experiment and observation. He did not see it—he was told it. In the material world the depth of an impression is in strict proportion to the force employed in making it, because we can fix the material to be impressed firmly and then strike. In the psychological world the reverse is the case. We cannot fix the boy's mind, because it is well-nigh impossible to hold his attention for many seconds together unless that attention is itself active through interest or some other cause. Hence in this case the depth of the impression is proportional, not to the force employed in making it, but to the force exerted by the boy in receiving it. Tell the mind a new thing and it may be more startled than if it had been on the track of the thing, but it will not be so deeply impressed as if the new knowledge had been the outcome of its own labour. How often does the schoolmaster exclaim "What I tell you goes in at one ear and out at the other!" Rightly does it go out. The fundamental canon of good teaching is "Tell the boy nothing. Let him find out."* This does not mean that a boy should never be helped, but that he should be skilfully guided along the paths which lead to the new fact, so that he comes upon it of himself instead of being told it at the very beginning without any effort at discovery on his own part. In many cases it is the master who does the work while the boys look on. The reverse process is the ideal of teaching. Teaching does not mean telling, as too many teachers imagine. It means leading to find out. The point of all this is that lists of exceptions are pernicious and illogical. An exception should be "come upon" after long familiarity with normal forms and fixed in the mind by the sensation produced on the mind of its extraordinariness.

I have already laid stress on the necessity of teaching "rules" in a manner calculated to draw "conscious" out of "unconscious" knowledge, so that "the mind comes down with a snap on the example and the rule, and it is no burden to retain them both."

---

* "In education the process of self-development should be encouraged to the fullest extent. Children should be led to make their own investigations and to draw their own inferences. They should be *told* as little as possible, and induced to *discover* as much as possible."—SPENCER.

VI. Method of Learning.

We may now, under the guidance of Preyer (pp. 305–330), pass to a short sketch of the manner in which a child learns its native tongue. Roughly speaking, the conditions are the same at the beginning of a foreign language.

In the production of single sounds vowels precede the consonants, those requiring the least exertion of the parts of speech * coming as a rule, but not always, first. The child rises slowly from sounds to syllables, from syllables to words, from words to sentences.

In the majority of children the capacity to understand spoken words precedes the power to reproduce them. In beginning a new language, therefore, the teacher must be content to give for some time before he demands anything in return.

The child learns to speak by associating ideas which it already has with sounds imitated at first without any regard to meaning. The meaning is coupled to them later by association.

The child obtains a complete mastery over the language spoken at home without the aid of grammar, dictionary, reading or translation, of which we see and hear so much in school. The language is learnt entirely by the ear without the intervention of writing. The child learns the language as a harmonious whole—accent, intonation, sentence melody, and dialect, as well as the single sounds and words. The memory retains what the child can understand and finds interesting.† All else is forgotten in two or three days.

In learning to speak, first the sound centre, then the syllable and word centre, and lastly the dictorium are gradually built up. By its own activity the brain grows (Preyer, 330.) We must reproduce a like activity in our children when they begin a foreign language, and this must impera-

* " Parts of speech" here = " elements of speech," *i.e.*, vowels, consonants, &c.

† So also Spencer.

tively take place through the ear, and not through the eye, as in teaching Latin. This leads us to the discussion of Phonetics.—Pp. 22, 23.

Extract.—Teaching consists of silence and of instruction. The skill to give each its due proportion is a delicate art. *Vox hominem sonat.*

The above section is mainly a statement of facts capable of ready verification by actual observation of the ways of children at home and at school. It is only necessary to insist on the point that our education should be based upon these facts and not on the traditional and empirical theories of mediæval grammarians.

Here, as elsewhere, the chief thing to be insisted on is that the child's mind should be first filled with that which is common and normal and afterwards brought into contact with the extraordinary and exceptional. This is the principle that should lie at the bottom of graduation. We should not make sentences easy by altering and emasculating idiom, but by keeping technical, scientific and otherwise unusual words and expressions in the background and teaching simply those which are in common and constant use for the purposes of daily life. New and difficult forms should become a part of the child's mental furniture as gradually in the school-room as they do at home and in the nursery, attaining of course a higher level and wider extent in the former, but proceeding as gradually and as naturally as in the latter.

As the child first "imitates" a sound as sound and afterwards attaches a "meaning" to that sound, so he should first acquire the raw material of language as language in the schoolroom and afterwards discover by analysis its grammatical structure and logical relationships, not attempt, as now, to acquire the two simultaneously. First teach him a sentence "through the ear" as a "harmonious whole" and then, when he has a wealth of sentences at command, endeavour to open his eyes and arouse his reason to a sense of the laws which knit that and those sentences into a "whole" and make that whole "harmonious." It is Nature's, therefore the "natural" and also therefore the only "right," profitable and effective method. Then only will the brain "by its own activity" *grow* and not, by the futile activity of the teacher who is no teacher but a "stuffer," be weakened, stunted and stupefied.

VII. PHONETICS.

Phonetics as such is not a school subject, but the master must be a phonetician, and happily a little phonetics goes a great way. Unfortunately our phoneticians are as little schoolmasters as our schoolmasters phoneticians.

The main objections against phonetics seem to be the learning of a new alphabet, and a vague sort of fear that English literature will die a sudden death if we alter our orthography. The latter objection finds no harbour in the mind of any true philologist, but flourishes among the half-taught, who, if the truth were told, would probably confess that they fondly imagined the spelling of their Shakespeare to be the same now as when he wrote.

Whether our object in learning a foreign language be to speak it or only to read it for purely scientific or literary purposes, the actual spoken language of to-day must form the base. For practical purposes, errors of accidence or syntax are of less importance than imperfect pronunciation. A language mispronounced is a language unrecognisable. For educational purposes, the spoken language is obviously superior to the literary as the starting point in our teaching. The vocabulary is limited in range, the words used have fixed definite meanings, the grammar is restricted, and, as

G

the facts lie well within the knowledge of the child, his attention is concerned only with the form, he translates from the very beginning in block, sentence by sentence.

The pronunciation cannot be "picked up." Each language has its own delicate shades of sound carrying distinct differences of meaning. Phonetics alone can enable us to pronounce them properly.

Throughout our language teaching, the study of English must always be several stages ahead, especially in phonetics, as our orthography is the worst in Europe, and consequently, English children have a confused sense of the connection between sounds and their written signs,* and hardly any idea at all of their true formation. This blurred feeling is carried into other languages.

Just as the infant lacks the physiological and psychologic means of speech, so too does the child lack them in the presence of a new language. For the physiologic side we need a thorough gymnastic of the organs of speech by means of our phonetics. For the psychologic side we need, by continued exercise *in* the foreign language, by repeating the conscious till it becomes the unconscious, to arrive at length at the *Sprachgefühl* of the foreigner.—Pp. 24–26.

Are we to begin with a phonetic transcription? Yes, decidedly, for French. The modern orthography is a very corrupt representation of the pronunciation in the seventeenth century, and is surpassed in badness only by the English, in which symbols mainly due to Anglo-French scribes of the Plantagenet period, and imperfectly adapted to an Elizabethan pronunciation, are retained in the reign of Victoria !—Skeat.

The magic simplicity of our inflexional system grows clear in its phonetic dress, and we proudly recognise in our tongue two of the leading attributes of advanced culture, simplicity

---

* In reading the syllable *fry* the pupil is made to say *ef, ar, y,* which invariably confuses him, the names of letters being mistaken for their sounds.—Arnauld.

and wealth. The swift grace and easy movement of English are lost because we make it wade up to the knee in caco-graphic mud.

Let us turn to French. Plump go all the plurals of nouns with the sole exception of the *cheval, chevaux* group, the singular of the verbs has very nearly given up every sign of person, the masculine adjective can be derived from the feminine by means of a few simple rules.—VIETOR.

All the apparatus that we fondly imagined to be grammar, turns out to be nothing more than the swollen hollowness of a bad orthography.

Finally a few words as to a very real fear on the part of many teachers. Things being as they are with an imperative demand on the part of examiners for correct spelling, shall we not hopelessly confuse our scholars and ourselves by the introduction of a phonetic notation? Experience alone can tell us, and, as far as we can judge at present, it is not unfavourable. According to Mr. Sweet, it has "certainly shown that children taught reading phonetically, will master both phonetic and ordinary reading quicker than a class taught unphonetically will master the latter only."

What are the advantages of beginning with phonetics? First and foremost, they compel the child to watch himself, instead of learning parrot-fashion what he is told.

As the ultimate element of language really is the sound and not the letter, we follow the method of Nature in placing the sound first. The grammatical forms are abstracted un-consciously from the spoken, and not consciously from the written language. When freed from orthographical confu-sions, they become few and simple.

A theoretic and scientific knowledge of a language cannot be obtained in the future except on the base of a genuine practical mastery over it.

The capacity to express one's thoughts freely and directly in another tongue, demands considerable intellectual activity. The effort to attain it affords far more "training" than an excessive occupation with grammar.

Suppose some innocent Spaniard had learnt English by himself in the belief that the spelling and pronunciation agreed as closely as in his own language, while another had confined himself to books written entirely in phonetic characters, which would be the more advanced after six months' residence in England?

In this first or phonetic stage our chief aim is to give a good pronunciation. "The pupil must hear the sounds frequently, have his ears, as it were, bathed in the sounds, so that he can recall them mentally when he makes the effort to repeat them. . . . . Subsequently the teacher should read frequently to the pupils, especially what they know, and do it in his best manner."—ELLIS.

The point to be insisted on is the correct reproduction of the *sounds as sounds*. The meaning can be put into them as soon as they are impressed on the memory and fall trippingly from the tongue.

As soon as a noun or verb occurs for the third or fourth time we demand the whole sentence in which it made its first and second appearance, thus getting all the help we can from the law of association. In this way the child will unconsciously be getting ripe for the strict scientific view of a word as the molecule of a sentence—the atom being, of course, the sound—and for a sense of the intimate connection between form and meaning.

These sentences will contain most of the future "irregularities" of the grammar, but as they are not yet recognised as such they will cause very little difficulty.—Pp. 30–34.

Extracts.—Language is not to be learnt by the eye for the eye but by the ear for the ear.

Since the ear is less discriminating than the eye, the ear must be addressed first by itself and the ear must not be allowed to shift its responsibility on the eye. The ear needs more repetition than the eye.

While asserting that phonetics as such is not a school subject, Widgery believed most firmly that the science of phonetics must some day be recognised as the essential basis of any intelligent and fruit-bearing study of language, and that is why he maintains that the school-master must be a phonetician. No teacher of modern languages can claim to understand the languages he teaches thoroughly unless he is acquainted with the phonetic laws which govern the growth of all languages. If he attempt to teach without this knowledge, he will be constantly hampered in the effort to deal with apparent irregularities of mutation, gradation and inflexion. The new science of phonetics has thrown quite a flood of light on anomalous forms.

Widgery's statement that a "language mispronounced is a language unrecognisable" is perhaps a little too strong. One of his critics remarks upon this point "Of course good pronunciation is of great importance, but not, I maintain, of the vital importance which Mr. Widgery assigns to it."—(W. F. DINGWALL, *Journal of Education*.) As a matter of fact it is a question of degree. A certain amount of mispronunciation—slight inaccuracy in uttering the vowel sounds, for example—even though it be constant and systematic, is quite consistent with making oneself understood. One—quite a common—instance will suffice. Having agreed once to converse with a colleague in French while out walking in the country, I was troubled by the great difficulty of getting him to correct my blunders. "Well," said he, when I remonstrated with him, "the fact is, you speak well enough for me to understand you and it does not strike me, consequently, to correct your mistakes." He referred chiefly, no doubt, to errors of structure and idiom, but also in a sense to slight inaccuracies of sound-production. Every one knows that it is quite possible

for an Englishman to pronounce French "well," as we
say, and yet be unable to reproduce those subtle peculiarities of vocalisation which constitute what we somewhat loosely describe as a "real French accent." This
is better described as the "real French quality" or
"timbre" that differentiates a born Frenchman speaking
French from a born Englishman attempting to imitate
him. Timbre becomes a real difficulty when a Frenchman speaks rapidly, but vanishes when he speaks slowly
enough for us to hear the vowels separately. But an
Englishman can speak French with a very considerable
English accent and yet be easily understood by a
Frenchman, provided his construction is correct, and we
can generally manage to understand a Frenchman who
knows English, however bad his accent. In short,
perfect pronunciation of a foreign language is a luxury,
not a necessity—an accomplishment to be proud of and
to be sought after as earnestly as a good elocution in the
vernacular, but it is by no means a *sine qua non*. Yet
any teacher who should advance this fact as a reason for
neglecting to inculcate correct pronunciation would be
worthy of the contempt of all who believe that the best
in anything is the least that should content the learner.

The importance of translating "in block, sentence by
sentence" has, so far as I know, been fully recognised
only by the "Prendergast Mastery Method" of teaching
languages. It will be best considered when we come to
the section on Translation, but a few remarks may be
made here. The chief advantage of translating "in
block" is that the connecting thread of sense helps one
to remember the relationship and order of the words.
This becomes most valuable when the time comes to
make use of our knowledge and again give it forth.
Then the words, once learnt in close connection, recall

and suggest each other, and come from the tongue in the same relative position as that in which they were first met. Consequently there is no time wasted in arranging the words and fluent speech becomes a possibility.

Widgery's remark that "the pronunciation cannot be 'picked up'" requires explanation. The best pronunciation always *is* 'picked up' in the sense that it is acquired by more or less conscious imitation of good speakers. Widgery does not mean to deny this. He refers to the fact that the capacity of close listening and accurate imitation is not a widespread gift. Some children cannot concentrate their attention quickly and easily enough to be good listeners and good imitators. Such children can often be materially helped by pointing out to them the phonetic structure of a sound, by analysing it phonetically and making them grasp the simple elements of a complex sound. A difficult diphthong, for example, can often be taught by making the child imitate the elemental vowels in slow succession and gradually increase the speed until the elements naturally coalesce and give the correct diphthong.

In the matter of orthography the "confusion between sounds and their written signs" should be most strenuously combated. A boy should never be allowed to say that "ess" is the sound of *s*. It should be pointed out to him that that is merely the "name" of the serpentine sign *s*. The "sound" represented by *s* is a long hiss . . s . . The distinction is not so trifling as it looks. It becomes important in connection with the manner of writing plurals like "dogs," pronounced "dogz," and it is a fundamental principle in phonetics. Many of the follies of our ridiculous orthography are due to our not having observed this distinction in times past.

The main reason of the difficulty experienced by

children in pronouncing foreign languages correctly is the small amount of practice they have in actual utterance. There is no such thing as " a thorough gymnastic of the organs of speech " in most schools. The amount of actual utterance of foreign sounds in a French class is utterly insignificant compared with what a little French child goes through in learning its native tongue at its mother's knee. Hence it is that I have in my lowest classes little boys of eight and nine who can speak German with a perfect German accent, though they cannot go through the inflexions of the definite article " der " correctly—speak with a far finer accent, in fact, than I could boast when I left the Sixth Form in the same school. This is simply because they have had far more practice in actual utterance, chattering at their mother's or nurse's knee, than I had in my whole school course under the modern system, which wastes so much precious time on the futilities of the grammar and the inanities of the exercise book. We cannot give too much time to oral repetition. Six years of that would produce boys of sixteen who could speak, read—ay, and write French and German perfectly, or at least as well as they do the same in their mother tongue (Has it not been often done already?) instead of the duffers we turn out of our Sixth Forms nowadays.

The advisability or inadvisability of beginning with a phonetic transcription can never be definitely settled until we actually make the experiment of training a class on such a transcription. Theorising is utterly useless here.

All that Widgery says of the simplification produced in grammar by the application of a few phonetic rules is perfectly true. Unhappily most of the men who write grammars of foreign tongues appear to be ignorant of the light which phonetics would cast upon their long lists of irregularities and their elaborately constructed paradigms of useless inflexions and fanciful conjugations seldom or never used in real speech. This paradigm business is a most unpardonable sin of grammarians. We force our unhappy children to commit to memory a large number of tenses of Greek verbs when not even examiners, those irresponsible tormentors of youth, dare ask one half of them, knowing well that no Greek, dead or alive, ever perpetrated the folly of writing, much less speaking, in the greater part of them. So it is with many of the tenses of French and German verbs.

The remark that "the effort to attain free expression in another tongue affords far more intellectual 'training' than an excessive occupation with grammar" might be enlarged by the insertion of the word " profitable " before "intellectual." I have already laid stress upon the fact that, if two methods of training can be proved to be equally good, *qua* training, that one should receive preference which is the least wasteful of energy and most facilitates the storing up of material that will afterwards come into use. (The equality of the training-value of grammar and language has been already discussed and demonstrated. Their relative wastefulness is the point in question here.) In training upon grammar we acquire a mass of learned lumber which nine out of ten of us fling into the limbo of forgotten vanities directly we leave school. In training upon language pure and simple, as directed in this treatise, we lay up in the course of the training, unavoidably and without special effort, a vast store of words and idioms that will be of life-long use to nine out of ten of us. Who then, if convinced of their equality in training-value, would fail to prefer mnemonic synthesis to grammatical analysis from the point of view of subsequent utility?

That it is well and necessary for the pupil to "have his ears bathed in the sounds" of the foreign language few will deny. Parents are always insisting on the necessity of foreign languages being taught by foreigners in order that children may be constantly hearing the exact foreign pronunciation. But whether this desirable result is best obtained by great activity on the part of the teacher in the way of reciting to the children, or by an equal activity on the part of the children in them-selves reciting the foreign sounds under the guidance and supervision of the foreigner, is matter of dispute. "I cannot," says Klinghardt in "Englische Studien," "ac-cede to the suggestion that the teacher should read frequently to the pupils, especially what they know. Occasionally that may be done, but the unlimited itera-tion of it, face to face (*auge in auge*), is not so efficacious as the question requiring an answer." "Hereby hangs a tale." The suggestion originates with Mr. Ellis, a great authority on language but, if I am not much mistaken, one who is without experience as a practical teacher. If Mr. Ellis knows by personal experience, he appears to have forgotten for the moment the extreme difficulty of holding the attention of children, even when they are interested and understand what is being read to them, for five minutes together. Now in this case, if the master reads a piece the children have heard only once before, they will not understand much of what they hear and their thoughts will soon wander away to the thousand and one trifles that are ever distracting the restless mind of youth. If he reads a piece they have often heard before, no matter how interesting it was the first time, at every repetition they will be more and more inclined to vote it "stale" and forthwith let their thoughts go a wool-gathering again, and failure and despair will be the teacher's only reward.* But if the children are com-pelled to recite the pieces themselves under constant correction of whatever they say wrong, or if they are required to answer a shower of questions, they cannot avoid a fair amount of active attention. This is a matter of practical experience, and Mr. Ellis's plan must fail with children and can only succeed with adults, where a strong desire to learn supplies the motive for attention which is lacking in children, who learn only because they are made to. But in a modified form Mr. Ellis's plan can be worked. Let the teacher recite to the children, but only phrase by phrase and sentence by sentence, and let these phrases and sentences be immediately repeated by the children after him, sometimes individually, sometimes in chorus. Then emulation will supply a motive for attention, and the constant tossing of the ball from master to pupil will leave the latter no time—no big blanks in effort—during which his thoughts may go a wool-gathering unchecked.

VIII. Reader.

We now pass to the "reader," the centre of our system, the *corpus vile* from which we learn our orthography, our vocabulary, our grammar.

We begin somewhat as follows. Let the teacher learn by heart the first piece, say Lessing's fable of "The Sparrows."

---

* The intellectual weakness of the child comes for the most part from his inability to fix his attention.—Compayré. The mind of the child is like a lighted taper in a place exposed to the wind, whose flame is ever unsteady.—Fénelon.

Then with voice, eye, and hand all active, let him declaim
the fable to the class, exaggerating just a little the sounds
peculiar to the German. After telling the gist of the story
in English, he will repeat the first breath-group of the
German sounds, and, after a slight pause, pitch on some boy
to repeat purely as a sound sequence. After a whole sentence has been thus repeated, the teacher will give again the
breath-groups and with them the English, *taking the words
in the German order*, this being the natural one for a German
—the object of the bald English is merely to give the
meaning.

When the piece has been finished in this way the books
may be opened, and one of the best boys put on to read and
to give the English translation with the words in their proper
order. Again the books are closed, and a lively shower of
questions, such as the native teacher would rain down on a
reading class of his own, must arouse interest and develop
fancy—things as important as the knowledge of genders
or the irregular verbs. Finally, an idiomatic translation
from the master is followed by another declamation of the
German.

As soon as a few pieces have been done in this way, a
systematic exploitation may be commenced of the material
acquired—first the orthography, then the grammar.

Preceding the reader should be a grammar containing
only the absolute essentials. Here let no "exception" or
list, even with the saving clause of being learnt as vocabulary, dare to show its head. "Single words and forms in
teaching are a clumsy breach of psychology and pedagogy."
—VIETOR. Later on come occasional lessons devoted
entirely to the grammar, the paradigms being taken with
the book open and each word embodied in a sentence. Boys
are not the only persons who cease to think when they say
paradigms by heart.

Another pedagogic error of lists is the juxtaposition of
closely allied forms. After *der* Band or *die* See has become
firmly fixed in the mind, we can safely confront them with

das Band or *der* See. To give them all at the same time must produce confusion.

Neither is the power to say the paradigms correctly of very great value, for the good of repetition lies not so much in remembering the same impression of a thing at different times as in the recognition of it as one and the same in different relations.—PERTHES.

The right hand side of the grammar should contain the syntax of the accidence on the left. The sentences must invariably be printed above the rule, and they, not the rule,* are to be learnt by heart.—Pp. 34–37.

As soon as the first dozen pieces have been read, and the vocabulary of the primitives occurring in them thoroughly mastered, a search can be made for derivatives. A sense of the connection between form and meaning is gradually aroused, and the child is being properly prepared for learning the accidence of a synthetic language.

As we work our way gradually through the reader, repetition must be incessant.

Together with many short pieces, fit for *intensive* reading, one or two easy tales of some length should be read *cursorily*, just for the fun of the thing, no more being demanded than a knowledge of the story.

Parsing at first must be very sparingly indulged in. A sharp look-out must be kept for idiomatic turns and phrases.

---

* "Children," says Comenius, "need examples and things which they can see, and not abstract rules." It is by use and by reading that Comenius would abolish the abuse of rules. Rules ought to intervene only to aid use and give it surety. It is by the reading of authors that the grammar of Port Royal completes the theoretical study of the rules that are rigidly reduced to their minimum. . . . . In this way the example, not the dry and uninteresting one of the grammar, but the living example, expressive, and drawn from a writer that is being read with interest, will precede or accompany the rule, and the particular case will explain the general law.—COMPAYRÉ.

They could be entered in an exercise book and learnt by heart.

Our main object being to concentrate the child's attention on the language itself, dictation will become important as a substitute for written translation. The almost forgotten art of listening is cultivated, as well as the power of grasping with the ear the foreign sounds—the first and most necessary thing when we put foot on foreign soil. The pieces already studied intensively are the best for dictation. The exercises when corrected form good material for repetition work, as the words can be freely underlined. After the piece has been thoroughly threshed out in this way, the papers are collected and the class left to give the substance in their own French or German, and to invent new sentences on the model of the old.

The main object of the reader being to give a thorough knowledge of the accidence and the first beginnings of the syntax, the number of pieces in it need not be great. Some of these may be read chiefly for vocabulary and syntax.

With regard to notes, lives of the writer, biographical data about unimportant persons, æsthetic disquisitions far above the heads of the children, scraps of etymology, often wrong in themselves, and when right of small value in making the meaning clearer, had better stay away. The notes must be worked out on a consistent plan for definite classes, explanations on things such as the foreign boy would need being kept distinct from points of language. In the latter we need the pronunciation of proper names, the leading examples in the book of any difficult construction, paraphrases in the foreign language of important words with their synonyms, and above all, the variations in the selected work from the modern prose of every-day life.

While the higher classes are reading the masterp.eces of the literature, they might also have very short accounts of the foreign history and literature given them, written in language easy enough to be understood without the need of translation.

For the future commercial man, a short chatty book written in the foreign language would be extremely useful. To the merest skeleton of the history, geography, and government of the country, should follow accounts of school life, the manners and customs of the inhabitants, the famous sights of the leading towns, the money and metric systems, hints on etiquette, art, music, and the theatre, everything in fact that bears on the life of to-day.

After three or four years' study of the vocabulary and grammar, entirely through the reader and easy prose texts, it is hoped the boy will be in a position to read literature as such, leaving all the paraphernalia of the earlier stages well behind him.*

The crown and summit of the language master's activity is to make some of his sense for the splendour and beauty of foreign literature—some of his sense for the warm breath of humanity glowing in its pages—pass into the souls of his boys. With our overgrown curriculum we lead or drag them up the steps of too many of the fair gardens of knowledge, but, after a brief glimpse through the gates, we turn them back into the turmoil and struggle of life, ill-fed and unsatisfied. " I've forgotten everything I learnt at school. I never found it of much use." Literature we must read as literature. Textual criticism, archæology, philology—these are the veriest handmaids of the school. Their work is over when they have left the best possible text at the school gates.

We often see papers set on " Literature," but the questions are almost invariably concerned with the language in

* Locke requires that Latin shall be learnt above all through use, through conversation if possible, but if not, through the reading of authors. As little of grammar as possible, no memoriter exercises, no Latin composition, either in prose or verse, but, as soon as possible, the reading of easy Latin texts.—COMPAYRÉ. Authors are like a living dictionary, and a speaking grammar, whereby we learn, through experience, the very force and the true use of words, of phrases, and of the rules of syntax.—ROLLIN.

which the literature is written—a very different matter.—
Pp. 39-44.

Extract.—" Mr. Widgery seems rather unfair when dealing
with the ordinary translation lesson. If the pupil is taught to
make the verb the cardinal word in the sentence, and therefore
to make sure of it first of all, next to look out for the nomina-
tive, and then (supposing the verb to be transitive and used
in the active voice) for the accusative, and to get his words
properly ranged in order before looking them out in his
dictionary, instead of taking them haphazard as they occur
without paying any attention to the terminations of case,
tense, person, &c., I think that the result will be quite as
satisfactory as that of the system advocated by Mr.
Widgery."—W. F. DINGWALL, *Journal of Education*, Jan. 1,
1889.

The difficulty, already pointed out, of holding the
attention of children when reciting to them what they
cannot yet be expected to understand again appears in
connection with Widgery's suggestion that the master
should learn a piece by heart and declaim it to his class.
Personally I am inclined to drop this step and begin
with the utterance of breath-groups by the master for
immediate imitation by the children. The final declamation which closes the "method" here elaborated is
desirable and, I think, sufficient for the purpose of giving
the boys an idea of what a piece of German really sounds
like when recited by a native of Germany.

In the extract from the *Journal of Education* we
have a synopsis of the method employed at present
by many language teachers. It is not without merits
and might, I think, be worked alongside the superior
method suggested by Widgery with good results. While
the analytic process of Mr. Dingwall's method can easily

be overdone by a mechanical teacher, its occasional use
in the hands of a thoughtful one in the habit of applying
Widgery's "block" method would be helpful. A little
analysis is good and strengthens the faculty of synthesis.
It is only unceasing analysis without any attempt to
acquire the units of language (*i.e.*, sentences) as coherent
wholes that is pernicious.

The suggestion that paradigms should be taken with
the book open and "every word embodied in a sentence"
is a most valuable one, but not too easy of application.
It implies an abundant supply of time, not at present
at the disposal of the language teacher and only to be
obtained by some such limitation of the languages taught
simultaneously as has already been suggested in the first
section of this treatise. Nevertheless it is undoubtedly
the ideal way of learning so much of declension and
conjugation as may prove useful. Considerable experience and experiment have convinced me, that the
amount of time spent in getting a child to repeat the
inflexions of *mensa*, "a table," for instance, or *Vater*,
"father," with anything approaching to accuracy and
speed is utterly incommensurate with the importance of
the result when success is at last obtained. Yet in these
foreign languages any attempt to embody individual
variations of word-inflexion in complete sentences, however short, implies an amount of ready ingenuity and
vigorous mental labour much beyond the capacity of the
average teacher, who is not a specialist, and absolutely
impossible to the average boy or girl. But in the case
of the vernacular, where both teacher and pupil have a
large stock of linguistic material at command, the plan
may be adopted with the happiest results. In teaching
English grammar to a class of small boys I teach

H

inflexions of gender and number in nouns, and of person in verbs, by giving sentences with blanks to be completed by the insertion of the noun or verb properly inflected. This can be applied more generally to the pronouns and anomalous verbs. I once had a striking proof of the fact that a child often knows the correct form of an element of speech when it is part of a complete thought, a complete sentence, though apparently unable to give it as an isolated element standing in a paradigm. In correcting an exercise on Pronouns I found a boy had written down the dative plural of the German pronoun *Ich* = " I " thus—

Uns = to we.

I turned to him and said "Look what you have written! Suppose you and Smith wanted to see a rare stamp which I had just shown to Brown, would you come and say 'Please, sir, won't you show that stamp to we?'" "Oh no, sir! I should say 'to us,'" he replied at once. This blunder tells another tale also, *i.e.*, that it is almost impossible to get a boy to appreciate the difference between the cases or attach any definite meaning to their names, even if you explain the origin and meaning of these names. This again carries us back to the manner in which a child acquires his knowledge of the vernacular. He learns it in sentences. Consequently, if you give him an incomplete sentence with a missing word, he can generally supply that word in its correct form by the association which it has in his mind and memory with the other words. But ask him to write it down in an isolated form and he has nothing to help himself with, nothing that calls up in his mind the correct form of the word by virtue of old association in a familiar coherence, which constant hearing has made him regard as normal. The moral is, try always to cover the skeleton which you take out of the Grammar with the flesh you find in the Reader. The bones of language are as ugly and unattractive as those which the anatomist handles. Attraction and memory go hand in hand. Therefore try to make your grammar attractive by clothing it in the æsthetic attractions of real language. Then only will it please and be remembered.

The sin of teaching "double genders" simultaneously is practically the same as that of giving long lists of exceptions to be learnt in connection with one normal form, instead of letting the exception be discovered to be such after the mind has become thoroughly familiar with the normal. Suppose we take *der* and *die See*. One means "the lake," the other "the sea." As it happens "der" goes with "lake" and "die" with "sea." But why should not "der" go with "sea" and "die" with "lake"? There is no reason whatever, and only a strong memory can avoid danger of interchanging the genders. But, when we have met "die" *See* half a hundred times, it becomes fixed in our minds as the normal gender of "sea" in German. Then, if we happen to come across "der" *See*, we are struck by the unusual gender and, the impression of irregularity being vivid, we remember the new meaning given to the familiar word by the change of gender. And so we learn "der See" in a manner that prevents our forgetting the distinction in meaning between it and "die See."

Widgery's suggestion for studying the history and literature of the foreign tongues being taught in the school should be noted. Far too little is done in this direction at present, again for lack of time—precious time wasted, as always, on grammar and exercises.

Such a book as is recommended for the "future commercial man" would be invaluable, and not merely to him. It would tend to widen the mental horizon of any boy and remove some of that narrow and mischievous insular conceit, miscalled patriotism, which is so common a characteristic of the adolescent John Bull.

The last paragraph but one strikes a very high note and is thoroughly characteristic of Widgery's broad mind and noble heart.

IX. Grammar.

1. *Historical.*

The beginnings of grammar spring from the discussion whether the relation between a thing and its name is one of necessity or agreement. But the true or the false, said Plato and Aristotle, lies not in the single word, but in its relation to the other words in a sentence. Philology thus became the handmaid of logic, and the parts of speech were determined according to its categories.

At the very outset we find two schools representing the two sides of that duality which we are always meeting in language, "analogy" and "anomaly," the regular and the irregular, the old and new, the conscious and the unconscious. The system recognising the two and allotting to each its proper place has not yet been worked out.

The terminology and system of the Greek grammar of Dionysius Thrax, the representative of the principle of "analogy" at Rome in the time of Pompey, have travelled for two thousand years over the civilised world.

Now this terminology was derived from Athens, where the "terminology of formal logic and formal grammar were the same." The categories of language, however, are congruent neither with those of logic, grammar, psychology, nor metaphysics.

Dionysius is the ultimate source of the grammars still in use in our schools. His method was founded on an empirical analysis of one language, and represents only one side of that language. Others followed him like the blind led by the one-eyed.

Since the discovery of Sanskrit and the rise of comparative philology, our modern scholars *know* a good deal more of the grammar than the Latins themselves did.

With the Renascence in Italy matters began to mend. Guarino da Verona and Vittorino da Feltre laid the first foundations of our modern school system. Lorenzo Valla first clearly stated the fact that the author rules the grammar and not the grammar the author. "Ego pro lege accipio quidquid magnis auctoribus placuit."

With the rise of Protestantism, Latin, the official language of the Romish Church, began to fall into disrepute, and we now begin to hear of its value as a formal study. Melancthon praised it for this purpose, as it clearly compels us to think.

In the explanation of the authors, the connection of the thoughts was quite neglected. It was all grammar.—ECKSTEIN.

The diversity of grammars then was no less a difficulty than now, and Henry VIII. attempted some reform. The conflicting opinions of grammarians are complained of.

The change to the system now in vogue seems to date from an address on the study of Latin and Greek delivered by Prof. Long in 1830. He urged the use of the inductive method of modern philology, that in the hands of Bopp and Grimm had achieved such brilliant results.

With 1838 came Dr. William Smith's "Latin Exercises for Beginners" and the change to the crude form system.

With the discovery of Verner's law, the investigations on the vowel system of the Aryan languages now made accessible in Brugmann's "Grundriss," and the beginnings of the study of comparative syntax, the whole aspect of our grammar has been changed.

The evil method of holding with persistent obstinacy to tradition has been applied to modern languages, and the

grammars persist in neglecting phonetics, in heaping exceptions upon rules—or shall we say rules upon exceptions—
and in keeping doggerel, that powerful aid to the production
of artificial stupidity.

The source of our troubles is making the *letter* and not the
sound the ultimate element of language. Until we have a
real living faith in the *spoken* language as the source of all
our literature, and as the starting-point of all our scientific
studies, we shall make no real progress with our language
teaching.

Can grammar teach us a language? Are the complaints
of its inadequacy to give a practical power to speak a foreign
tongue confined to our modern reformers?

" I had rather a scholar should remember the natural and
received position of a clause by keeping the words always
all together than understand the particular correspondence
of the words, and thereby lose their proper places. For
discretion and comparison of clause with clause will at length
bring the understanding of the words, whether we will or no;
but nothing will bring the true position of these words again
by reason that our own doth therein still misguide us."—
Petition to Parliament by JOHN WEBBE. 1623.

" Boys of good parts spend five or six years in a Grammar
School, without attaining so much of the Latin Tongue as to
make sense of half-a-dozen lines in the easiest of the classic
Authors."—J. CLARKE. 1720.

In the present century, from Grimm downwards, complaints of the powerlessness of Grammar to teach a language
effectively have grown in bulk and loudness, and the change
they demand must come soon.—Pp. 11-19.

I would lay particular stress on the last words of the
quotation from Webbe—" Nothing will bring the true
position of these words again by reason that our own doth
therein still misguide us." Teachers do not appear to
realise with sufficient vividness the fact that the grammar

never teaches us *how to arrange words* in order to make
up a sentence. We have only our notions of the order
of words in the vernacular to go upon, and the order in
the vernacular seldom corresponds exactly with that in
the foreign tongue.

2. Critical.

All the reformers from Ratke down to Grimm have grown
eloquent in combating the mistake that grammar can teach
a language.* Not an exact knowledge of all the rules of the
grammar, nor some skill in their application, will give the
power of speech. There is no time for conscious reflection,
the thought and the word must spring up in the mind simultaneously. And this power, this readiness, will never be
acquired by the conscious method of reflection, but only
by the unconscious method of imitation and incessant
repetition.

The task of the grammar is a purely subsidiary one—it
must classify *known* facts by making clear what the child
has already felt, half seen in his reader. The rules must be
simply short and concise statements summing up the facts
of the language. It might, perhaps, be a wise thing to put
in the hands of the children a grammar containing only
well-selected sentences *without the rules,* and to leave their
induction to the teacher.

We must learn to think *in* before we think *of* the language.
Grammar is not elementary in the teaching of languages,

* I will give it (grammar) no attention, or, at least, but very
little.—FÉNELON. The grammars in use are intended simply to
teach correctness in speaking and writing. By their aid we are
able finally to avoid a certain number of faults in style and orthography. . . . . This instruction becomes a pure affair of memory,
and the child becomes accustomed to pronounce sounds to which he
attaches no meaning. The child needs a *grammar of ideas.* . . . .
Our *grammars of words* are the plague of education.—
PÈRE GIRARD.

and what we now ask from the lowest classes we ought to postpone to the highest.

As soon as the reader has been finished and the study of works of literature begun, a large grammar, arranged somewhat like a dictionary, may be used. The paradigms given in the reader should be met here in the same type. In making groups for the nouns and verbs, only those that have at least fifteen or twenty examples should be given, all others being relegated to alphabetical lists.

As far as possible the grammar should, by means of different print, distinguish clearly between the logical and idiomatic sides of the language.—MÜNCH.

The teacher will find it advisable to limit himself very strictly as to the main points of grammar to be insisted on during each month. Examples for the accidence may be denoted by dots, and for the syntax by lines drawn under the words.—Pp. 38-40.

Extracts.—Do we begin to teach a boy carpentering by an elaborate description of the tools carefully arranged in compartments? Take up a tool, do something with it and then show how it is fashioned to do its work. The work and the tool enter into the memory together and mutually strengthen one another.

"Mr. Widgery points out that the teaching of English is wofully neglected and above all the teaching of grammar is little short of an infamy. A man may be stuffed with all the rules of syntax that exist and yet be unable to write one sentence of good idiomatic English. He may string words and phrases together, but his construction is faulty and at variance with the taste and canons of the best writers."— Tacoma *Morning Globe.*

We dress up the skeleton of grammar with a few rags that scarce hide his nakedness and hope that in the twilight he may pass for a human being, but we fervently pray nobody will ask him to move. In him there is neither flesh nor blood. When the cock crows for the actual labour of life he falls to pieces.

Most of the points raised in this section have already been illustrated in the course of my remarks upon other sections. All the objections already brought against relying on grammar are summed in the sentence "There is no time for conscious reflection."

The suggestion that we should use what might be called an "Illustrative Grammar"—a collection of "well-selected sentences *without the rules*"—and help the child to draw the rules out of the sentences is a most excellent one. Many teachers would rejoice to have such an aid to rational teaching. The great difficulty of inductive teaching, such as Widgery suggests, is the extempore composition of sentences that will exactly illustrate the rule we wish to teach. This implies considerable quickness and originality on the part of the teacher, and not many teachers have those qualities in abundance. But a book such as Widgery describes would remove this difficulty. It is really not such a very formidable work. The best grammars give plenty of examples in illustration of the rules they codify. We only want to extract these illustrations and add half-a-dozen similar ones to each of them and we shall have the book we need so much. Will not some teacher, blest with leisure and industry, give the profession this boon? Many blessings would light upon his, or her, head, I am certain.

"We must learn to think *in* before we think *of* the language" is a golden rule that ought to be painted up on the door of every language-teacher's class-room. The whole of this section, full of the profoundest wisdom, is worthy of the deep and earnest attention of all who busy themselves with the education of the young, and especially of those who have the good fortune to be at the head of great public schools with a free hand and unlimited power to bring new theories to the test of practical application during a period sufficiently long to yield results that may be trusted.

X. Translation.

What has become of translation, of exercises? Their limitation and partial extinction we shall endeavour to justify below.

The native speaker, we may reflect, uses his grammar unconsciously, and never employs translation at all. And yet around these two our method of teaching centres. Our whole system seems planned to give a self-conscious knowledge about the language and not the language itself. We rate a knowledge of the visible signs of a foreign tongue much higher than a practical power over the audible, spoken language, in fact the very language itself.

If our object is to think and feel as a Frenchman thinks and feels, then surely this will be accomplished the quicker the more the English is kept out of sight.

Theoretically we do, indeed, look on the capacity to speak as one of the aims of our teaching, but it " doesn't pay " in examinations—as little as the examinations themselves " pay " in after life—and, worst error of all, the power to speak is put at the end of the school career, or more correctly outside of it, instead of at the very beginning.

Let us try to see a little more closely what happens with the ordinary boy.

He has, say, twenty lines of Latin to do. After reading the first sentence through, he picks out the subject and then the verb. He turns up the dictionary for his noun, and after sensibly skipping the dubious or antiquated etymology, begins to wonder whether the meaning is under I.A., 1a, or II.B. (b). On the road he has to turn back sometimes to the three pages of abbreviations at the beginning. However, he gets a meaning at last, and the process is repeated with the verb and the other words, with a flying reference, perhaps, to the grammar for some irregular gender. Then comes a hunt through the index—and, at last, the meaning is fairly clear. Frequently, however, this is by no means the case, and he dives into the dictionary and grammar again. This is a danger to which conscientious boys are liable. By patient and misdirected ingenuity, they arrive at a false construction, but the labour of finding it was so great that the first impression remains stronger than the later correction.

The good boy works in this fashion. The ordinary boy leaves his grammar at school, skims through the lines as quickly as he can, writes down the words that are utterly foreign to him, turns up the dictionary, puts down the first meaning he comes across, and is quite happy next day if he escapes the Task Book.

In class there is a raking fire of questions directed apparently on the principle of "take care of the grammar, the æsthetics will take care of themselves." After vivisecting the author in this manner a translation is made, and the child does all he can to prevent his weak English from being twisted quite out of shape by the foreign idiom. So we creep on towards the examination. Then one morning a strange thing happens. The master touches the acme of absurdity by saying, "We haven't time to read the Latin (or French). Get on with the translation." What is the lesson— Latin, French, English? Not only must the boys read the French aloud as a connected whole after the details have been discussed, but the teacher must declaim it to them in the finest style he can master. For if we really desire to teach French, the French must be the first thing to be heard, and the last thing must be a memory haunted by the clear thoughts and the clear sounds of the French.

Another branch of the translation method is the veritable "night side" of our system, I mean the exercise-book. The merest common sense is surely enough to see the impossibility of making anything homogeneous out of such disparity in difficulty as the two parts of an exercise.

The form in which to clothe a thought is given at once in the mother tongue, and we need know little more than the meanings of the separate foreign words to translate them with fair accuracy. But with the converse the form is almost entirely lacking. To obtain even a feeling for it we must first and for some time insist on attention being paid to it as embodied in sentences in the foreign language.

The fundamental error at the base of this system is the belief that language can be reconstructed *a priori* on the model of certain types, or by the exercise of the logical faculty in the correct application of the rules of grammar. This, as we have seen, leaves entirely out of view the portion retained purely by memory, and the mind, lost in a mass of details where thought must wait on form, when suddenly confronted with the lively interchange of thought in conversation, finds itself unable to use the material acquired.

(In making up exercises) when some remark not wholly foolish has been found, the noun or verb turns out to be irregular or not yet given, and in changing the forms sense vanishes.

Translations from English into a foreign tongue lie really outside the school, and, if exercises must be done, they should not come till at least after two years' reading, and then only in aid of the study of the syntax. It is impossible to translate into a foreign language unless the mind feels in it more or less at home.

I would seriously urge on all in authority to try at least the experiment of putting the exercise-book at the beginning of the second year.

Translations, at first, we must of course have, but they should be idiomatic. "The English boy says *this*, the German *that*, when he wants anything."

As soon as possible, however, we must begin to use paraphrases * in the foreign language, rather than send the child to a dictionary with English meanings, our object all through

* See reference on p. 125.

being to transplant ourselves into the method and manner of thought of the foreigner.

However swift the process take place, there must be a great psychologic gap between the conscious arrangement of elements and the unconscious flow of real speech.

Occasional written translations into English are in their proper place only in the highest classes.*

The most interesting way to teach composition is by means of short stories. Of course, in French and German, more discussion and help must be given. This exercise would make an excellent substitute for *Unseens*. In the higher classes a variation can be got by giving a free English translation of some foreign original for retroversion.

In close connection with this exercise stands the art of letter writing.† The introduction into schools, even for "commercial boys," of actual business letters, is a grave mistake—they belong to the counting-house. Neither do we

---

* "It may be doubted whether the schools furnish a better 'intellectual gymnastic' than translation. Three high intellectual attainments are involved in a real translation—1. The separation of the thought from the original form of words. 2. The seizing or comprehension of the thought as a mental possession, and 3. The embodying of the thought in a new form. A strictly analogous process, of almost equal value in its place, is that variety of reading in which the pupil is required to express the thought of the paragraph *in his own language*. This exercise involves the three processes above stated, and may be called 'the translation of thought from one form into another in the same language.'"—PAYNE. This is all very true, but, as Widgery points out, only the highest classes possess the condition of mental development which can undertake with profit the separation, comprehension and embodiment described by Mr. Payne.

† The pupils of the Jansenist solitaries at Port Royal were set to compose little narratives, little letters, the subjects of which were borrowed from their recollections, by being asked to relate on the spot what they had retained of what they had read.—COMPAYRÉ. So also Locke.

want the letters of the great literary men of the last century, but the easy unaffected style of the present day.—Pp. 43-50.

Extracts.—In every case the English required in translation must be below the standard obtained in the specific English class.

The walls of the pedagogic Jericho are built all of paper. Around is the moat of ink and on guard inside is the paper-master. But if we blow the trumpets of common-sense long enough and loud enough the walls will collapse and the paper-master with all his paper exercises will be blown into the desert and the land he cumbered filled with the fair fruit-trees of knowledge.

"Let me express my cordial assent with Mr. Widgery's remarks on the system of exercises. Any teacher must know that, however carefully an exercise on one particular rule of syntax may be gone through with a class, and however diligently the rule itself may be explained, yet the ordinary pupil will simply translate the sentence literally in an examination, when no hint is given of the rule which is to be applied. In spite of this a pupil's time and patience are still wasted on turning bad English into worse Latin, French, &c., instead of his being set to translate easy sentences from the foreign language, as soon as he has mastered the most ordinary terminations of verbs and nouns, and has perceived for himself that the "concords" are simply a matter of common-sense after all, and equally applicable to all languages."—W. F. DINGWALL, *Journal of Education*, Jan. 1, 1889.

Widgery's point in the second paragraph is that we should try to put the learner of a foreign language into the position of the man who speaks it as his native tongue —put him into an attitude of looking at the language from within, not from without. The same point is made in the well-known maxim that a man cannot speak a language until he has learnt to think in it. And Widgery contends that the analytical method of learning to translate advocated by Mr. Dingwall and very generally practised in schools tends to keep the learner outside the language and make him regard it objectively, while the method of translating "en bloc" recommended by Widgery forces the learner to throw himself into the language, as it were, and practise it subjectively.

"Rating a knowledge of the visible signs of a foreign tongue much higher than a practical power over the audible, spoken language, in fact the very language itself" is one of the numerous sins which must be laid at the door of examinations and especially those held by the University of London. This University distinctly states in the Regulations for its examinations that the examiners may, if they please, examine candidates *viva voce*; but, except in the case of treatises written for the Doctorate and in the Honours examinations, such *viva voce* questioning is almost unknown. Certainly it is possible to *pass* in French and German without being called upon to utter a single word in either of those tongues! Could anything be more ridiculous? No doubt the chief reason for this pedagogic absurdity is the facility with which written papers may be marked and the difficulty—one might almost say, the impossiblity of marking *viva voce* work in any manner that will yield a satisfactory classification in order of merit. And then the delightful ease of marking grammar questions! Is it any wonder that translation is dreaded by examiners and oral work discarded in favour of grammar? It is high time that the University of London set a better example in this respect and made oral work a very strong feature of language examinations. No doubt such a change would be resented by the patrons of this

University, and the length of the language examinations would have to be much extended in order to test every candidate in actual speaking. But some such test is a matter of pressing and vital importance, and educationists should not allow it to be shirked. So long as the ability to speak is not a necessary qualification for passing examinations in language no one will spend time on acquiring this power. No one ever has "too much" time for preparation, and therefore no one will sacrifice any of the little he has to a subject that "does not pay" in the examination. What matter if "the examination does not 'pay' in after life?" It "pays"—nay, it is indispensable at the moment of entering that "after life." It is the "Open Sesame" to almost every profession, and therefore every one will struggle for it, even though it may be utterly worthless once the magic door is passed that gives access to a post and pension.

Widgery's picture of the "good boy" at work upon his "translation" for the next day's French or German lesson is drawn from the life and true in every feature. How many hours have I spent, alas, in similar labours— for I always ranked as one of these "good boys," which means that I spent the greater part of four hours in the evening, after my five hours in school, hunting in dictionaries and grammars for a not intolerable mis-translation of some ten or fifteen lines of French, German, Latin or Greek, as the case might be, or in the effort to make up an utterly unforeign rendering of some piece of doctored English, a very disproportionate part of the four hours being devoted to English, Mathematics and Science. Doubtless my cleverer school-fellows did not all work so long. But every school is full of "good boys" who, being like myself dragged back by illness and a variety of causes, make up, for inability to " cram " the grammar without effort and " spot " the translation without grubbing in the dictionary, by this Herculean effort to arrive analytically at a recondite meaning or build up synthetically a form which they ought to acquire by much reading and more oral imitation. Another fact, sadly overlooked by modern education, is the superior ease of imitation as compared with construction. The latter requires an adult brain, and the capacity for it is developed much later than for imitation. Even unreasoning brutes are capable of learning by imitation ! Hence the " brain fag," of which we hear so much nowadays, produced by imitative studies is far less than that produced by constructive effort. Certainly the reasoning faculty must be trained and fostered, but it should not, when it has just begun to grow, be suddenly called upon to work with the facility and circumspection it attains in adult manhood and womanhood. Most youthful effort should be imitative, and constructive effort should only be introduced gradually and continued only for short periods. Has any teacher, who believes in the exclusive use of the method described above by Mr. Dingwall, thoroughly and clearly realised what it means to ask a boy to proceed in this manner ? It means that the boy, with his undeveloped brain and unpractised concentrative power, is to assume the same mental attitude towards the sentence to be translated as his adult teacher, who has had years of practice and possesses a fully developed brain ! It means that the boy is first to remember that he must first look for the verb—then, that the verb has different forms for person, number, tense, mood and voice—then, that it may be active or passive, transitive

I

or intransitive—then, to reflect that, if transitive, it will have an object—then, that these forms will correspond to similar variations in the subject—then he must think out which of these forms fulfil the demands of the laws of concord—then he must think yet further, if an adjective happens to complicate the subject or an adverb the verb—and then the question of connectives! All this the teacher, by virtue of long practice and a strong and fully-developed brain, does instinctively and with little effort, and then—O acme of pedagogic fatuousness!—he expects the poor little half-formed brain, in a skull whose interlocking bones are perhaps not yet completely closed, weak, hazy as to reasons, distracted in attention by a thousand wandering fancies and altogether unfit, to think and plan and so produce a translation, or an exercise-sentence, as perfect as those which the master reels off his tongue in a few seconds with a wealth of æsthetic alternatives that fills the "good boy's" mind with mingled wonder and despair! When will the perfection of the man understand the imperfection of the child? *

"We haven't time to read the Latin (or French). Get on with the translation." "What then," asks Widgery in despair, "is the lesson—Latin, French, English?" It is not any of these. It is a lesson in EXAMINATION LANGUAGE! "Where is this strange dialect spoken?" "Spoken!—no one dreams of trying to speak it! We only write it on paper and have it marked." (!)

I have already pointed out that "declaiming in the

---

* Comenius gives to education a psychological basis in demanding that the faculties shall be developed in their natural order : first, the senses, the memory, the imagination, and lastly the judgment and the reason.—COMPAYRÉ. Note the word *lastly*.

finest style," though highly desirable, is difficult to practise with any effect and should therefore be done in
moderation and not too often. It is hard to hold the
child's attention, and, if the child is not listening, where
is the use of declaiming to him? It would be as profitable to declaim to lay-models, after the manner of Mr.
Punch's stage-struck shop-assistant.

As for Exercises, I would earnestly commend Mr.
Dingwall's remarks in the extract from the *Journal of
Education* to the serious consideration of "the powers
that be." No more disastrous and disheartening truth
was ever stated than that, "however diligently the rule
itself may be explained, the ordinary pupil will simply
translate the sentence literally in an examination, when
no hint is given of the rule which is to be applied."
And it is the ordinary pupil whom conscientious teachers
have to consider. The extraordinary pupil—"the clever
youngster" who learns without apparent effort—does not
want much teaching. He will get on under any master.
Indeed he is the delight and the consolation of the bad
teacher, for he will always do well in examinations and
give the ineffective teacher a spurious reputation, that
will often stand him in good stead when the rest of his
class is proved to be a mass of failures. The reason for
this inability to remember the necessity of obeying rules
is simply the undeveloped condition of the ratiocinative
faculty in the child, as I have endeavoured to show above.
To produce a correct exercise in the examination room
a boy must have the full-grown and fully-trained mind of
the teacher who set it, and only the mind of the "clever
youngster" ever even approximates to this condition.
The "stupid" boy never comes within a hundred miles
of it, and the "ordinary" boy only knows of it as a hope-

less ideal lost in the dim distance of his master's "awful" learning.

The "disparity in difficulty" between the "French into English" and "English into French" parts of an exercise, pointed out by Widgery, is worthy of note. Every teacher knows how much "easier" children find the "French into English" part and how gladly they turn to it from the insurmountable and vexatious difficulties of the "English into French." The reason is tersely stated by Widgery. The merest inkling of the thought embodied in the French words is generally enough to enable the English child to give a fair translation *of the thought*, for he immediately clothes it, without difficulty, in the English words which convey the same thought to him in English. But in the opposite process, where he wants to transfer an English thought into French, he is at once at a loss how to express himself. He does not know what French words would convey the same thought to a Frenchman, or if, as happens in the case of easy sentences, he does know the words, he is generally at a loss to know in what order they should be arranged. No grammar can tell him. The exercise book only helps him in the case of certain typical sentences, generally of a stiff, un-literary, non-idiomatic and altogether artificial nature. How then can he transfer his thought into the foreign language and clothe it in an idiomatic dress, in which it will be recognised by a Frenchman?—only by saturating his mind with the spirit of the French language and absorbing the genius of its idiom. This he can only do by reading great quantities of real, not doctored, French and repeating still greater quantities of French sentences orally, till they become a part of his own thought—till, in short, any thought that may come into his head can be run off, at will and with equal facility, into a French or an English word-group, and find an equally perfect æsthetic expression in a French or an English sentence.

"It is impossible to translate into a foreign language unless the mind feels in it more or less at home" is another golden sentence worthy of inscription over the door of the language-master's class-room. No candid linguist can deny its truth, no conscientious teacher dare ignore its teaching.

"Retroversion," recommended by Widgery for the "higher" classes, should, I think, be confined to the "highest" class. It is a very difficult exercise and cannot be attempted with success till long practice has produced very considerable familiarity with the language into which the "retranslation" is effected. Only the best boys in the school should attempt this task.*

XI. Vocabulary.

Vocabulary lessons we must have as a regular part of school work. For practical use after leaving school a vocabulary is most important. On what principle are we to classify the words—by the alphabet, the things around us, the parts of speech, etymology or psychology?

The first plan hardly needs any discussion. The second somehow grows very dull in practice, nor can it be consistently carried out.

Now, since the primary office of words is to carry meaning, they must be arranged, as far as possible, in those groups which analogy forms unconsciously in the mind. For this we need very much a small edition of Roget's "Thesaurus of

* I must set beside my own experience the opinion of a colleague, who tells me that he constantly employs this exercise even in his lower classes and has no reason to be dissatisfied with the result.

English Words and Phrases." The groups of this ideological dictionary should then be sedulously worked over in the English classes by forming sentences with them. The corresponding French and German vocabularies should be printed in precisely the same way, so that, with the English vocabulary open before him, the child could tell at once from its position in the page the meaning of the French or German word.

Later on, when we wish to drop translation as much as possible, the foreign vocabularies can be taken alone, and cross associations will be avoided. How are we to acquire these groups? First and foremost we must never ask the child to learn a word he has not already seen as an integral part of a sentence.* A single word by itself has no more meaning than a single bone.

After a fair number of primitives have been mastered, in the manner explained in the Reader above, the words should be ticked off in the vocabulary parallel to the English. As soon as any particular one has a majority of ticked forms, the teacher can make up easy sentences for the others, and the whole group may be learnt by heart.

As soon as the higher classes have acquired a fair store of words, they may be gradually rearranged on etymological principles, so far as these are applied to showing the *inner* construction of the language.

By this time a number of derivatives will have been unconsciously absorbed, and, as soon as a clear feeling for some of their formative elements has been obtained, we can work over our primitives again by making words (*e.g.*) ending in -*able*, -*ung*, -*eur*, compound verbs in *be*-, *er*-, &c. &c.

A useful plan for saving the time of the children is to work through the author set with a note-book cut step-wise into an alphabet, and to enter the leading derivatives as they occur under their respective primitives. Then we can either take one page and explain the family of words on it, or we

---

* Père Girard makes it a principle always to have the conjugations made by means of propositions.—Compayré.

can work through the note-book and pick out all those that have the same formative element. In this way, by preparing for the coming words, we can read faster.—Pp. 51–53.

Nothing need be added to this section. I would merely draw the reader's attention to the importance of the statement "A single word by itself has no more meaning than a single bone." The truth of this has been sufficiently illustrated by numerous remarks in the preceding pages and we may now pass on to consider the utility of philology in school-teaching.

XII. PHILOLOGY.

Like phonetics, philology is not a school subject save in English. The teacher should know a great deal about it, and the children should hear uncommonly little. Our statements on language should be made as far as possible in that form in which the pupil, if he advance far enough, will meet with them in philology.

We should keep to the principle of restricting philology to showing the *inner* formation of the language. This is not, however, the method most in vogue. Some of our grammars and readers present us with something over which they are pleased to put " Grimm's Law." A mnemonic formula ASH, SHA, HAS is to help us. The sounds apparently are divided, like boiled eggs, into hard and soft. *A* stands for aspirate and, as we learn by the way, for spirant too—that is *father* and fa*t h*er are the same ! Unfortunately this pleasing law breaks down when we compare *father, mother, brother* with *Vater, Mutter, Bruder*. Of course, boys soon get to believe that etymology is a game where the letters of the alphabet are shaken up in a bag and you take out what you like. Another firm conviction, which always rouses the wrath of Mr. Skeat, is that English "comes from" German. They cannot believe anything else.

A curious defence for the retention of Latin in schools is sometimes put forward on etymological grounds. "To understand the English language thoroughly it is necessary to have a knowledge of Latin." It may be pointed out that the same holds true for half the languages of Europe.

One point of capital importance is altogether overlooked by these classical philologists—the change of meaning. Even our professed etymologists subordinate it far too much to the changes of sound. A month's study at vowel gradation in Old English would teach more etymology and philology than years of school Latin. It is often easier to learn the meaning at once than to follow the various changes from Latin to modern French. We stand a chance, too, of blurring the scientific sense for language, by putting side by side changes in form that it took centuries to bring about. We set up cross associations, and they are the one thing to be avoided in teaching language. Let us not confuse the practical mastery of a modern tongue with the scientific study of its origin.* We must learn things as they are before we begin to investigate how they got to be what they are.

The intrusion of comparative philology into school work is positively harmful.—Pp. 53–57.

This, curiously enough, is the section that excited most comment and opposition. Though it appears to me the least important in the book, the assertions of Widgery's opponents are interesting. I shall quote them in extenso and then offer some criticisms tending to show that Widgery's opponents have, in one sense, begged the question and, in another, appear to be playing at cross purposes with him.

Extracts.—"The paper on the Teaching of Languages is very valuable, but Mr. Widgery's objections to philology do not prove any necessity of failure. They do not touch the bulk of the language; moreover, they are applicable just as well to the 'inner construction' as to philology.

* In Condillac's system the real knowledge of the language precedes the abstract study of the rules.—COMPAYRÉ.

"Difference in the meaning of cognate terms is not necessarily an objection ; nor is cross association always a consequence of it. Most generally the difference is merely one of width, and the present, apparently different, meanings can easily be reconciled. Why should we, for instance, teach *Lager=camp*, when we can explain hundreds of terms by tracing *Lager* to *layer* and *lair*, comparing the present with the past meanings ? Delay occasioned by tracing the meaning of a term is not always unprofitable.

"As for the more general objections of Mr. Widgery, I can only say—

"(1) That we do not necessarily blur the religious sense of a savage by teaching him the Bible, nor the 'scientific sense for language' of a boy by showing him that the words he has to learn are the very ones he uses himself every day.

"(2) We do not usually tell a man who forges a tool for his work, that he should not try and 'do two things at once,' and that he should first finish his work and then forge the tool. As a tool we regard, of course, philology.

"(3) Depreciation of comparison of any kind, as long as it does not go beyond the capacity of pupils to grasp it, would be folly.

"Finally, allow me to mention a few points which, in my opinion, go far towards assuring success in regard to philology—

"(1) All the theory required is an idea of the formation of vowels and consonants—not more than that amount of phonetics which most teachers, especially abroad, would consider necessary in any case. It will enable boys to realise that there is similarity between certain words. We need not say one word of Grimm or Verner.

"(2) This knowledge we do not try to exploit in order 'to strengthen weak vocabularies' of boys for examination. We only want to facilitate future recognition of terms already examined. Such recognition increases the chance of retention tenfold.

"(3) Discrimination in language as well as in music lies

with the ear. Sight comparison cannot be much else than
vanity.

"(4) If it is found that a certain boy cannot remember
words the similarity of which with others he knows has been
pointed out to him, then we may be sure that no such
similarity, however clear to his master, has ever been clear
to *him*.

"Thus, to keep comparison within due limits and check all
foolish pedantry, we have only just to remember—similarity
must be *understood*, it must be *heard* and must *facilitate*
acquisition."—F. G. Z. in *Journal of Education*, Jan. 1, 1889.

" Suppose I have succeeded in making a word sink into a
boy's mind by the help of some stray light which philology
may lend me, what have I done? I have by comparison
established connection where there seemed none before. I
have thereby made association natural and remembrance
easy. I have also by my comparison collected material for
a possible future law, or have brought a certain fact within
the range of an established law. I have established some
true relationship which is a meritorious piece of education
quite apart from any practical advantage."—F. G. Z. in
Journal of Education, March 1, 1889.

"Mr. Widgery looks upon philology as only a *science*,
whereas F. G. Z. regards it only as a *tool*. It is unquestionably
both ; but, for school purposes, it can never, except in the
highest forms, be more than a tool. Mr. Widgery seems to
ignore the fact that philology and analogy in their simplest
forms are an immense aid to memory, and any tool which
will sharpen a boy's faculties is surely perfectly legitimate.

" Show boys that hundreds upon hundreds of little words
are identical in the two languages, or differ so slightly that
there is no real difficulty in retaining them, that the hundreds
of difficult big words are very often only small words to
which are joined certain prefixes and suffixes, and that, if we
split them up, we get little words they use daily without
thinking. All this can be done by simply and intelligently
comparing and explaining German words with English, and

laying down a few broad rules for the boy's general guidance. The word philology need never be mentioned.

"Is it true, as Mr. Widgery asserts, that 'there is nothing elementary in philology'? I think the statement most misleading. We must not trouble a boy with Grimm's Law, or the modifications and discoveries of Verner and others. But give him his few simple rules with dozens of examples, and we shall strengthen his vocabulary, which is the one thing needful above all others in a language."—W. S. M. in *Journal of Education*, March 1, 1889.

Now all this indignation, it seems to me, is rooted in a very simple misunderstanding. Widgery possessed a considerable knowledge of philology and no little skill in the art of philological investigation and, when he deprecates the use of philology in schools, he is thinking of those elaborate comparisons and those deep investigations with which the professional philologist busies himself. Both F. G. Z. and W. S. M., while talking nothing but sound sense and making the most valuable suggestions for the use of what they call philology in schools, seem to me to beg the whole question. *Is* this simple common-sense comparison, which they so well and wisely use, philology in the sense understood by the specialist? I think not. At any rate, if it *is* philology, then it is the very elements of the elements of that science. Would not Grimm, or Verner, or Skeat be scandalised to hear that "simple and intelligent comparing and explaining German words with English, and laying down a few broad rules for the boy's general guidance" is teaching philology? Surely F. G. Z. and W. S. M. are merely playing at cross purposes with Widgery! He deprecates any attempt to introduce boys to the subtleties of comparison and philosophical

generalisation which constitute the science of philology
in the hands of a specialist, but nowhere, so far as I can
make out, does he object to such elementary comparison
for purposes of recognition as F. G. Z. and W. S. M. propose to employ and affect to dignify with the name of
philology, which does not, in Widgery's mind, include
such elementary comparison. Widgery is thinking of
the higher flights of comparison indulged in by the adult
specialist. F. G. Z. and W. S. M. agree with him in
saying that such high flying is not for the schoolboy's
wing. Then they proceed to accuse him of deprecating
those easy comparisons which they, very rightly, employ.
He does no such thing, for the simple reason that, when
he deprecated the teaching of philology, he never
thought of such common-sense observation of similarity
and difference as being a part of that science at all !
This is what he means, I think, by saying that "there is
nothing elementary in philology." No more there is in
what *he* called philology—the unearthing of roots and
the life history of derivatives and linguistic construction
in general. F. G. Z. and W. S. M. would not recom-
mend such "digging" for schoolboys nor such historical
investigation. Neither does Widgery. They approve
of making a child use his eyes while he is busy in the
linguistic field, as well as when he is wandering over the
green meadows and through the wooded lanes of the
material world, in order that he may compare one thing
with another and, by registering the differences he observes, store up the means of recognition. So does
Widgery. Indeed no one inculcated this elementary
observation and comparison more systematically and
earnestly than he did. But—and here is the root of the
misunderstanding—he did not call such elementary

comparison philology. F. G. Z. and W. S. M. do—*hinc illae lachrymae.*

The heart of Widgery's objection is to be found in the two sentences " Let us not confuse the practical mastery of a modern tongue with the scientific study of its origin " and " We must learn things as they are before we begin to investigate how they got to be what they are." In the first he strikes at the prevalent idea that a study of the grammar of a language will enable a child to speak it. In the second he once more gives expression to his deep regret that we persistently waste, in prying into the processes by which a modern language has been developed out of a more ancient one spoken a thousand years ago, the precious time that should be devoted to acquiring a practical fluency of speech in the form in which we happen to find and must use it now.

XIII. Need for Reform—Obstacles.

Our present method needs a thorough reform. The hindrance lies in the exaggerated respect paid by the British public to examinations,* while it takes no trouble to see that they will test the capabilities it wants or that the examiners are specially fitted for their work.

We shall not teach either foreign languages or other subjects adequately till scholarships can be freely gained for them at our Universities, and the graduate feels that his future chance for a headmastership is as good as if he had taken up classics, mathematics, or science. Or rather, the particular subject he is to teach ought to be made subordinate to his knowledge of pedagogy. In the past the school-

---

* Our purblind prejudice in this matter is only matched by the gigantic stupidity of the Chinese, among whom life itself, one might almost say, depends upon a competitive examination.

master has been confused with the scholar. Now we run the risk of confusing him with the specialist.

The scholar lacks intellectual detachment, the specialist a right sense of proportion in estimating the value of his subject. With each the main occupation is with a thing. With the schoolmaster it is a mind. The true doctor is an artist with his skill based on science. He sees instinctively what the particular individual patient before him wants at that particular moment. We should be artists in the souls of children, but as long as we are allowed to offer great knowledge of a single subject joined to a rough empirical experience, instead of a profound study of the child's mind, we shall rise in matters of teaching, in spite of all our enthusiasm, devotion, and hard labour, no higher than the level of the herb-woman and the bone-setter.

Considering the large number of men and women engaged in education, and the intrinsic value of the subject, is it too much to ask our Universities to give us *Schools* or a *Tripos for Teachers?*

At present our method in examining for foreign languages is little short of ludicrous. In the great majority of cases the highest honours *can* be won by the deaf and dumb! Of the four elements of language, hearing, speaking, reading, writing, not a single one is adequately tested. The weight is thrown on translation and the exceptions in the grammar. The former the native speaker never wants, and the latter he absorbs unconsciously. So far can false views on the nature of language mislead us.*—Pp. 58, 59.

Extracts.—The actual amount of knowledge we can hope to instil into a boy of sixteen must of necessity be small: but habits, above all the habit of independent investigation, the habit of accuracy we must instil.

The teacher must keep one eye on practice and the other on theory.

* Compare Section I. of Theories.

In future the writers of our text books must keep the right eye on the child and the left eye on their subject.

Instead of spending weary hours in correcting papers the teacher's work must be more intensive in the class room : all must be alive, questions right and left, one boy improving on another's answers,* and all to be done in the foreign language.

Do masters ever sit down and try to form some sort of not altogether inadequate conception of what is going on in the brains before them ?

It is so much easier to say a boy is stupid and lazy and cane him than to confess an almost total ignorance of his psychology. The first requisite in the artist is to know the capabilities and limitations of the material he is working in, but then teachers are not artists—yet.

What shall be added to this heavy indictment ? If parents knew !—if teachers cared !—half the schools in the kingdom would be emptied in a day and a giant stride be taken towards the perfection of educational methods. There could be but one result—a wiser, broader-minded, nobler race of men and women sprung from children trained up by rational methods to a profitable and effective knowledge. But three huge obstacles block the way—lack of information on the part of the parent, lack of imagination in the teacher and lack of courage on the part of headmasters and the scholastic world at large. The parent knows not how little the methods in vogue in the schoolroom are calculated to secure the results after which he or she is longing—the training up of the child, in whom the parental hopes are centred, on whom the parental anxiety is so richly lavished, into a perfect man or woman with a sound

* Active and animated co-operation of all the members of the class, rapid interrogation.—Père Girard.

mind in a sound body acting upon the dictates of a
sound heart, capable of discharging the duties of life
with success and building up an honoured name. The
teacher, not always but too often, knows not what a
mighty power he wields for good and ill, and cannot
project his mind by the help of imagination into the
distant future and see how faulty teaching in the child
sitting before him, young, innocent, helpless, in every
way at the mercy of his superior knowledge and wider
experience, will be reflected in faulty success in the man
who will one day issue from the school gates and go out
to add his influence and his learning, whether his teacher
shall have given him much or little, good or bad, to the
shaping of the destinies of the world and the sum of
human knowledge. Could the light-hearted merchant of
worthless knowledge see so far ahead, cold and callous
as he might be, he would weep for very shame at the
thought of the possibilities for evil that the so-called
" stupid " boy carries silently out of those same school
gates, whence the last scholarship-winner went out but
just now amid cheers and handshakes. And this because the " stupid " boy was not " stupid " but " ill-
taught," while he to whom the teacher owes his reputation and the school its prosperity won that scholarship,
not because his master was so good a teacher but
because he himself was so gifted as not to need " good "
teaching ! So much credit may wrong methods claim
unreproved for a right result in no way due to them.
The headmaster, harrassed by the difficulties of an
organisation that must respond to the fads of ill-informed
and injudicious parents and the crotchets of masters who
forget that they are assistants and not chiefs, that their
duty is to carry into effect the conceptions of the prin-

cipal and not amuse themselves with their own hobbies, is also hampered ceaselessly by the consideration that every boy removed by an unsatisfied parent means money, strength and reputation lost to the school. He *dare* not tamper with tradition or strike out along the new paths indicated by a more enlightened pedagogy with that boldness and thoroughness which can alone ensure the success that can silence the clamour of a timid and ignorant conservatism. And the scholastic world at large takes its inspiration from the heads of schools, reposes in a sweet apathy of irresponsibility, leaving all innovation to the head who would be held responsible for its possible failure, or, if aroused by any cry of indignation from among its own ranks, doubts tremulously where he doubts and stops where he stands still. But

> " Our doubts are traitors,
> And make us lose the good we oft might win,
> By fearing to attempt."

So child after child comes into the world, is seized in the day of his weakness and ignorance by the ruthless Giant Grammar and his henchman Exercise and syste matically maltreated and abused, till the attainment of manhood gives him strength to fling the "loads of learned lumber" he has carried so long at the bidding of these tyrants into the silence of the irrecoverable past. Only when he goes out into the great world and tries his strength against the giants Time and Opportunity does he realise—too late, alas!—how little he has been trained to grapple them with success, and discover suddenly, with indescribable humiliation and a regret that often amounts to despair, that the time for training, so misapplied, is now for ever past away.

K

CHAPTER IV

SUMMARY OF SYSTEM

LET us, before we pass on, summarise briefly the main points of the system of language-teaching elaborated in the preceding pages.

The system at present in vogue attempts at once too much and too little. Too many languages are taken in hand at the same time and every one is studied too superficially.

The claim of the classical languages to superiority as a means of culture cannot be sustained. Modern languages have an advantage in the possibility of effective criticism by living exponents of their native pronunciation and æsthetic qualities and, being nearer, can be heard and felt.

In future time must be saved by limiting the teaching of the Classics. Our teaching should centre around English. We ought by a good preliminary training in our own tongue to acquire a general framework into which we can place afterwards as many languages as we please.

In the study of English, grammar should be taught inductively and for language we should work back to the age of Anne, thence to Shakespeare, Chaucer and Old English. Between thirteen and fourteen bifurcation should begin, the future classicist turning towards

Greek and Latin and the future modern linguist towards French, German and English, with the last always in the centre.

The chief defect of our language teaching is the neglect of the capacity of the mind for unconscious activity. By beginning Latin too early we encourage the formation of various prejudices detrimental to a correct method of learning languages. It requires considerable time to be able to reproduce exceptional forms, and "lists of exceptions" are therefore psychologically unsound. Rules should invariably be derived from the language and enough examples should be given to make the rule spring up as it were by itself.

The child obtains a complete mastery over its mother-tongue at home without grammar, dictionary, translation or reading, learning it as a harmonious whole. We must learn foreign languages in the same manner, and through the ear, not the eye, as in learning Latin.

Phonetics is not a school subject, but the master must be a phonetician. The actual spoken language of to-day must form the base of all learning. Accidence and syntax are less important than pronunciation. Phonetics alone can enable us to pronounce properly. Sign must never be confused with sound. For the physiologic side of speech we need a thorough gymnastic of the organs of speech by means of phonetics and for the psychologic side we need to repeat the conscious incessantly until it becomes the unconscious and we arrive at the *Sprachgefühl* of the foreigner. A great part of grammar is merely bad orthography. Grammatical forms should be abstracted unconsciously from the spoken and not consciously from the written language. The pupil should have his ears "bathed" in the sounds of the foreign

language. The point to insist on is the correct reproduction of *sounds as sounds*. Meaning can be put into
them later when they fall trippingly from the tongue.

The centre of our system should be the Reader. From
it our grammar and orthography should be drawn inductively.* Grammatical paradigms should be taken with
the book open and every word embodied in a sentence.
Examples and not rules are to be learnt by heart.
Parse sparingly at first. Look out sharply for idioms.
Substitute dictation for written translation. The main
object of the Reader is to give a thorough knowledge of
the accidence and the first beginnings of the syntax.
After three or four years study of the Reader, the child
will be in a position to read literature as such, leaving
all the paraphernalia of the earlier stages well behind
him. The crown and summit of the language-master's
activity is to make some of his sense for the splendour
and beauty of foreign literature pass into the souls of his
boys. Literature we must read as literature. Textual
criticism, archæology, philology have merely to prepare
the best possible text and leave it at the school gates.

The source of our troubles is making the *letter* and
not the *sound* the ultimate element of language. Until
we have a real living faith in the *spoken* language as the
source of all our literature and as the starting-point of all

---

* The pupils ought, from beginning to end, to assist themselves in constructing a grammar of their own.—PÈRE GIRARD.
"Jacotot," says Doctor Dittes, "has incited a lasting improvement
in the public instruction of Germany. The reform which he introduced into the teaching of reading is important. He started with
an entire sentence, which was pronounced, explained, and learnt
by heart by the children, and afterwards analysed into its consti-
tuent parts."—COMPAYRÉ.

our scientific studies, we shall make no real progress with our language teaching.

Not an exact knowledge of all the rules of the grammar, nor some skill in their application, will give the power of speech. There is no time for conscious reflection, the thought and the word must spring up in the mind simultaneously. And this power, this readiness, will never be acquired by the conscious method of reflection, but only by the unconscious method of imitation and incessant repetition. We must learn to think *in* before we think *of* the language.

The native speaker uses his grammar unconsciously and never employs translation at all. Our whole system, centring around these two, seems planned to give a self-conscious knowledge about the language and not the language itself. The power to speak is put at the end of the school career, or outside of it, instead of at the very beginning. If we really desire to teach French, the French must be the first thing to be heard in class and the last thing must be a memory haunted by the clear thoughts and the clear sounds of the French. The Exercise Book is the veritable "night side" of our system. The fundamental error at the base of this system is the belief that language can be reconstructed *a priori* on the model of certain types, or by the exercise of the logical faculty in the correct application of the rules of grammar. As a matter of fact the mind has no time for this process when suddenly confronted with the lively interchange of thought in ordinary conversation. The Exercise Book should be put at the end of two years reading. However swift the process, there must be a great psychologic gap between the conscious arrangement of elements and the unconscious flow of real speech.

Vocabulary lessons we must have as a regular part of school work, but we must never ask the child to learn a word he has not already seen as an integral part of a sentence. A single word by itself has no more meaning than a single bone.

Philology is not a school subject save in English. The teacher should know a great deal about it and the children should hear uncommonly little. We should keep to the principle of restricting philology to showing the *inner* formation of the language. Let us not confuse the practical mastery of a modern tongue with the scientific study of its origin. The intrusion of comparative philology into school work is positively harmful.

Our present method needs a thorough reform. The hindrance lies in the exaggerated respect paid by the British public to examinations. The schoolmaster is confused with the scholar and the specialist. With each the main occupation is with a thing. With the schoolmaster it is a mind. We should be artists in the souls of children. We require in the Universities a *Tripos for Teachers*. At present no one of the four elements of language—hearing, speaking, reading, writing—is adequately tested, and, in the great majority of cases, the highest honours *can* be won by the deaf and dumb ! So far can false views on the nature of language mislead us.

This comprehensive and apparently revolutionary scheme is but the logical development of a few simple fundamental conceptions.

The first of these is a smaller field and a more intensive study of it. Widgery does not ask that Greek and Latin should be banished from the field of intellectual culture, as a hasty conclusion might suppose. He merely pleads that they should be put later. First lay a firm foundation of the practical languages—French, German and English—and then take up the more ornamental Greek and Latin.

The second is the dominant importance of " unconscious activity." The chief consequence of this is the substitution of imitation for construction. Imitation is the process natural to adolescent mind. Construction belongs to the adult intelligence. At present we try to make the half-grown child assume the mental attitude of a full-grown teacher. This is a fatal mistake.

The third is that language is learnt naturally as a harmonious whole by imitation, not put together *a priori* on the model of certain types by the conscious logical arrangement of elements drawn from a classified list previously committed to memory. This implies the substitution of oral recitation for written grammar.

The fourth is that grammatical forms should be abstracted unconsciously from the spoken and not consciously from the written language, whence it follows that the centre of our system should be the Reader, grammar and orthography being drawn out of it inductively.

The fifth is that the sound, and not the letter, is the ultimate element of language, and that therefore the spoken language is the real source of all our literature and the starting point of all our scientific studies.

The sixth is that conscious reflection is inconsistent with fluency of utterance, and that such fluency can only be acquired by incessant iteration resulting in unconscious imitation.

The seventh is that a single word by itself has no

more meaning than a single bone.   Hence a child should never be asked to learn a word he has not already seen as an integral part of a sentence.

The eighth is that the practical mastery of a modern tongue is entirely separate from the scientific study of its origin.   Therefore comparative philology has no right to enter into school work.

Lastly he conceives that, while the scholar and the specialist are occupied each mainly with a thing, the schoolmaster has to deal with a mind.   Therefore teachers should not be scholars in grammatical form, but artists in the souls of children.

Generally Widgery holds that language is to be learnt by the unconscious imitation of a harmonious whole, following Nature's method with an infant, not built up by conscious effort of the logical faculty working after artificial models in accordance with the custom of the adult intelligence.   And he believes that the base of all linguistic study must of necessity be the spoken language of to-day.

CHAPTER V

POSITION IN HISTORY OF PEDAGOGY

I SHALL close this part of the memoir with a brief estimate of Widgery's contributions to the progress of
pedagogic science and his position in its history.

" By dint of wide reading and ingenious experiment he
had made himself an authority both at home and abroad
in the infant science of Phonetics," now generally
acknowledged to be the base of all language teaching.
His "knowledge of the literature of education was very
extensive." The valuable bibliography at the end of "The
Teaching of Languages in Schools" affords ample proof
of this. "If he had been spared, there is little doubt
that he would have attained a distinguished reputation
among educational writers." "What Widgery accomplished was little in comparison with that of which he
gave such brilliant promise. It was rather the man
himself, with his inspiring love of literature and philology
and art, which counted for so much "—counted none the
less because their influence lies hidden in the minds and
hearts of men, working in a thousand secret ways
unknown to the more open art of books. "Living," like
all original minds, "to a great extent before his time," he
"did a great service to a great cause" and his death was
"a very serious loss to education."

He was distinguished from other educational reformers

of like boldness by the faculty of organisation. No charge brought against him by shallow and hasty thinkers was falser than that of unpractical theorising. Lapses into chimerical dreaming and ludicrous sophistry and mysticism, such as disfigured the sublime inspirations of some of the great educationists of the past, were impossible to his sane intelligence. Something of this he owed, of course, to the scientific spirit of the age in which he lived.

Widgery follows Pestalozzi in the application of the " natural method" which " makes the child proceed from his own intuitions, and leads him by degrees, and through his own efforts, to abstract ideas." He acted upon Morf's Pestalozzian maxims "that intuition (*Anschauung*) is the basis of instruction," "that instruction ought to begin with the simplest elements, and to progress by degrees while following the development of the child, that is to say, through a series of steps psychologically connected," "that instruction ought to follow the order of natural development, and not that of synthetic exposition," "that to wisdom there must be joined power; to theoretical knowledge, practical skill." The Pestalozzian watchwords of Froebel and his pupils Langethal and Middendorf at Keilbau, "intuition, personal initiative, proceeding from the known to the unknown," dominated Widgery's educational methods.

"There are two categories of educational reformers. Some see a goal by reason and reflection and lay out a logical route to it which they may or may not traverse, but some one ultimately will. Others, dominated by an intense feeling, grope their uncertain way towards a goal whose outline and position are only dimly discerned through the mists of emotion. With some, the motive is intellectual, with others, it is emotional; and in their higher manifestations these endowments are mutually exclusive."—(W. H. PAYNE.) Nevertheless, perhaps because in him they were not manifested in the very highest degree, Widgery possessed both these endowments. He saw far and clearly and he followed passionately to the end. "Tested by the simplest rules of order, symmetry, and economy, the schools organised by Pestalozzi were failures." "Pestalozzi was a poor teacher, but an unsurpassed educator."—(PAYNE.) Widgery was the reverse of a poor teacher and, in his narrower sphere, he gave promise of being a great educator. Order and symmetry characterised all his thoughts and actions. He possessed a mind at once philosophical and practical. And this in its highest development is the greatest mind.

Let us turn somewhat more particularly to Widgery's contributions to the progress of pedagogy. Combining "Comenius's desire for widening the realm of positive knowledge" with "Pestalozzi's enthusiasm for heightening the intellectual powers," and so "wedding the formal education of the Middle Ages to the spreading science of the moderns," Widgery did not exclude the Classics, but reduced them to their true character as a luxury of education, an ornament of the highest culture.* He

* Locke does not disparage the beauty of a language (Greek) whose masterpieces, he says, are the original source of our literature and science ; but he reserves the knowledge of it to the learned, to the lettered, to professional scholars, and he excludes it from secondary instruction, which ought to be but the school which trains for active life.—COMPAYRÉ. The classics, being fancy studies, so to speak, are fit only for a small minority of pupils, and have no right to the first place in a common education, destined for men in general.—DIDEROT.

defended the superiority of the living over the dead languages as a " mental gymnastic," and he would have the study of the Classics limited to acquiring the power to read them. In this he ranges with Descartes, Locke, Condillac, La Chalotais and others against the pernicious formal system of the Jesuits. So with Ratich, the Jansenist solitaries of Port Royal, Locke, Rollin and Père Girard, he lays immense stress on the importance of the vernacular and advances beyond these greater exponents of pedagogy in making it the centre of all teaching. But perhaps his most original contribution to the science of language teaching—a proposition, so far as I can discover, unique in the history of that science— is the notion of studying the mother-tongue in reverse historical order, working back from its latest developments to its primitive form. His idea of working upon the conscious till by incessant iteration it becomes the unconscious has its germ in Pestalozzi's insistance upon the necessity of studying the psychology of the child. The method of teaching, according to Widgery, must be based on psychological considerations, not upon philological classifications. He makes a valuable distinc- tion in asserting that the scholar and the specialist are occupied each mainly with a thing, while the teacher busies himself with a mind, and he has crystallised the highest conceptions of previous educators in the demand that the teacher should be an " artist in the souls of children." A profound truth, too little recognised, too little appre- ciated, underlies his theory that a language should be learnt, not analytically, but as a harmonious whole, and also the other theory that the conditions in face of a foreign language resemble those of a child beginning to learn its mother-tongue. Still more important and original is his contention that languages must be learnt through the ear and that therefore all linguistic study must be based on a knowledge of phonetics. He rises again above the majority of educators in placing a practical mastery of a language before a scholarly command of its ornaments and an antiquarian insight into its origin. But he is not a mere utilitarian. His contention is— "use" first, and then (for those who are equal to it) "ornament."

With Skeat, he makes a strong plea for a deeper study of English by Englishmen. He repudiates analytical grammar—an artificial creation of antiquarian scholars— and would teach grammar only inductively, following the natural method, as exemplified in a child learning the vernacular. With grammar he denounces translation as unnatural methods, so joining issue with the academic (and not, be it observed, the popular) practice of centuries, while he pleads for the most natural of all methods—oral repetition, which has ever been the method of the free student, the ordinary man outside the university in his daily intercourse with foreigners upon the mart and in the counting-house. Most valuable, too, and bold, liberal and original, is his repudiation of a mere knowledge of linguistic structure and his exaltation of the practical ability to speak a foreign tongue. What reproach could be more keen than his statement—too true, alas!—that in our present system of examining in foreign languages the highest honours *can*, in a majority of cases, be won by the deaf and dumb? A deaf and dumb master of speech!

But, in thus pleading for the methods of Nature,

Widgery never falls a prey to the delusion which beset some of the greatest educationists, who fled from the extreme of mechanical artificiality into the licence of the natural wilderness. With Widgery "natural" means "rational"—natural methods mean the fostering of a rational and well-ordered, not an unlimited and disorderly, growth.

He sounds, too, a valuable warning against the danger of working from theories without watching whether they result in good when put into practice—against, that is, the reformer's overmastering inclination to become the slave of an idea. "Less theory, more practice!"* was his constant cry.

Finally, we cannot claim for Widgery a place at the side of the great reformers. To him was assigned a humbler task, but he discharged it as nobly and with far less error. Within the limits of his own sphere, indeed, Widgery had all their boldness and enthusiasm, while he far excelled them in practical sense and in method. They were idealists who had to get others to adapt their ideas to practical use. He was an idealist who could and did apply his own ideas. Their ideas were greater, more original, and helped to solve profounder problems, when others had pruned and shaped them into rational coherence ; but Widgery's ideas came clean-cut from his brain, ready for immediate use. He worked in a more limited field but with a saner intelligence. Less original, his mind was better balanced and his work more perfect. In a smaller sphere he stands forth a greater man. He suffers from the relative perfection of his age. The pioneers of the day of small things appear giants in the

* Few precepts and much practice.—RAMUS. Few rules, many exercises.—PÈRE GIRARD.

eye of posterity. In the noon-day of knowledge tall men
are too plentiful to arrest attention and achieve renown.
Time and opportunity might have raised Widgery as far
above the average of his age as the early reformers rose
above theirs: facts point in that direction. But to him
both were denied.

PART III—CHARACTER

" To live in hearts we leave behind
Is not to die."

CHARACTER

LIFE is not merely a chain of conscious acts, it is also the nest of a vast number of unconscious impressions. In striving therefore to form a true estimate of any man it is not enough to know the history of his deeds, we must examine also the reflection of those deeds in the minds and hearts of his fellow-actors. Shakespeare's dictum—

> " All the world's a stage
> And all the men and women merely players "—

is but a half-truth, since he omits to add that in this terrestrial theatre the stage and auditorium are one, and every player, playing his own part with heart and soul, has yet both eyes and all his mind bent on the performance of every other occupant of the stage. For this abnormal curiosity Fate, with fine irony, has provided a singularly appropriate retribution—that no man shall be able to form a just estimate of his own performance, in direct consequence of his deep engrossment in that of his neighbour. But a biographer stands in a more hopeful situation. If he can but rein in his own critical faculty—save in so far as its action is helpful to correct the prejudices of bad judgment and the errors of ignorance—the double rôle of player-audience will help him to a far more accurate estimate than any he could form by his own insight and observation. He has but to chronicle faithfully the deeds and—whenever he can seize them—the thoughts of his chief actor and then depict, as far as his information goes, their reflection in the minds and hearts of the other actors in the particular scene at the time upon the boards, and the soul of the prime actor will be laid bare to the public eye. Much depends, however, on that saving clause—as far as his information goes—and it constitutes a loophole through which the tricksy spirit of truth will do its best to escape. Many allowances must therefore be made for the partial failure of a system undoubtedly the best that lies to the hand of the would-be honest biographer.

In the first part of this work the mere facts of Widgery's life have been stated chronologically, with such additions only as were necessary to give them the coherence produced by an occasional glimpse of character and motives. The second part dealt more particularly with the work which was the outcome of that life. This last part is an endeavour to illuminate both the previous ones by the strong light thrown from the opinion created by his acts and work in the minds, and to an even greater extent in the hearts, of those who knew him most intimately and best. My part here is merely to weave the scattered thoughts of many minds into a coherent whole, correct any wrong impressions wheresoever my personal observation enables me to do so, and round off the story of his life with as perfect a revelation as may be of that which, after all, was the most important and impressive part of his entity—the man himself.

Once more, ere I enter upon the most delicate and difficult portion of my task, I repeat that the opinions here gathered together are not merely my opinions.

They are, in the first place, the written expressions of many who knew Widgery personally. I have sifted and classified them, and woven the material in each class into a coherent narrative. But the opinions are mine in so far as I accept and record them without comment. Where I could not accept, I have still recorded the opinions, but with the addition of my own view and my reasons for dissenting from the views recorded. In a work like this the constant insertion of chapter and verse would be merely irritating. Let it suffice that this "character" is founded upon the collation of written opinions drawn from many sources.

Teacher.—Whatsoever Widgery may have been, he was, beyond question, first a teacher. We begin then with his characteristics as a teacher. And here we are tempted to ask—"What led him to become a teacher?" For those who do not believe in a "Providence their guide," there can be but one answer—"accident"—the accident of his being fitted with a conscience "too nice" to enter even the most liberal pulpit of his day.

It would be natural to suppose that the first thing observed in a good teacher is ability. But that is, on the contrary, a subtle qualification requiring long and close observation to detect. What does strike one at once is the presence or absence of enthusiasm. Widgery's enthusiasm overflowed. Whether the class were high or low, he gave to it his whole soul, and gave it for the highest reason—a passionate zeal for the art of teaching. Of this zeal the most remarkable instance is his pilgrimage to the chief temple of education in Europe— Germany. Unlike the greater part of educational enthusiasm, his was not merely acquisitive but productive. He had in him little of the so-called scholar, the

University Casaubon, searching lamp in hand among the dust of learned lumber with the sole ambition of filling every cranny of a capacious cranium with barren facts. He learnt that he might teach. He filled his mind with details that he might pour them out to others less gifted with leisure or less ripe for information. This kind of enthusiasm belongs to what one of his German critics called the "catching sort." The natural consequence of such devotion was a "singular success in stimulating his pupils" to a conscientiousness of like character. His interest in teaching and, what is more rare, in school life generally had the keenness and intelligence found only in the teacher who "lives to teach." His constant aim was to lift his pupil to a higher vantage ground. In the attainment of that object he never spared himself. His own immediate interest—his own desire for leisure and more congenial occupation—stood always second to the public good. Such was his enthusiasm for teaching.

But this quality is seldom—doubtless it would be quite safe to say, never—separated from the gift of energy. Widgery's energy never failed—unhappily for his own welfare. The subtraction of a tithe of his energy would have added ten years to his life. He had a wonderful power of continuous and determined work. Hardly anything he undertook failed altogether, almost everything attained a respectable success and many things surpassed it. He was one of those rare and invaluable members of a teaching staff who can be relied on to fill a gap at a moment's notice and fill it creditably. He possessed in a high degree that uncommon common-sense that enables a man to get a firm grip of an entirely new subject the moment he lays hands on it. He was one of those men who are always called to the front

when pioneer work is in hand. Vigorous, capable, original,
he was never content with a commonplace standard—
the standard of the teacher, so called, who shuffles
through the day's time-table and leaves his class-room
ere the last notes of the last bell have been drowned by
the shouts of noisy boys stampeding to the playground,
He had a most untiring perseverance in digging for
"origins" in the fertile soil of books of reference and
learning, that he might woo the interest of his boys by
quaint and curious lore concerning the hackneyed facts
of grammar and the exact sciences. It was not enough
to talk of sonants and consonants, he must unearth the
mother of letters, the hieroglyphic, from the dust of the
Pyramids and bring her with her remote offspring, the
Germanic rune, to brighten the eyes of sluggish boyhood
and entrap its absent ears. All this painstaking work in
the by-ways of learning for the removal of the greatest obstacle of the teacher, inattention, had its
natural result in marked success with the major part
of his pupils. The same industry distinguished the
preparation of his public lectures. With his own
hand he prepared, for his lecture on Beówulf to the
Exeter Literary Society, huge diagrams (several feet
square), maps and other graphic representations that
must have cost him days of hard work—all for an
hour's lecture to amuse a local audience and receive
perhaps a dozen lines of ignorant praise in a sub-
sidised provincial weekly! This last consideration
never entered his head. He lectured to and for his
art and no labour was too great a sacrifice to that art.
In the same way, when his attempt to apply the
metrical test to the First Quarto of *Hamlet* was balked
by the chaotic condition of the text, where verse and

prose are ignorantly mingled, Widgery set to work and
copied out the whole of the Quarto, correcting gross
blunders in spelling and the division of lines and filling
up gaps with the aid of the Second Quarto and the First
Folio. Again, in order to test the possibility of pirating
a play of Shakespeare without the aid of shorthand as
now perfected, Widgery made a determined attempt to
pirate the play of *Macbeth* from the pit of the Exeter
theatre. Such was his thoroughness in whatever he
undertook.

Few of the highest Honour Men of the elder Universities, who have undertaken teaching, trouble to go so
deeply to the root of educational methods as Widgery
did. One little specimen of the readiness of his energy
may close this paragraph. It throws a side light on his
manner of maintaining discipline in the case of foolish
boys. Many men would have stormed and so increased
the enjoyment of the culprit in his crime. Widgery simply
crushed him by the energy and readiness of his wit. "The
boys were doing Schiller's *Ghostseer*, wherein the prince is
described as one who had remained indifferent to the
fair sex. One boy made a noise with his lips intended
to imitate kissing. As quick as thought I wrote the
word 'Laletik' on the board and, although I wasn't
quite sure, pounced on the right boy for the meaning.
Of course he didn't know it.

"'Nobody know the Greek Laleô?'

"'Yes, sir. "I talk."'

"'Right! "I talk or babble." "Laletik" is the study
of the sounds made by savage tribes, babies and others
devoid of reasoning faculties.'"

But neither energy nor enthusiasm will avail much, if
the faculty of interesting, attracting and inspiring be

absent. That Widgery did attain the result usually following from the possession of this faculty seems certain, but there is some difference of opinion as to which of its three agents named above most contributed to that result. Some say that his power of interesting boys was much above the average. He certainly had the power of making boys think. They had a lively remembrance of him after he had ceased to take them. Their eyes brightened at the recollection of his teaching and the methods he employed to captivate their attention. "Oh, sir," they exclaimed to one of his successors, "why don't you tell us some stories as Mr. Widgery used to?" They meant life-like stories about famous characters by which he won their interest for the dry annals of history. One who spent some hours in his classes and watched him teach declares that "he had that sure characteristic of genuine pedagogic skill, the power of assimilating himself with the mental standpoint of his pupils and carrying them along with him and yet holding, at the bottom, a scientific view of the subject taught." Personally I incline to accept the opinion of another old friend and intimate of his, with whom he had frequent converse on educational methods—that Widgery did possess interesting, attractive and inspiring power, but that it was not universal in its effect. He succeeded often, but he also failed sometimes with some boys. I agree also in the opinion that of the three elements Widgery possessed inspiring power in the highest degree. His hold on his class was emotional rather than mental or æsthetic. Given a boy who had any heart of nobility in him, Widgery could play upon him as Orpheus upon Pluto. But with boys of shallow sentiment and mean calibre, who can be held only by the sensation of a tickled fancy (such boys abound), he was unsuccessful. Perhaps little blame can attach to failure in this direction. One source of his hold on boys appears in his habit of allowing them to question him with the utmost freedom. He knew the evils of such license in the hands of a weak teacher, but, for the sake of the good that may be brought out of it by judicious management, he "didn't like to check it." Naturally the boys were "all alive" in his class.

A similar diversity of opinion, again with a share of probability on both sides, prevails with regard to his expositive power. Merely to state the truth that his teaching was clear, as it certainly was, and that he had expositive power, would be insufficient. Some of the elements of clearness—care in arrangement, accuracy in detail, painstaking marshalling of material—he possessed in a high degree. A general lucid fluency of thought and expression appeared even in his conversation, which often conveyed the impression of being original, independent, clean cut, acute, almost brilliant. But his expositive power was always hampered by an impatient energy, which hurried him on to a conclusion obvious to himself without perhaps sufficient consideration of the difficulties of the audience in following him. An intelligent mind kept pace with him easily and with pleasure. But his intellectual march, as in the case of almost all original and strong thinkers, proceeded by long strides which often covered controversial hedges and ditches that proved impassable to less gifted pedestrians. 'Tis a vice that is born of the virtue of unusual excellence. We cannot be hard upon it, though it would be foolish to deny its existence entirely.

I have called his energy impatient. His was the impatience of a strong man eager to reach his goal. From the impatience of the incapable teacher, who is too idle to take the trouble to understand the mental attitude of his pupil and diagnose his intellectual disease—commonly called his difficulty, but rather to be termed his incapacity, his mental ineffectiveness in some particular direction—Widgery was eminently free. No trouble was too great that would enable him to arrive at the weak spot in his pupil's brain and devise a means of strengthening it. He never met a typical difficulty in class without jotting it down on a slip of paper to be thought over at leisure and met, on its subsequent appearance, with some well-considered remedy. Of pedagogic impatience he was quite innocent. When he first left college and was yet uncertain whether the ministry were not his true vocation, one of his friends dissuaded him from it with the opinion that he "lacked the patience and long endurance in the most adverse and uncongenial surroundings, which a Unitarian minister's calling made inevitable." Possibly his friend was right, for the adverse and uncongenial surroundings in such a calling are largely the creation of human narrow-mindedness and prejudice, and those two foibles of humanity Widgery loathed with a hot loathing. When he encountered them in his scholastic campaigns for the conquest of headmasterships, there was certainly no patience in the outpouring of the vials of his wrath. But of the patience which wrestles ceaselessly with fate and rises again and again from the dust of disaster to a renewed encounter he had no lack. And of the patience which can endure the cruellest pain in silence, rather than publish it to the hurt of another, he had an abundance. I shall have occasion to return to this quality later.

Concerning communicative faculty his last head-master said that "Widgery had the power of bringing boys face to face with principles. In algebra he took the greatest pains to keep his lessons from degenerating into mere practice in manipulation. But English was his favourite teaching subject and he managed, some-how, to make it a real discipline even to a class of unscholarly boys."

But Widgery's greatest success was in his personal influence over the boys with whom he came into contact, and on this point there is no divergency of opinion. In the opportunities for the exercise of such influence there is a remarkable difference between School and College—the schoolmaster and the professor. The latter recites to an audience of individuals, whose characters are already more or less completely formed or in a fair way to maturity, for a definite time a connected thesis from which they extract in the form of notes what instruction they can. Then he may pass from before them, if he choose, without censure or remark. The schoolmaster and his boys talk to each other and the former, if he be of the true mettle, endeavours to enter into the secret recesses of a horde of adolescent intelligences and unripe characters and reduce the chaos of crude fancies and unripe principles to some semblance of order, ex-pelling such as are pernicious and fostering the growth of such as promise to aid the perfect development of the full-grown man. And, unlike that of the professor, the best work of a schoolmaster is often done in the play-ground after school hours are over. For it is there, in the open air of athletic liberty, that he gets into closest touch with the heart of the boy. The professor aims only at the head, the true schoolmaster looks rather to

the heart of his pupil; for only when he has the heart
under complete control can he hope to act upon the
head with any chance of success. Personal influence
therefore plays a distinguished part in the schoolmaster's work. Widgery's personal influence was exceptional.

He was thoroughly in sympathy with the boyish
nature. He had a strong moral influence over his own
pupils. He managed to win not only their affection
(lenience in class, athletic excellence in the playground,
will make the most worthless schoolmaster popular) but
their respect. As a result "he gave the boys fibre and
made them more manly." By the force of his own
example he drew out the energies of the dullest and led
them to take an interest in study. Let a master work
hard for his boys and sooner or later, however lazy and
indifferent they may be at first, they will catch the
infection of industry and be shamed into more vigorous
application. Many a teacher who complains of the
idleness of his boys has only to thank his own perfunctory
supervision for their perfunctory work. Widgery seemed
to maintain discipline without serious effort. Always
firm, he nevertheless won the respect and regard of his
scholars by his evident anxiety to further their interests
in every way. His firmness was never tinctured with
unkindness. Boys detect this rare distinction in a man
very readily, and any man in whom it is marked soon
becomes popular, for the sense of justice is abnormally
developed in the schoolboy mind. But it was not only
his pupils who felt the invigoration of his energy. His
own headmaster said of him after his death "His enthusiasm for knowledge has been a good example to us."
The most interesting testimony to this quality is found

in the voluntary remarks of his pupils when death
had removed him from their midst. A parent wrote to
Widgery's father "My boys are very much upset by
your son's death. One of them exclaimed 'We shall
never get another master like him.'" An old boy of the
school wrote "I can never be sufficiently grateful for
Mr. Widgery's teaching, especially for his teaching in
good principles, and for the advice he was always giving
his boys to guide them in their work and conduct
throughout their life. I look back with pleasure at the
way in which he taught and regret that I did not follow
his advice. As is often the case, his teaching has done
me far more good since I left school than when I was
there. I have to thank him more than any other master
for forming much of my character and opinions. His
kindness to boys out of school and his interest in their
pursuits were well known. I always entertained for him
a profound, though somewhat secret, admiration and
respect. I feel as if I had lost a dear personal friend,
such as I know he would have been to me, had I chosen
to make him so." Still more interesting is the letter of a
friend who accidentally overheard the conversation of a
few of his pupils. "Some time last autumn I got into
the train with six or eight schoolboys about twelve to
fifteen years of age. I soon learnt that they belonged to
University College School. They were eagerly discussing
the merits of various masters, among them Mr. Widgery.
It was evident from the tone of the boys' talk that he had
won their affection and strongly impressed himself on
them. Amongst other things they talked of his knowledge, especially of mathematics, and eagerly decided
that it was first-rate. But not in that subject only did
they agree that Mr. Widgery's attainments were striking.

They spoke of his teaching of English subjects in such a way as to show that his care to teach well and his enthusiasm had touched them really. They looked as though they could be abundantly 'naughty and larky' in their schoolboy fashion; but what struck me most was the strong influence their master had established over them and their affectionate trust in his goodness and knowledge."

To sum up Widgery's qualifications as a teacher—in the three important points of ability, enthusiasm, expositive and communicative power, there is a consensus of opinion in acknowledgment of his excellence. That he lacked a certain kind of patience—the patience to go leisurely to the goal of his explanation—must be admitted. That he succeeded in holding his pupils and carrying them along with him, and in filling their minds with such information as he thought fit to impart, is obvious; but whether his success was due to intellectual and æsthetic captivation, or to the emotional stimulus of personal example, is matter of dispute. His personal influence was great and predominant.

Lecturer.—Let us look at him now in the capacity of a lecturer. Here, unfortunately, the evidence to my hand is of the most meagre description. Few of his intimates seem ever to have heard him lecture. Those who did hear him agree that his enthusiasm and fire were as great as in his teaching. We might have divined this, even if all evidence had been wanting; for lecturing is in many ways only a specialised form of teaching under the conditions which obtain in colleges as distinct from schools. Enthusiasm in the one would naturally remain in the other. With regard to the power of persuading or captivating his audience the same remarks apply that were

made upon Widgery's use of these qualifications in the
class-room. Though his pleading was often brilliant in
respect of thought, it won its way rather by dint of
earnestness than by æsthetic attraction. In other words,
as in teaching, so in lecturing, he seems to have inspired
rather than delighted. His lecture at Exeter on Beówulf
was frequently applauded. But applause is far oftener
the expression of emotional excitement than intellectual
gratification, which is usually restrained because the
capacity for it is so much a product of deliberate culture.
In fact it was not so much the interest excited by the
way in which Widgery handled his subject that aroused
the enthusiasm of his audience as the conspicuous nobility
of the man himself and the grandeur of his conceptions.
He had a way of linking the most dry-as-dust investigations of philology with the noblest conceptions and
aspirations of the human soul. He himself was almost
as keenly moved at the addition made to the sum of
human knowledge by the discovery of some little fact in
philology as the author of the Venus of Milo may be
conceived to have been when that divine creation stood
complete before his eyes, or Mozart when the first sentences of "The Requiem" broke upon his mental ear.
And this was because Widgery's broad mind took in at
once the vast unity of the universe. Nothing was trifling
or mean in his eyes because everything was an integral
and honourable part of the sublime. This mental
attitude produced a personal atmosphere which was immediately perceptible to all who approached him whether
in the capacity of scholar, student or public audience.
And it was this atmosphere that exhilarated and inspired
those who breathed it in the schoolroom or the lecture-
hall. Once this fact is grasped, it is easy to understand

why it could be said with perfect truth that he was not a popular lecturer, that he lacked the power of stooping to his audience. He did not stoop—he would not stoop—he soared. He was always struggling upward, striving to reach higher educational ground, loftier educational conceptions, nobler educational attitudes. He hated all truckling to educational hobbies. He would not bind his soul in the fetters of educational conventions. His aim was intensely utilitarian. In his constant desire to be useful to his audience, to give them something to take away, he often forgot to be pleasant to them, to ease the strain of attention with a little of the lubricant of fancy. Thus too he often offended the scholarly mind by a lack of literary polish. But this was due to the absorption of intense earnestness, not to any puritanic contempt or dry disregard of the light play of fancy or the keen edge of wit. In his reviews of other men's performances he never failed to single out for praise and encouragement these very qualities of popularity which he was said to lack. However that may be, if he was not a popular lecturer, he had enthusiasm and force and, in this direction, attained no mean success.

Writer.—When we turn to consider him as a writer, we stand on firmer ground. Though his written work is not abundant by reason of the short period during which his pen was active, it is sufficient to form the basis of a very fair estimate of his powers of literary expression. But it must be borne in mind that he was only just beginning to feel sure of his ground and write with the ease and confidence of a recognised authority when Death struck the pen from his hand. Another decade would have put a warmer colour and a finer finish on his composition. Signs of this are apparent in his latest productions. In

M

this connection his premature death lends a peculiar
pathos to his saying "I think I would rather write a
great book than do anything else."

One of the chief qualifications of a reformer, whether
his sphere be social or intellectual, is independence of
thought and vigour of expression. Widgery had both
these qualities in a marked degree. Thoroughness of
investigation, resulting in complete mastery of his subject,
characterises his writings. Nowhere is this so apparent
as in his reviews. He never reviewed a book without
working conscientiously through it from beginning to
end. He jotted down every point he intended to dwell
upon and many he knew he would have neither space
nor time to deal with. Only when he had the salient
points of the book at his fingers' ends did he sit down to
give his opinion of it. But perhaps the chief agent of
force in his reviews was the breadth of the regard he
directed upon them. With most reviewers the book
itself is all in all, and whatsoever they say is drawn from
it, and their commentary is but a reflection of the book
upon itself. With Widgery the book had merit only so
far as it served to illustrate some phase of education or
add another step to its advance. Often the book itself
was the mere stimulus that produced an outpouring of
original suggestion and valuable theories—the text of a
suggestive original discourse on the subject handled by
the book. Such treatment, possible only to an original
mind, at once lifted Widgery's reviews out of the sphere
of the common-place literary hack and gave them an
individual educational value. To the force of a grand
conception was added the keenness of a trenchant
aphoristic expression and the weight of a passionate
nature. His review of Stopes' book on the Bacon-

Shakespeare question is a case in point. Believing firmly in the conclusions he had formed, he was a formidable opponent in argument. "I have known him," says a contemporary and friend, "impatient with arguments he thought absurd, but don't remember his becoming angry, as impetuous young men often do. He reserved his indignation for an unrighteous cause, not the paltry upholder of it." But much of the force of his mental impact was due to the momentum of his passionate desire to reach the root of the matter. He says himself " To stand by and watch the evolution of a gas fills me with wonder, and I am a little put out that the mind cannot be knife-like enough to cut into the division of things and see what really happens when the elements rearrange themselves."

But the rush of a steam-engine would be merely ruinous were it not for the clear guidance of the rails which conduct it with unerring certainty to its goal. So mere force of expression is little worth unless it be guided to its aim by the indispensable quality of lucidity. In his earliest work Widgery seems to me to lack this quality, doubtless just because it is early work, student's work, done amid the rush and swirl of ill-digested thoughts, dreams, aspirations, hopes. These break in a torrent of confusion upon the student mind when it first awakes out of the narrow interests and childish self-absorption of boyhood into the realisation of the worth and wonder and insoluble mystery that fill the boundless field of an immense past, a far-reaching present and an infinite future. Widgery's Harness Essay is smothered in the wealth of its suggestion. The prime element of lucidity, careful arrangement, which he practised so consistently in later work, is here neglected or managed

with but little success.   In this work Widgery is in the
first stage of literary development.   His mind is teeming
with a wealth of ideas, but the faculty of selection, the
sense of proportion, are not yet fully developed.   For
six years after its appearance he was silent, crushed by
an adverse criticism which he took deeply to heart.
When he resumed his pen, the impress of a new spirit was
upon his writing.   The confusion of an undisciplined
imagination had passed away, but the strength of an
original mind remained.   There is not a sentence in his
reviews which is not clear in its perfect simplicity and
striking in its directness.   The imagination is under
perfect control, the idea is clearly grasped and trans-
parently expressed.   The force is carefully calculated to
produce the requisite impression and nothing is added
in excess at the bidding of an injudicious imagination.
This characteristic of well-balanced thought continues to
become more and more marked as we pass through the
reviews and reach his most ambitious work—the booklet
on "The Teaching of Languages in Schools."   Here all the
qualities of a clear, vigorous and not unimaginative prose
writer are apparent.   It would be absurd to imply that
this book is the production of a literary artist, but the
style is admirably adapted to the needs of the work in
hand.   Such work gives little opportunity for the highest
flights of imagination or the brightest colours of eloquence.   But the lucidity, force and directness of expression required to convince and captivate are plentifully
present, nor is there any lack upon occasion of the light
play of fancy, the subtle suggestion of humour, the keen
edge of sarcasm, or the passion of earnest persuasion,
when the appeal to intellect requires the reinforcement
of an appeal to the heart.

Force and lucidity are the chief agents of argument. But there are times when the perversity of prejudice or ill-judgment is proof against conviction and then success may sometimes be won by the charm of brilliancy. The neat snap of an aphorism will appeal to some minds that would look contemptuously upon the substance of its contention expressed in commonplace paraphrase. If Widgery's brilliancy was not perhaps of the highest order of originality, he had considerable facility in aphorism, and there was a certain glitter, as of a clean cut facet, about the manner of his expression when he was in his happiest mood. Whatever he said deliberately was well said, and he had a knack of adding a fresh tint to the commonplaces he was obliged to use. This freshness is an enviable possession, since the major part of the material of expression must of necessity be commonplace. Incessant brilliancy would soon bring on a surfeit. There are passages in the Harness Essay, in his later papers and in his speeches, which have the warm glow of true eloquence—that which springs from the fire of noble conception and the passion of genuine sensibility.

Looking then at his best work as a writer, we may say that he had great force, lucidity and eloquence, and brilliancy in a high, if not the highest, degree.

Thinker, Philosopher, Man of Parts.—I have dealt here with the simple qualities which one might describe as the body armour of the literary man. But there are a number of other forces—side arms, as it were—which the well-equipped mind has at its disposal, belonging more intimately to the personality of the man himself and yet permeating his work in every direction—in writing, speech and thought. We may better judge these forces if we dismiss from our minds what I shall call the objective aspect of the man—the revelation of him in his formal writing and set speeches—and regard him in his subjective aspect, as a thinker, philosopher and man of parts.

Widgery's intellectual power was acknowledged on all hands to be keen and vigorous. His mind appeared to "flash with light and faculty." Something of his intellectual nature, his literary faculty, he inherited from his mother. Both his parents were given to aphoristic expression. But his intelligence was not merely keen, it was extensive. His attainments were varied and he possessed a wide general culture. I wish it were in my power to catalogue here the more notable of the books he read in the process of self-education. But unhappily I have not been able to get any information on this point. Widgery is said to have been capable of turning his attention successfully to any subject of study. His versatility gave increased extent to his sympathies and he had the valuable faculty of transmitting his own enthusiasm for the inspiration of all who came in contact with him. One of his German critics remarked that he united sound scholarship with clear practical insight and enthusiastic devotion to his subject, and added that the beginnings of his activity announced a brilliant development. Widgery devoted a good deal of time and energy to philology, but unfortunately left no tangible proof of his attainments in that science. The vast quantity of MS. notes found in his rooms are too incoherent to be gathered into literary form. It will therefore be interesting to hear the high opinion expressed by an authority on the subject, and I have to thank Mr. Henry Bradley for the following statement of his opinion. "It is difficult for me to give any definite grounds for the profound conviction which I certainly entertained that Widgery had great capacity for fruitful original research in philology. My opinion of him in this respect is based, not on anything he actually achieved, but on the remarkable precision of thought and independence and soundness of judgment he exhibited in his conversations with me on philological subjects. He had a very modest estimate of his own attainments, and an almost oppressive sense of the vastness and complexity of the science, so that I could not judge very exactly how much he knew. But it is easy to distinguish a real thinker from a mere passive absorber of the results of other people's research ; and a thinker Widgery unquestionably was. He was never satisfied without understanding the full bearings of every fact of the science which he knew ; and he never rested content with any of the mere pretences of explanation which so often pass current even among those who are accounted experts. That kind of man goes far when he fairly takes up a study ; and I think it quite certain that if Widgery had lived and enjoyed fair health he would have attained a distinguished position among philologists. I think every one who knew him well must have felt that he had in him a great reserve of intellectual power; but he has left nothing behind him to bear witness, in any adequate degree, to the ability which he possessed. Considering how short my acquaintance with Widgery had been, I feel surprised at the keen sense of loss which comes to my mind when I think of him even now."

It is always a thankless and dangerous task to attempt to give examples of mental quality culled from the speech or writings of a man. The nature, the classification, of such examples depend so much upon opinion that one can scarcely hope to escape the charge of mistaken definition and ill-judgment. Nevertheless I shall venture to cite some sayings of Widgery's which appear to me to give evidence of mental keenness and penetration. Should any reader object to the connection, let him distribute the examples among Widgery's many qualities as his fancy prompts him.

" The desire to show ' power ' must show a fundamental weakness somewhere."

" Our best work is usually what we do unconsciously. And we are apt to nourish dreams of an earlier age."

"Others judge us by our acts, we judge ourselves by our thoughts."

" ' I have no respect for experience ' I once told an old man in one of my cantankerous moods. ' If you can't put your experience into words for other people, it's a selfish and useless knowledge.' That was too harsh, but it had some truth in it."

" Life after all solves itself and is slipping by while we are reflecting how best to spend it."

Though Widgery's abilities were of an "all-round" nature and his best work was done in English, he at first considered his forte to be mathematics. He seems really to have been an able mathematician and it was in that subject that he took his degree. This mathematical skill he carried into the discussion of difficulties and problems of a more general character.

From his student days onward he always gave evidence of a philosophical turn of mind. He had a habit of connecting the smallest things with the greater issues of life and thought. The foibles of humanity set him constantly thinking on the fundamental principles of ethics.

An earnest nature, aided by a fairly vigorous imagination, was chiefly responsible for this.

He generally gave one the impression of being a versatile and brilliant talker and his conversation bore witness to wide reading and original thinking. Both found expression in a keen and sarcastic wit, which, however, contained no taint of malice. Whenever there was a sting in it, the hand of righteous indignation had placed it there for the confusion of petty pedantry or unscrupulous meanness. It was never levelled at the weak and helpless. Here again I shall brave the frown of opinion and appeal to the generosity of tolerance while I endeavour to give some specimens of Widgery's wit and sarcasm.

" Popular reforms are like a medal of which we can see only one side at a time, *e.g.* in France great superstition was the obverse of free thought."

" Great men, as proofs of certain training, are like one or two remarkably fine ears in a corn-field overgrown by poppies."

" People with tips seem to think it is more blessed to give than to receive."

" To arrive at the right through the wrong does not seem less foolish than to seek vice to attain virtue."

" Intellect is the blade of a knife. It is no use without the heft and the heft is hard work."

" The coldness not of granite but of putty."

" His soul seems to have been boiled till the residue comes out as a heap of red tape."

The next quotation throws a curious side light upon his mind and his own estimate of one feature of his character.

" It is curious how strong a distaste I have for anything

I have done.   Once the shot has been delivered even the gun fails to attract me any more."

Three others I shall give in which the wit is edged with sarcasm.

"Had Sanskrit been a new 'line' in business we should probably have worked it, but it was only intellectual, so we left it to the Germans."

"Others followed him like the blind led by the one-eyed."

The next is a good instance of his habit of flashing the light of humour upon the dark places of educational science—into the dusty recesses of bibliography. It is taken from the bibliographical list appended to his booklet on "The Teaching of Languages in Schools."

"The author (Alexander Allen : "An Etymological Analysis of Latin Verbs") apparently imagines the primitive man as one day making up his mind to have a language, and then glueing it together in this fashion—

Preposi-tion.	Redupli-cation.	Connect-ing vowel.	Root.	Flection syllable.	Tense vowel.	Plural sign.	Person sign.
con	*d*	*i*	*d*	*er*	*u*	*n*	*t*

We talk of wit *and* humour, as if there were some essential difference between the two. Yet no one, so far as I know, has discovered any satisfactory test for differentiating them.   I suggest the following, not as a conclusive and satisfactory test, but as a working gauge. Wit is cleverness of thought or expression that lies upon the surface of the words and is obvious at the first glance. Humour is a sensation of the ridiculous, not present in the words themselves, but contained in some collateral thought indirectly suggested by the words in question. Wit is bold, barefaced, obvious smartness. Humour is shy, subtle, elusive, evanescent comicality. The one is masculine and robust. The other is feminine and delicate. The examples I now cite seem to me to belong to the latter class. The first seven are culled from reviews and speeches and have something of an academic savour. The rest are taken from letters and are less formal and more general.

" The two introductory chapters take thirty pages, so that the front doors are larger than the house."

" It used to be the fashion to treat Keltic as a refuge for the destitute, for whom a respectable Latin derivation could not be given."

Dealing with some arguments concerning the Cradle of the Aryans based on the names of animals, Widgery says

" The Indians and Persians had ample time to forget the eel and his name. Did the Scandinavians, who had staid at home all the time, forget him too? They surely should have kept him in tender remembrance."

"Teachers cannot hope to come out as a sort of Bob Acres and ooze literature."

"The admirable quotation on page 96 might with advantage be read as a sort of pedagogic grace at the beginning of our educational conferences."

" Loading the reader with a mass of worthless bibliographical and other details till he almost feels as if he were labelled 'Intellectual rubbish shot here.'"

"The heaped-up genitives that stuck to Pestalozzi like his debts."

Walking to Lynton he passed unawares through the Valley of Rocks. Afterwards he exclaims "They ought not to keep the valleys so high up!"

"I feel like a regular old broody hen; ideas, plans &c. for books seem to grow up spontaneously in my perfervid old noddle, but it's the sitting, my dear, what costs the time."

In the midst of a serious letter we come suddenly upon the paragraph "One of the salts of zinc is waiting for me and I must be polite to him."

"Mrs. R——'s brother is stroking the Oxford boat (I have not heard if the boat purrs) and of course, &c."

The following is from Widgery's *Hamlet* Essay. "Should the Council disbelieve Hamlet's story and bring him to a trial, he would find some difficulty in getting a subpœna served on the ghost; or, if he could, a ghost giving evidence in an ancient Danish or a modern English court would considerably puzzle the councillors or lawyers as to the value of his evidence."

One of Widgery's contemporaries says "He was always the most jocular man present in any company that I knew at Cambridge." Whenever he was well he overflowed with kindly good-humour, fun and frolic, and he was fond of the broad comedy of practical joking whenever it was harmless.

But whatever Widgery may have had of wit and humour, they were among the externals of his nature. There was another quality that sprang from the very heart of the man and permeated his whole being—his passionate love of Nature in all its aspects. This he inherited from his artist father. He never took a walk of any extent through the country without a road-book which was at once sketch-book and log. Here he recorded his experiences both in words and in the more graphic eloquence of rough and ready sketches made upon the spot. Several of these books exist. His verbal notes show a keen appreciation of the beautiful and especially the sublime in Nature. He constantly describes them and jots down the ethical and æsthetic impressions made upon him by lovely scenery, sweet-scented flowers and the singing of birds. But his drawings were not confined to the representation of natural objects. Anything novel and interesting that he happened to come across in his continental tours was at once committed to paper for future enjoyment, reflection, or use in illustrating his theories and opinions. These sketches, rough and ready as they necessarily are, show real ability and no small appreciation of form. Indeed he was one of five children, three of whom possess considerable artistic ability. One or two specimens of the jottings in these books will illustrate his passionate love of Nature and his habit of connecting its aspects and activities with the ordinary phenomena of human life.

" The sea with its eternal bass to the multitudinous music of the earth." (Written in the Park at Clovelly.)

" As tender as the amber green of budding poplars."

" The clouds were spread out like a huge fan, the handle hid somewhere below the horizon. The extreme edges were blown straight out into yellow flakes suffused with a tinge of orange, all on a background of steel cold blue."

The next one touches on that constant sense he had of his personal unity with Nature. "The glories of the heavens and the soft sweetness of the earth grew part of my being."

" It was 'a lovely night. The clouds hung like

gossamer fleeces in the sky. The moonlight was not strong enough to light them into gold, but a yellow flushed up the tender gray pearls as they moved slowly among the stars."

The dreamy stillness and intangible evanescent witchery of Nature's supreme hour of fertility, when ripeness reaches its limit and begins to pass into decay—a late autumn noon—breathes in the following passage.

"'Tis a cool morning fit to usher in the ripe wealth of October. The silence is broken only by Nature's own sounds. The birds are twittering in dreamy tones. Soon they will burst into full song. The sunlight sways over the bending branches of the willow or warms the deep glow of the fir. The chesnuts are ripe and begin to burst their prickly armature. The grass plot of the garden looks greener than the surrounding common that stretches away into a pearly gray mist. Across it runs a gravel path glowing ruddy in the sun. The faint sound of the horses' hoofs comes mingled with the baaing of the sheep. The small pool looks silvery with a steadfast gaze at the high overarching blue, through which the fluffy clouds sweep slowly upwards as they are touched with the fervour of the sun."

The next two again touch upon his feeling of kinship with Nature and his love of clothing its operations with a distinct personality. " The purest tears are those that spring from beauty."

Lydford House, Dartmoor, December 31, 1885.—"All day long the clouds have been gently weeping, bowed low over Mother Earth. Funeral wraiths shrouded in long white robes have silently stolen towards the moor, and there at midnight in a pool of light will they bury another yearling heavy as all his ancestors with sorrow and joy, the child of much hope and father of many disappointments. With him too let us bury all vain regrets and attune all our sorrows to the vague half-forgotten melody of some sad song. We are in eternity, let us enjoy our rights therein."

" I soon tire if I cannot meet with Nature in her remoter spots where man is not needed."

Often his love of Nature enabled him to throw a tinge of æsthetic beauty upon the dry mechanical operations of language. " The rain falls upon the earth, sinks and is seen no more. So words sink into unconsciousness. But the roots beneath sprout and issue in the promise of fair flowers."

This keen appreciation of whatever is ennobling in the material world was extended to the intellectual world of science, art and literature. Widgery's literary taste while he was at college is said to have been broad, robust and sure, though not very delicate.* In poetry it seems to have been the thought of the poet and his power of clear expression rather than the music of the verse that attracted him. This preference † for what one might call the poetical philosopher over the artist in verse is apparent in the following extract.

" What a curious contrast Browning and Tennyson make: one weighted with thought beyond his power of music to express, the other melodious without any great body of thought. Once I started to become a Tennyson student, but I began to read him chronologically and stuck at the juvenile poems. The spring is usually my time for reading poetry." The last curious phrase again suggests the intimate connection between Widgery's emotional susceptibility and the phases of Nature.

---

* " More fastidious then than later."
† Disputed by some.

Referring obviously to Shakespeare, he says "Once again have I bathed my soul in the mild munificence of him whom I most reverence among the sons of men—whose soul was indeed shaken with passion but (in whom) high over all reigned the same will, shaping and fashioning things rare and beautiful. By none but born Englishmen can the full flavour and weight and the divine beauty of thought wedded to immortal verse be wholly felt." The last is a curious statement to come from a man of broad mind and cosmopolitan sympathies. I cannot but believe that there was in his mind some qualification which does not appear in the words. I rather fancy he made this reflection after witnessing a continental performance of one of Shakespeare's plays. In that case he may merely have referred to the natural difficulty a foreigner has in interpreting an English dramatist.

In the following highly poetical conception Widgery sounds once more the note of Nature's union with man. "Keats is my especial favourite. I read all the poems twice in two days. Whenever I read poetry like his I get a bit horrified, wondering whether my incessant work at knowledge has not a little overlaid the artistic temperament. If I think of doing anything wrong, the very stars seem to grow uncertain in their orbits and the blades of grass lift up their heads in mournful warning against me."

"I suppose, when English has its proper place, men will awake to the fact that Shakespeare really does require as much study as Cæsar, say? With me he is a part of elemental Nature, and I gaze on him with the same awe as I do the sun."

In spite of his leaning † towards the "thoughtful" or

† See reference on p. 191.

" philosophic " genre in poetry, Widgery was fastidious about form and style.

" If the author is an artist the way in which he says a thing is precisely the best way. To change one phrase is to take an axis out of the crystal."

An old and intimate friend of Widgery's thus recounts his first impressions of him. " I described my newly-found kinsman by sympathy as a modern Greek—a very Achilles—in might and strength (so I thought) and more a Greek in his love of beauty in thought and form. . . . . As I came to know him better I learned to feel he was rather of the race of man, desirous in an unusual degree of passing beyond the limitations of even nationalities."

Some specimens of the strength of Widgery's imaginative faculty will complete the consideration of this aspect of the man.

" This afternoon " (in class) " a boy kept asking me sensible questions " (on chemistry). " This started me and the warm impetuous words kept tumbling out till there came that solemn hush of absolute quiet in the room. In the midst of it a door seemed to open and shut and, while my lips were busy with acid and base, I felt myself sink sudden and swiftly down to the unfathomed depths of the sea, while the waves in angry storm leapt up with hoarse voices to drown the stars."

" I began reading some of Swinburne's ' Studies in Song ' and, after some time, almost fancied I was physically on fire."

(Speaking of Hamlet and Ophelia) " When the pitiless blind storm uproots the forest kings the clinging trusting ivy is foreordained to death, and the emblem of marriage grows dark with the shadow of the grave."

" The warm love-languorous air of Verona, where

Philomel in some melodious plot singeth of summer in full-throated ease : the cold bright stars that glitter on the battlements of Elsinore, weird-lit with shadow and the moon's pale beams, where the barren sea beneath moans against the rocks or drags the pebbles down with angry rauk : Hamlet and Romeo that live in meditation or the thoughts of love : the lovers that clasp hands and souls at the meeting of the lips : the lovers that unclasp hands and souls in the parting with their gifts : ripe Juliet, filled with passion pure and vehement, cleaves to her husband and leaves her father and her mother : sweet maid Ophelia, that cannot bourgeon and blossom in Danish air, yields to her father's deception and slips alone to muddy death : Mercutio, instinct with wit and lyric lilt, whose light is quenched : Horatio the prudent and grave, who lives to tell of the sad tragedy—these are births and these are twin births of the self-same soul."

" The mind at times seems to me like a vast cathedral. Down the aisles wanders the common crowd of thoughts, but around are still chapels of the heart opened only on high festivals and solemn ceremonies."

Yet another aspect of the thinker—breadth of mind. Widgery appeared to be totally free from professional and national prejudices. Naturally a man of large mind, he made thoughtful use of his experience and shrank from no opportunity of adding to it. He was never afraid of putting his opinions and theories to the test of new circumstances or under the light of fresh argument. He delighted in "rubbing" his mind against other minds. In one of his letters he says " Intellectually I seem to starve if I am not acquiring new material. My fault so far, I see very clearly, has been hasty digestion. I mean I have not endeavoured to co-ordinate or concentrate my discursive reading. That too has a good side : it leaves you more open to a greater range of human sympathy." In another, referring doubtless to some one's narrow-mindedness, he complains "The alterable margin of people is wofully small." Perhaps Widgery's breadth of mind is most apparent in his ability to throw off the cramping conservatism of academic occupations. Well acquainted with the noblest productions of the mind of antiquity and giving them the full due of their surpassing merit, he was yet able to exclaim, in his review of the "Harvard Studies in Classical Philology," "Was there not room for one article breathing a larger life than all this intense specialism—not for one article bearing on the things of to-day? "

To sum up this aspect of the man—wit and intellectual power he had in abundance. He had considerable neatness in aphorism and no small sense of suggestive humour. His æsthetic sense was correct and catholic and his æsthetic sympathy was a striking and dominant feature of his character. He had a considerable imagination and great breadth of mind.

I pass on to consider him in another capacity—to speak of his sympathy and helpfulness, his tact and tolerance, as a colleague.

Colleague.— He had a ready sympathy, which won the hearts of his colleagues at University College School. It was perhaps this quality more than any other that prompted them to say in their letter of condolence to his parents, " Although Mr. Widgery's reputation extends far beyond the walls of University College School, it is there that his memory will be most affectionately cherished by his colleagues and pupils." But, though his sympathy was unusually great, it was in one sense restricted in

its application. For the helpless, for the deserving,
it was always ready and inexhaustible. Where he
esteemed and liked it was boundless. But the fountains
of his goodwill could be readily and effectually sealed by
personal dislike.

> " He was a scholar, and a ripe and good one ;
>   Exceeding wise, fair spoken, and persuading :
>   Lofty, and sour, to them that loved him not ;
>   But to those men that sought him, sweet as Summer."

He would not waste his sweetness on the mean and worthless. But this by no means implies that he was incapable
of that noble magnanimity which knows how to make
allowances for the faults and failings of others. It was
deliberate selfish meanness and perverse folly that he could
not tolerate. Nor is it difficult to sympathise with the
righteous indignation that steeled his heart. Though it
may be possible to criticise his attitude, it is difficult to
avoid assuming it oneself in the face of the provocation
offered by what he used to call " scholastic tradesmen,"
wherein, it may be well to explain, he meant no insult to
the honest merchant, but merely censure of the dishonest
teacher who " teaches to live," and solely to live.

Widgery's helpfulness to his fellow-workers was always
generous. He loved to share his abundance of experience and knowledge with all who chose to ask a
portion, and to add to what he could give plentiful
encouragement in that which must of necessity be left to
the recipient's own energy and resource. But in this
direction also the note of qualification must be sounded.
He would help the worthy only and the wilfully worthless
might go beg elsewhere. The confessions of two well-
loved colleagues will show what he was capable of giving
to those who deserved and asked it—more perhaps

indirectly through the influence of his personality than directly by word of mouth, but in both cases a gift of great value, for sympathy is the crown of gifts. "One brother teacher at least owes more than he can tell to Widgery's professional enthusiasm, his eagerness to discuss method, tell and hear of experiment." "We were," says the other, "in matters of our profession strugglers together, and I joyfully and thankfully recognise that Widgery's ready sympathy was a real help to my life. It was a joy I cannot express in words to have him dropping in on his 'chance' calls, or to look him up. . . . . He was ever the 'sweet presence of a good diffused,' and his joyous, spontaneous temperament accomplished more than he was even himself conscious of—for those who were within his reach."

If one were to ask what human foible might be expected to afford the most abundant food for melancholy mirth to a nineteenth-century Jaques, one might safely say—want of tact. Every one accuses every one else of want of tact, and yet no one is always and under all circumstances tactful. Of course Widgery was accused of great want of tact—upon occasion. Yet, to those who knew him most intimately, he appeared to possess both tact and good sense—at least to an average extent. "In his relations with those whom he liked and loved, he was always trying to use tact. But, if he disliked any characteristic in any one"—any trait of meanness or frivolity—"he could never really and wholly hide his dislike. He was too transparent. If he thought 'truth' would suffer from 'tact,' he had no 'tact.'" So says one who knew him as intimately as any one on earth. It seems to have been the outspokenness of his opinions that gave offence at Dover College to some one or other of the senior masters. He appears not to have been liked there because he would not conform to all the conventionalities which play so large a part in public-school life. His intolerance so-called, his habit of going straight for anything he thought wrong, was strikingly shown when he was quite a boy. His father had painted a life-like head of a lion. The finished picture stood on an easel in the studio. One day the boy went quietly into the room, took up his father's brushes and smeared the whole picture out of all recognition. "Whatever made you do that?" exclaimed his mother, when the mischief was discovered. "What right had a lion in our house?" was the prompt and indignant retort of the youngster, all unabashed. Let us look into this question of tact. Every one has noticed that all the known specimens of the human mind can be divided roughly into weak and strong. Many people too have observed that the strong minds are generally active and aggressive, just because they are strong, while the weak minds are passive and compliant. Now if, as constantly happens, one of these strong minds, full of original theories and decided opinions, happens to meet one of its weaker brethren, the strong mind (like the strong man who delighteth to run a race) delights to use his strength upon the weak mind—nay, cannot refrain from using it. For he is overflowing with earnest conviction that his opinions and theories are of vital importance to the stability of the intellectual and moral world, and he must proclaim them upon the housetops and drive them home into the minds of all whom he may chance to meet. The weak mind resents this, because it demands a great exertion of mental effort on his part, it unsettles his comfortable unreasoning unquestioning repose, it flutters the dove-cotes wherein his dear old hobbies are at roost, and lo ! he has but one defence, but one missile o offence, and he hurls it—want of tact ! Such tact—the complaisancy to leave his scholastic neighbour's beloved hobby at roost—was conspicuously absent from the composition of Widgery's character. He had transcendental conceptions of truth and sincerity, transcendental notions of the enormity of error. The most trifling flaw, the most harmless delusion, assumed enormous proportions in the eyes of his earnest and exalted nature. This common characteristic of strong and pure minds guided by a vigorous conscience is generally—we must in justice confess that it was in Widgery's case—accompanied by a certain deficiency in the sense of proportion between error and error, crime and crime. He was apt to exaggerate the significance of a small philological blunder in a discourse otherwise of great merit and cause pain by a criticism that, to the less enthusiastic and earnest minds of the friends of his victim, appeared hypercritical and ill-timed. This form of want of tact, which is but a slight flaw, after all, in the great virtue of earnestness, we cannot deny to Widgery. But from that kind of want of tact, absence of consideration for the feeling of others, which is more appropriately described by the word— that dense insensibility which springs from the incon-sequence of a stupid intellect and a callous heart, he was utterly free. Something too must be credited to the frankness and transparent simplicity of a character that sees no harm in many things and sayings, to which the prudish temper of shallow conventionality often attaches exaggerated meaning and imaginary consequences.

The intolerance charged against Widgery is but another variant of the same characteristic. He had strong

beliefs, deliberately formed, sincerely held, and he fought
for them with all the persistence of an indomitable
nature. What wonder if the hasty resentment of those
who differed from him mistook strength of conviction
for the bigotry of narrow incapacity to understand the
possibility of another conception, the rightness of another
theory than his own? Hasty and superficial judgment
often mistakes deep and deliberate conviction for the
fatuity of vacuous incompetence, which alone is rightly
termed conceit, and earnest loyalty to such conviction
for the spiteful hatred of difference, which alone is
rightly stigmatised as intolerance. Let it pass! The
penalty of virtue is misunderstanding, and ignorance
must have its toll of knowledge. Widgery had a strong
mind and a vigorous nature, and he would not have
exchanged them at any price for the everyday intellect,
that never sails out into the open sea of invention to
encounter the storms of criticism, and the complaisant
character, that takes its daily shape from the fickle
fingers of soi-disant tact.

As a colleague, then, he had the essentials of sympathy and helpfulness under the restriction of righteous
desert. He had the tact of love, but not the tact of
expedience. He was tolerant of honest opinion where
he respected the mental stature of the holder. But he
proceeded *vi et armis* against all opinion that he considered mean or pernicious, and cared not how cruel the
wound inflicted provided it were delivered by the hand
of righteous indignation. And it must be confessed that
his virtue of earnestness was not regulated by a sufficient
sense of proportion in the estimation of human error.

Friend.—Before we sum his characteristics as a man,
we have yet to consider him as a friend. Here he

stands forward in a most amiable light. His personal qualities gained him the warm affection and cordial esteem of a large circle of friends. When he was a candidate for the headmastership of Reading Grammar School, twenty-three of his colleagues at University College School signed a joint testimonial in his favour. It is easy to see whence he drew the capacity for inspiring so general an affection—from his warm heart, his affectionate nature, his good-humoured self-sacrifice, his lovable genial disposition, the frank expression of his eyes,* his cheerful spirit (whenever he was not depressed by his mortal disease), his unaffected kindness and impulsive generosity, which embraced all mankind in the sphere of its consideration and regard, and

> " That best portion of a good man's life,
> His little, nameless, unremembered acts
> Of kindness and of love."

He had a wide circle of affectionate friends, and an inner circle of devoted intimates to whom he revealed the finest possibilities of his noble nature. They knew his foibles, but were ever forgetting them by reason of the wealth of his excellent virtues and the kindling warmth of his pure-hearted affection.

Outside the limits of ordinary friendship Widgery was a thorough cosmopolite. One instance is enough. A Swede came to see him with no other introduction than a copy of " The Teaching of Languages in Schools " in his pocket. A few minutes sufficed to convince him that no other introduction was needed, and this is what he said of Widgery when he heard of his untimely death—

* I shall never forget the way in which he smiled at me and the warmth with which he shook hands, when I walked into his classroom and approached him for the first time as an utter stranger.

" He was a true gentleman and friend, one of that rare kind who brighten our path, warm our heart and make us feel at home in a foreign country." What greater, what more eloquent, testimonial could be given than the creation of such a feeling in the heart of a stranger in a strange land within a few moments after he had come suddenly upon a representative of that land till then unknown to him?

But the best friend is he who can best sympathise. Help may be impossible, encouragement may be mockery, yet sympathy is always open to friendship and is always acceptable. Widgery possessed this faculty of assimilating himself with the situation of his friend in need to a high degree. Perhaps the most that can be said in this direction is summed in the remark made to me that "he would do anything to share one real sorrow."

As a friend Widgery had a rare capacity for inspiring friendship. His friendliness was not limited to a certain circle of intimates and acquaintances. It embraced the inhabitants of the whole world irrespective of nationality or creed. The unity of man with man was as deep a conviction of Widgery's mind as the unity of man with Nature. He had in abundance the all important qualification and the supreme virtue of the highest friendship—sympathy.

We have now considered what I call the objective qualifications of Widgery's character (his capacity as a teacher, lecturer and writer) and his more subjective attributes—his capacity as a thinker, philosopher and man of parts, as a colleague and as a friend. I shall finish the portrait of his individuality by considering him in a more intimate sense "as a man"—saying something of his manliness and moral courage, his tenderness and chivalry, his child-like simplicity and modesty, his religion, his incorruptible honesty and sincerity, and last the constant nobility of his conception, motive and thought.

Man.—Widgery's manliness and moral courage were unusually great. "I feel," he said, "an elation of spirit at the mention of difficulties." "If we are the sport of circumstances, then one of the determining circumstances is my intention to fight the rest." His life was characterised throughout by this determination to

> "Breast the blows of circumstance
> And grapple with his evil star."

But his manliness was not merely of that common kind which appears in the ability to push one's way through apparently insurmountable obstacles and is so often associated with a reprehensible callousness to the suffering not seldom caused by such pushing. It possessed that rarer capacity of passive endurance which distinguishes the genuine manly nature. While he was engaged on the *Hamlet* Essay, he bore for a month in cheerful silence a secret which he feared would hurt his sister. And when his first engagement was broken off he bore "the horrid secret" for several weeks alone, not merely because, as one might naturally suppose, his pride was deeply wounded, but again for fear of hurting his sister. "I wish I could blot it all clean out and spare you the pain of reading the letters." The same capacity for passive endurance appears in his remark "If anything pleasant happens to me, I generally save it up until something unpleasant comes along and then we can cry quits." That this was not merely the callousness of a selfish mind, worshipping the *carpe diem* of gay indifference to the weightier issues of life, appears in the noble note struck in the following extract. "Life seems a mighty gift! Shall we complain, after we have drunk the strong wine, if a few drops are tinged with the bitter salt of tears?" In this spirit the pain of the last sad days was bravely borne and the strenuous battle for life was not demeaned by one cry of impatience or complaint.

This inborn strength found a fit expression in the contagious cheeriness which distinguished him when the shadow of suffering was not lying darkly across his sunny spirit. For one oppressed by ill-health his temperament was wonderfully buoyant. He was never long depressed —a sure sign of a strong, as well as an affectionate, nature that brightened up when friends were near and served to cheer them perhaps more than himself. Under such circumstances a quaint remark he once made upon the action of a friend was most applicable to himself— "He has sent his grief below and battened down the hatches." The same buoyancy of spirit appears in the fact that he *enjoyed* a holiday in Switzerland during the year of his greatest trouble. "It was like him—the great trouble underneath, the sunshine on the soil, if possible."

One instance of a quality not seldom associated with manliness—presence of mind—I shall give here. "I was showing my class an experiment, when the top of the methylated spirit-lamp suddenly fell off and the desk and my hands were covered with flame. I proceeded with the experiment, quietly talking all the time, and finished it. Then I put out the flames on my hands and asked the boys, amidst much hilarity, whether I did not smell like a singed goose!"

Widgery possessed unflinching rectitude. His courage in standing by his sense of right was as great as his honesty. Whenever, in the cruel temptations of competitive existence in the nineteenth century, worldly prudence called upon him to tamper with his conscience, he struggled most manfully against the weakness of human nature. He was ever possessed by a strong determination to fight against all injustice, no matter on whom his blows might fall.

But if he recked nothing of the pain he caused at the command of righteous indignation, in the presence of the weak and helpless he displayed the tenderness of a true woman and the most refined chivalry of sentiment. Warm-hearted and generous by nature, so full of *gemüth* (as a German friend said), his greatest tenderness was reserved for children, in whom he took a passionate delight. In his tour through Devonshire and Cornwall he met two little children near Tannacombe. They walked some way with him and he notes with delight the charm their naïve and innocent prattle cast upon the beauties of the scenery through which he was passing. Once again on this walk he stopped at a farm called East Dizard and asked for water. A comely young girl came to the door and insisted on his having milk. He closes the account of her youthful charms with the exclamation "delightful little episode !" As soon as he entered a room children instinctively went to his arms. They have a rare shrewdness in detecting at a glance a man who loves their fresh innocence and childish naïvety. But he extended the same tenderness to all helpless things. He was an excellent nurse, with the touch and sympathy of a woman. But it was not necessary to be sick in order to excite his tender solicitude. He

happened once to hear that the "brother-friend" of his
boyhood was out of employment and wrote at once—
"Sorry to hear you are out of a situation, hope you are
not hard up. If so, I have a sovereign saved and you
are to send for it (if it is any use) as if it were your own."
This practical kindness was a strong feature of his
character. He might know a man to be foolish, but, if
that man wanted help in any way, it was given most
sincerely and ungrudgingly. On one occasion he came
across a man of brilliant parts who was cursed by a
strong tendency to licentious living. This man he
induced to live with him, in order that he might watch
over and save him, and only abandoned the task when
he found that the tendency was incurable and that the
poor fellow could only be influenced while under actual
surveillance. Another time a family he knew fell upon
evil days and had to leave their native town. He durst
not openly offer them help for fear of hurting their feelings, so he went to a friend, who was about to visit the
place they had gone to, put a cheque in his hands and
instructed him to employ the money, at his discretion, in
making things smooth in the new settlement, strictly
enjoining on him not to betray the donor. So anxious
was he to be good to his neighbours in life that he was
quite distressed when he suspected himself of having
given pain unintentionally. "I am by nature strong-
willed and have lived by myself for twelve years, and
can't help drifting into ways that may at times quite
unconsciously give others pain. I don't wish to, indeed
I don't!"

Tenderness towards other people is usually accompanied by great sensitiveness to other people's unkindness to oneself. It was so in Widgery's case. He

suffered keenly at the beginning of his career from an adverse criticism of his *Hamlet* Essay. Years afterwards he writes, "In turning over one of the German books I caught my name and found that the essay is quoted as being well-known and making with others a new departure and advance in the study of *Hamlet*. When I read things like that I always feel wistful at having let seven years slip by without another sign of life. That wretched man —— cut me up in the *Academy* and I shrunk up like a mimosa plant. I wish I had known then as much about him as I do now. I should have taken his criticism as a compliment." Widgery's friends little suspected how much he suffered from stage fright. "Appearing in public is very horrid. I get so very nervous that I have to jump on my nervousness and then you get the reputation of being as cool as a bed of cucumbers!" It is to his credit that he had the will-strength to apply the athletic remedy he describes. The constant desire to help and comfort naturally resulted in his being looked up to and leant upon. That gave him great happiness, but it had its disadvantages also, since it deprived him of the comfort of himself leaning upon others when he happened to need such support. "As long as I can remember," he says," "people have in a way looked up to me and told me all their secrets. Sometimes when they are gone I think with some bitterness, ' so they imagine that I am all strength and need no tenderness myself?' Their woes and their sorrows hour by hour—does it ever flash across them that I too feel the need sometimes of confession and expansion?"

This tenderness sprang from an innate spirit of unselfishness. On one occasion some friends of his happened to be passing through Exeter by the night mail. So he sat up late, made some tea and carried it down to the station in a jug to meet the train at 2.30 A.M., to the great comfort of his friends and a porter who finished what they could not manage. His sympathy for all in distress was extended to every class irrespective of birth or station. His last touch of burning indignation was for the poor pay of hospital nurses. Not even illness could induce him to disappoint a friend. "Do come," he wrote once when he was hardly in a condition to receive visitors, "with your whole party!" They came. "When we left, there was not one among us but felt that he had enjoyed a quarter of an hour with a rare man." I have noted Widgery's wit and sarcasm. But they were never employed in petty malice for mere delight in annoyance. A Cambridge contemporary says Widgery only once hurt a man, and "he was a rather gloomy old-fashioned man, who had been invited to meet Widgery." Two delightful stories are told of Widgery's chivalry and they will serve to close this account of that most excellent virtue in him. One day in the depth of winter, as he was travelling home to Exeter, there happened to be a poor dressmaker in the carriage, who seemed to be but ill-fortified against the inclemency of the season. He soon got into kindly conversation with her and no doubt learnt something of her narrow means. As he rose to leave the carriage at Exeter he drew off the long warm gloves, which reached up beyond his wrists, and offered them to the poor girl. We may imagine what she thought of this "gentleman" as she gratefully accepted them. She asked for his address and it was not long before the gloves were again in his possession. While he was at college there came into residence a poor little puny foolish fellow who was utterly unfit for the rough and tumble conditions of University life. He soon fell into the hands of a set of bullies and was nearly frightened out of his life. They persecuted him even at the dinner table. When Widgery discovered him he was on the point of falling ill with worry and nervous anxiety. Widgery at once communicated with one or two friends. They formed a vigilant association that mounted guard and kept the bullies at a distance, till something occurred to take the responsibility out of their hands. This action involved being continually for days in company with a nervous man driven almost mad by his apprehensions. We may imagine the self-sacrifice it meant. But the task was cheerfully undertaken and effectually accomplished.

Another quality of Widgery's character—his almost childlike simplicity—was not at once obvious. But a very short acquaintance sufficed to reveal it. For a grown man of good education and considerable knowledge of the world, his simplicity was singularly pronounced. It was much to his credit that he retained this natural innocence so late in life. Utterly devoid of guile, his life was pure and blameless from an ethical point of view, and the exclamation of one of his friends when he heard of the untimely death—" how perfectly good he was ! "—did not exaggerate the moral purity of the man. There was about him something of an atmosphere of truth and simplicity, which on two occasions made two different women involuntarily exclaim, " I *do* want to be good when I am with you ! "

I have noted above the charge of arrogance and stated my opinion that it was merely the persistence of strong conviction, not the vanity of vacuous incompetence.

o

Petty conceit he had not. But he knew his own capacity
and was glad in the perception that he had some merit.
This, to my mind, is a perfectly legitimate delight.   If
the labourer is worthy of his hire, the wise man has a
right to enjoy the consciousness of wisdom and there is
no meanness in the strong man's eagerness to run a race.
All this is perfectly consistent with the possession of real
modesty. The fact is well illustrated in Widgery's almost
prudish shrinking from any effort to push his own educational theories. He knew them to be worth consideration and, if any man chose to criticise them, was
prepared to defend them to the uttermost. Yet, when I
suggested to him that he ought to send copies of his
work on "The Teaching of Languages in Schools" to the
leading educationists of the time in order to make his
views more widely known, he replied "I would rather
starve than attempt to advertise myself! My views are
there, let those who choose to consider them, do so."
"But how," said I, "are the leading educationists to
know your theories, unless you bring them under their
immediate notice?" "I have published them," he
replied, "and it is the business of educationists to make
themselves acquainted with new theories." It did not
strike him that people are too busy with their own pet
theories to go a-hunting for those of other people. He
only saw in my proposal a dangerous similarity to the
puffing placards that disfigure our walls and hoardings,
and his soul loathed any process so immodest. Some
may say this was mere morbid pride. I concede the
morbidness, but I do not think that in Widgery's case
there was any element of pride in the sensitiveness I
have described. It was modesty, tinged, if you will, by
a lack of power to discriminate between the puff of the

quack and the honest publication of the educational philanthropist, yet genuine modesty. Something of this modesty, mingled with the simplicity already mentioned, appears in the remark "You gently surprised me at the time by looking on me as an educational reformer."

With regard to Widgery's religion, after a careful study of the meagre data and conflicting evidence to hand, I have come to the conclusion that no definite opinion can be formed, no indisputable statement made as to the real state of his mind on this subject. It seems to me therefore unprofitable, if not undesirable, to attempt an argumentative inquisition into his religious views. We are rather concerned with the effect which the holding of views stigmatised as heterodox by the comfortable complacency of an established and stereotyped religion had upon his career. This I shall notice in due course. At the point we have now reached I shall merely make a series of quotations from Widgery's writings, and then add a summary statement of observations made by myself and his other friends. In this I shall try to avoid argument and leave the reader to draw any conclusion that may seem obvious.

I will now give a number of quotations bearing on Widgery's religious views. The first two show him in a caustic and somewhat contemptuous mood.

"The eighteenth century looked on God as a banausic worker in star-dust."

"Theologians hanging on to the tail of time."

"Can God make two and two equal to five? If the scientific conception of law has fully worked itself into a man's brain, a miracle is as unthinkable as that contrary bit of arithmetic."

My next quotation well illustrates Widgery's inde-

pendence of mind with regard to tradition whether
religious or artistic. "The pluck to fight the gods if
necessary is peculiarly Aryan and would possibly be
impossible to a Semite. Mohammed finely called the
Jews the 'people of the book.' Now, the appeal to a
book is the predominating trait of the Semitic mind and
means ultimately its subjection to the Aryan, who goes
for his inspiration to the source of all books—Nature.
As long as we have Bibles we shall have the priest and all
the deadly influences that spring from that deadly person.
Goethe made a magnificent beginning to a Prometheus.
My will is part arbiter in my fate. The only good point
about Jacob was that he wrestled with the Almighty. I
came across a fine passage in Michelet's 'Nos Fils' the
other day on the coward counsel to be on the winning
side. 'Young man, stick to the true. Who knows
whether God's broom may not go through the unrighteous to-morrow?' Who knows? It is something
to be above fear and fate."

The following is in a noble key. "Surely people who
belong to a sect and believe that they alone are the
guardians of the truth must be terribly deficient in
imagination. A real pervading belief in the loss of the
majority of souls around me would make life unendurable
and turn earth into a hell. God has not dawned in
patches, nor has he left mighty nations unillumined to
burst in all his splendour on the Jews and on the Jews
alone. Let us clear ourselves of our prejudice of class,
of country, of continent. Religion envelops the world
like air, better in some places than in others, but still
universal and life-giving."

The last I shall quote is in much the same tone as the
foregoing and as noble. "What is the key-note of the

last three centuries? What central fact will supply us with a thread to trace out the labyrinths of modern thought, of modern action? What is it that cuts us off in feeling, in colour of thought, from the past? The change springs from the mighty audacity of Galileo, who, distrusting the obvious evidence of his senses, distrusting the unanimous voice of antiquity, the authority of the church, dared to affirm that the earth went round the sun. This conception has now become such an integral portion of our intellectual life, that we require a strong effort of the mind to picture the effect of this startling doctrine on Galileo's contemporaries. The earth was displaced from its proud position of pre-eminence. It was reduced to the rank of a planet and was not even allowed the satisfaction of being the first among them. The starry host was not made to throw an uncertain light on the darkness. That could have been far better done by three or four moons. This dislocation of authority, this shifting of centre, has been carried further in our time into the kingdom of man. Now he does not stand apart as the lord of creation, differing from the rest of the animal world not only in degree but also in kind. Now he takes his stand as the apex of the animal kingdom in this world. He is not sundered and kept aloof from the other animals that live and move and have their being beneath the sun. Again, after the first pain of the change of thought, we find that there has been no loss but gain in man's dignity, in man's worth. 'It is inexpedient,' says the Bishop of Gloucester,—' It is inexpedient to compare the Christian religion with the other religions of the world.' Yes, if your reverence for early training, your prejudice in favour of historical Christianity, be greater than your love of truth, then is it highly inexpedient. For, as surely as the world and man have been taken from their isolation and made links in a chain, so surely has the Christian religion been placed at the head of all other religions, immeasurably superior to them in degree, if you will, but not different in kind. Again, the change opens our horizon, widens our sympathies. God hath not dawned in patches. The terrible wastes of Sinai, the olive-clad slopes of Olivet have felt His awful power. Have the teeming myriads of India and China been left without some spark of the divine light?"

"What he could not grasp by reasoning Widgery's sympathies sometimes brought home to him. Having occasion to go into a Catholic church, he there saw a girl wrapt in silent prayer with such an expression of religious devotion in her face and attitude as profoundly impressed him. 'Since then,' he said, 'I have been able to understand religious people better than I did before, though I am no less an agnostic than before.' The girl's expression so roused his sympathies that the condition of mind of religious people became intelligible to him—his imagination, and through it his thought, was set to work by fellow-feeling."

" He combined an entire absence of religious conviction with a great capacity for religious sympathy and a decidedly religious tone of mind. Intellectually his tendency was to be in an extreme of some conviction, but his unusually strong sympathetic nature made it impossible for him to harden himself in any extreme conviction."

One who knew him very intimately says: " Everything which he could not believe thoroughly with the *whole* of his being he put aside utterly. That

was his mission in life—the ultimate reward of the sacrifice which would not believe with only one part of himself, even when a probable half-belief would have brought
him ease and many things he dearly loved—that was his
voice to tell the orthodox that there is martyrdom on
the side of free-thought. For no worldly consideration
whatever would he assent to a thing which he might have
believed with the emotional side of his nature but could
not say he believed with his mind because his reason
did not see it. It was part of his character to be thorough
in that way. He was ready to risk the comforts of this
world, his chances of success, eternity itself, rather than
insult the Deity with the offer of half his being—the
heart without the head."

I have already mentioned that he had the usual boyish
troubles about atheism when he was in the critical transition stage between boyhood and manhood. At Cambridge too he worried himself a good deal about his
religious difficulties. He seemed at one time to have
found rest in Unitarianism, but not, I believe, for long.
He had, as we should imagine from his extremely independent nature, a very strong dislike to any and all
pressure from the authorities in religious matters. At a
later period we find him saying in one of his letters " My
acts are my religion." In his review of the "Ethics of
Aristotle " in the *School Board Chronicle* he distinctly
denies that the voice of conscience is the expression
of an absolute truth independent of the individual.
"Aristotle," he says, " clearly understood, what the
majority of students of philosophy do not appear
to know to-day, that conscience itself is blind—an
impulse to do not that which is right, but that
which the subject deems to be right." The

remark that "death is a beautiful rest" may be a poetical expression of his mental impression of death, but says nothing further one way or the other.

The impression created by the information now before the reader is certainly one of no great complexity. There is nothing in it inconsistent with the theory that Widgery was—not perhaps a Christian, a believer, that is, in the divinity of Christ, but—a Deist. Some of these extracts, however, are of an early date. He started life as an orthodox Christian. Very early he was pulled up by that most pernicious of all doctrines *not* preached by Christ—the doctrine of eternal punishment. The ferment aroused by this poisonous dogma brought him to the region of Unitarianism about the time he left College. How long he tarried in these parts of the spiritual field it is impossible now to say. Probably he himself could not have told us. This only is certain that a time came, when he recognised or thought himself to be outside the boundaries of Unitarianism and wandering in the pathless and bewildering desert of universal doubt. This much appears to be incontrovertible fact. But just here begins a conflict of opinions. Did he, in the midst of his spiritual gropings, at length come to a dead stop and exclaim "God and a future life are absolutely *unthinkable!*"? One of his friends, who enjoyed much of his confidence in religious questionings, most positively asserts that these were his very words upon one occasion. Within the last year of his life—I believe even within the last six months—he asked one who was very near to his heart whether she ever prayed for him. This might be passed over as a mere display of curiosity, if it ended there. But, when he received an affirmative answer, he remarked that he was "glad." Had Widgery been another sort of man, one might have felt inclined to put this down to the feeble cowardice, that does not believe yet deems it well to provide against the possibility of a day of doom. But with a man of his moral and intellectual courage, it is difficult to account for this question, and the subsequent expression of pleasure, in accordance with the theory of absolute negation of all belief on his part.

Widgery was a rare combination of the poet and the scientist. The scientist in him cried out "Let us express God in an equation, of which faith shall form one member and proof the other." The poet in him replied "God is not a mathematical abstraction! He is the essence of the heart of Nature, whereof your heart is an integral part, as you have always felt, and He is revealed in those wonderful manifestations of Nature's workings which fire your heart and fill your soul with conceptions of immortal beauty. You cannot express Him in an objective equation, because your subjectivity is itself a part of Him whom you would fain examine from without as you do a crystal or a salt." This was the conflict that raged ceaselessly in Widgery's soul, as it does in these latter days in the soul of thousands of others, who feel but cannot prove God. To my mind Widgery did not believe in the existence of God, but he worshipped Him all day long. This is only a paradox so long as we forget, that man is neither wholly mind nor wholly heart but a composition of the two in proportions that vary for each individual. The conclusion I have come to—and I give it as a personal one for what it is worth—is this : that to say Widgery was an absolute infidel, because his mind denied the existence

of God and a future state, is as incorrect as to say that
he was a true believer, because his heart was ever worshipping the manifold manifestations of a God whose
name he could not read upon the forehead of the Morning Star nor hear in the surging thunder of the eternal
sea.   Like all of us, Widgery had two parts—one was
religious and the other sceptical.   It might—to some—be
a satisfaction to be able to claim him for the ranks of
positive infidelity.   To others it might be a joy to
number him among the avowed Sons of God.   The
judgment of facts, so far as I can interpret it (and here I
hold no brief from either claimant), decrees that neither
shall be wholly satisfied.   What consolation then for
those who alone are likely to take the judgment to heart
—the believers who loved him even as themselves and
more?   Only this.   If there be indeed a God, which
means the Soul of Ideal Good, it is inconceivable that
he can be other than the Soul of Ideal Justice, and, that
being so, it is equally inconceivable that a man, who,
with all his natal weaknesses and all his freedom from
the stimulus of future reward, did nevertheless live a life
so essentially Christian and (in its degree) Godlike, could
possibly be rejected by such Justice and such a God.

Whatever conclusion the reader may draw from the
above quotations and from statements made here and in
other parts of this Memoir, one thing was obvious to
those who knew Widgery, that he was saturated with
the instinct of worship.   " He suppressed this side in
himself because he could not fit it in with his intellectual
conceptions, but it had its expression in sympathy with
others and in his whole feeling about Nature and life."

Closely akin to the worshipping instinct are the
virtues of honesty and sincerity.   A man can hardly

be honest and sincere in any noble sense, unless he holds
certain principles of rectitude and worships them in
the good old sense of worship, which was "honour."
Widgery's honesty and sincerity were unusually great,
both in the limited possibilities of school and in the
larger sphere of life in the great world. Even in boyhood he was held to be the soul of truth and honour.
Absolutely upright by nature, he never found his integrity
in question. His rectitude was so unflinching that it
constantly hindered him in attaining a position more
worthy of his powers as a teacher. "His tongue answered in utmost exactness to the thought of his mind,"
said one of his friends, and his pursuit of truth, beauty
and freedom was utterly fearless. He could never
tolerate ignorance that aped taste, and eagerly joined
in any scheme that made for its exposure. But he did
not, as so many censors habitually do, exempt himself
from the rigour of the standard he applied to others.
He made an honest estimate of himself and was not
afraid to publish it. Being praised for his mathematical
power, he replied that it was much overrated while he
was at school in Exeter. "There he counted as a small
wonder, while at Cambridge he was quite ordinary."
With the same frankness he criticised his own temper.
" I am rather of the slowly kindling sort, and I am afraid
(my indignation) takes some time to burn out again,
except I am asked and then I must perforce yield at
once. I infinitely prefer not to have to forgive or be
forgiven."

Essentially genuine and thoroughly true-hearted, sincere in every thought, word or deed, Widgery's directness
of manner disarmed all affectation. Men instinctively
behaved naturally to him and the regard he won was

deepened by experience.   But where regard was out of
the question, this outspokenness did him no little injury.
It proved to be an almost insuperable obstacle to his
rise in the career of a public-school master.   But that in
itself was no small satisfaction to a man of Widgery's
mental calibre—apart from its injury to his hopes of
material happiness.   For every rebuff meant a wound in
the battle against sham and narrow-mindedness, and the
scars of such a conflict he regarded as the good-service
medals given him by his empress Truth.   In the same
spirit he drew a lofty consolation from his religious position, comforting himself in the bright radiance of his
soul's honesty amid the dark and dreary mists of doubt
that swathed him in their chill embrace.

But this passionate worship of truth was not confined
in Widgery to the higher walks of the soul.   He was
equally conscientious in the petty details of bread-winning
work.   Studiously exact and always thorough, he had a
most profound loathing for the shirk, the sloven, the
consciously incompetent, the brazen "tradesman," as he
called a master who cares only for his own profit and no
whit for his pupils'.   "The steward that buried his talent
in a napkin was punished, but what punishment," he
asked, "shall be meet for the steward that uses his talent
to do evil?"

It may well be supposed that a man holding such
views would often be called upon to offer up his dearest
hopes on the altar of Conscience.   It was so with
Widgery.   In such cases it is easy to mistake probability
for fact.   Circumstances have a knack of tricking them
out in shapes and hues so strangely similar.   But
Widgery was on the point of getting an assistant-master-
ship at Harrow when this same inflexibility of truth cast

him out. I believe he was asked to sign some statement of religious conformity of a purely formal nature, which would in all probability never have been practically applied. But the mere signing would have sullied the spotless escutcheon of his spiritual honour, and the very insignificance of the blot would, to his mind, have magnified a thousand-fold the disgrace of its presence on a field he strove to keep as white as the lap of a high and lonely Alpine dale. Could he have purchased this appointment by a reluctant conformity, his material comfort would have been assured and his mind would have been relieved of the corroding anxiety which preyed ceaselessly upon his physical vitality. Is it too much to believe that the same conformity would have purchased at the same time a considerable prolongation of a valuable life? Is it too much to say that his death was ante-dated for conscience' sake? This aspect of his character is well reflected in the lofty and serene severity of the following noble censure of an unworthy deed. "Somehow I feel that this action of his will some day come home to him and be ruinous to his dearest hopes, for the world is founded on honesty and neither can outward seeming, nor orthodoxy, nor heterodoxy, endure for any, but this only—white truth and its passionate pursuit."

We have now considered Widgery's character in the capacity of teacher, lecturer and writer, and in the more subjective capacities of thinker, philosopher, man of parts, colleague and friend. All these are transfused with certain other more spiritual qualities, that characterise the entity we call " man "—manliness and moral courage, tenderness and chivalry, childlike simplicity and modesty, religion, honesty and sincerity. These in their turn are dominated by a comprehensive and general nobility of motive, thought, conception. A brief consideration of this last dominant feature will complete the full-length portrait of the man before us.

As nobility is the last and crowning virtue in manhood, when it is present in a high degree of excellence we are willing to overlook the absence of many minor virtues. Earth's darkest dens are tolerable in the glare of noon, and the failings of conspicuous greatness cannot but seem insignificant in the bright shining of a rare nobility. We have found little to apologise for in Widgery's character, and that little glimmers faint in the white splendour of his surpassing nobleness. In this aspect the qualities of his mind and heart were uncommon and he was, as one of his friends exclaimed, "a rare man." Mediocrity had no satisfaction for him. In whatsoever he undertook he must needs excel. This legitimate ambition was deeply rooted in his nature. His view of life, or life's progress, was "a spiral passing over the same ground, but always on a slightly higher level."* "Novelty," he said, "has a great charm and I want always to get to the bottom of a soul or the reason of a thing."

Even in boyhood he detested with his whole heart anything mean and contemptible. In later life the same loathing of littleness appears in many a caustic aside amid the full course of scholastic argument. One specimen must suffice. "As long as our schools prepare directly for examinations which permit a man to obtain a better living 'with his coat on' than he can get with it off—as long as society pays more respect to those social parasites, who do no work save to spend

* I believe this idea is not original, but cannot trace the author.

the money others have made for them, than it does to an honest and skilful carpenter—so long will the poorer classes strive to 'rise.'"

His character had a massive back-bone of the highest principle, his mind was carved on a noble scale, and his ideal of life and duty was a transcendental one. "About all he attempted there was the stamp of that earnestness which carries double conviction to those who witness it, bearing evidence alike to the truth of the cause and the high purpose of the advocate." Widgery's purpose was never a commonplace one. He always aimed high. "The successes of society seem to me no more worth than the shadow of dust." All his work, no matter how trifling and temporary it might happen to be, was characterised by deep fervour. In his letters he constantly mentions the inflammatory effect of the best prose and poetry upon his sensibility. Sometimes a poet like Swinburne would work him up to such a pitch of nervous excitement, that he became incapable of doing anything until he had tranquilised his mind with the antidote of several pages of an official or statistical register. Occasionally the recollection of another's wish that he should spare himself had the same calming influence. The fact that this fervour was to some extent physical does not diminish the dynamic effect of it upon the vigour and smartness of his action when those qualities were most valuable. Side by side with this fervour was an optimistic hopefulness, which had its basis in a wise philosophy that looked ever to the ultimate victory of good and right. "Take life quietly and vex not your soul because of evil-doers." "Years roll on and regrets are vain, so take life gladly." It was this perennial fount of hope that gave his eyes

their "vivid glance." " In every sense a gentleman,"
he possessed all the magnanimity of that best product
of heart-culture. "I can barely understand and not at
all sympathise with that mental attitude, which feels it
can only show itself to be right by making everything
else wrong." Such narrowness is contemptible to the
broad sympathies of the truly gentle soul. Nobler yet
and louder is the protest against all snobbery and caste
prejudice in this—"People forget that they create an
atmosphere as well as say or do things. They think
that you draw your conclusions from their words alone,
whereas the effect of their atmosphere tells more on your
feelings. How much nobler to say and feel in the last
thoughts of the heart 'Behold, we two walk our
life in the palm of the Almighty. I may have more
money or less than thou—that concerns me not. I am
neither above nor below thee and, if there is aught of
good in me, take it—take freely, take abundantly. The
things of the spirit alone last and give peace."

From no very different source sprang Widgery's public
spirit, which was of no common measure. His unselfish
zeal for the good of others was early manifested in the
determination I have already quoted to enter the
ministry chiefly because "a minister is better able than
a layman to influence people for their good." It appears
in the form of disinterested study of science for its
own sake in the remark " The ultimate peace of going
far and deep into a subject and then brooding over it
till it shines seems to be a pleasure unknown to the rich.
Their life consists of an infinite number of infinitely
small quantities, but whether the integral amounts to
much may be doubted."

There was a "splendour in Widgery's nature," which

shines forth in the central idea of such a statement as the following—"There must be somewhere some quickening breath of spirit in my subject, or it cannot detain me long," and in his feeling of " kinship with the stars." It burns brightest in the prayer and vow " Thou helping, shall the world be better for my advent and I will carve my name among the noble workers." Whom he meant we see in the confession " One of my dreams is to read the seven or eight great works of the world each in its original language : Homer and the Bible in Greek, Dante in Italian, ' Don Quixote ' in Spanish, Molière, Shakespeare and Goethe, with perhaps the Rig Vedas in Sanskrit."

But, alas, these were aspirations. Hope painted a fair canvas before his spiritual eyes, but Death drew a dark curtain across it. Was it in mere mockery, or that in the purer light of a new and yet nobler life he might create a picture yet more sublime? We know not. But for us also, when the mist of mourning clears, the same subtle and airy spirit of Imagination paints a living dream, wherein " our wonder, reverence, love " seem to " mount up the tideless unresting stream of time and touch with glad joy the soul of him whose stature," in that perfect life, " grows with the growing years—whose soul is as tender as a moon-dawn on a summer night, or the opal heavens that usher in the sun—as just in her movements as the ever law-obeying stars—as strong as death, or love, or the unsubduable spirit of man !" What if Hope's creation proved but a figment for him ? Work is not the only proof of worth, and well might he exclaim in the Rabbi's immortal words—

" Not on the vulgar mass
　　Called ' work ' must sentence pass,
Things done, that took the eye and had the price;
　　O'er which, from level stand,
　　The low world laid its hand,
Found straightway to its mind, could value in a trice :

　　But all the world's coarse thumb
　　And finger failed to plumb,
So passed in making up the main account ;
　　All instincts immature,
　　All purposes unsure,
That weighed not as his work, yet swelled the man's amount :

　　Thoughts hardly to be packed
　　Into a narrow act,
Fancies that broke through language and escaped ;
　　All I could never be,
　　All men ignored in me,
This I was worth to God, whose wheel the pitcher shaped."

His own example is indeed the greatest thing that
Widgery has left us, the rich legacy of a life most nobly
spent. And who shall estimate the effect of such lofty
sentiments as dominated Widgery's scholastic activity,
when infused into the humdrum pedantry of ordinary
scholastic life? Who shall say what sloth he startled
into eager strife, what diffidence he galvanised into
effective courage, what mean conceptions he inspired
with the warm breath of noble instinct and lofty aspira-
tion? They are lost to us, scattered in the many brains
that passed beneath his moulding influence for a brief
space and then sank into the general mass of competitive
humanity—lost to us, buried in the many hearts that
came for a moment, in all the soft susceptibility of youth,
within the warm rays of his glowing nature and then
passed out into the cold disillusions and material aspira-

tions of the great world—lost to us. And yet we know that, in the great sum of human effort one day to be told and weighed and valued, they have their part and shall not be forgotten, nor discarded, nor in any wise demeaned, but laid up to his renown and the world's lasting good. And what if amid these noble strivings sometimes his hand grew weak and, his heart failing with weariness and despair, the deed of his hand was marred and the purity of his heart took on the taint of bitterness? These are the spots upon the sun, the seeming wavering of the stedfast star betrayed by the restless shifting of a too gross atmosphere. There are faults that spring from the absence of all worth and there are failings that cling about the trailing skirts of Nobleness, struck from the brazen front of wrong, like sparks from flint, by the ruthless sweep of her strong arm. For she is ever essaying to destroy at one blow what only the slow tooth of Time may grind to dust—longing to consume with the white rays of her burning eyes the cherished foibles of inert and purblind Prejudice, that only the slow heat of growing wisdom can avail to burn away—battling ceaselessly to tear suddenly from the reluctant hand of Knowledge what only long years of Promethean anguish amid the chill Caucasus of fate can slowly earn for man—the sweet boon of heavenly light. Widgery's errors were the little failings which the weakness of human nature renders inseparable from great virtue, resulting from the strenuous and sometimes perhaps too rigid application of noble principles. Of those lamentable faults which spring from the ineffectiveness of a mean understanding, or the poverty of a shallow heart, he was utterly innocent. Shall we weigh the faults of meanness against the failings of worth? If there be one who can pronounce them equal, or in any sense comparable, his eyes are surely blinded by "the motes that people the sunbeams" and to him the clear shining of the sun is lost for the darkness of the spots that cover its face. The truly noble heart will be ready and eager to cast the failings of worth into the secret holds of memory and bow his spirit in admiring reverence before effort that is earth's noblest, albeit imperfect, groping after the sublime.

Widgery's soul was essentially noble and the noble words he applied to Pestalozzi may well be our last words on him. "As we close the story of his life we feel anew the irresistible power possessed by a man who has really seized some side of the truth. Neither war nor poverty, neither neglect nor the bigotry of sects miscalled religious, neither sickness nor the loss of friends, can quench the flame of him who strives after truth in the service of man."

APPENDICES

APPENDIX I

LIST OF WRITINGS

1880—The First Quarto Edition of Hamlet, 1603. Two Essays to which the Harness Prize was awarded, 1880. I. by C. H. Herford, B.A. Trin. Coll., Camb.; II. by W. H. Widgery, B.A. St. John's Coll., Camb. (The above were declared equal in merit.) 1 vol. 8vo, 204 pp. London : Smith, Elder & Co. *Out of print.* (Essay.)

1882 : Nov.—Beówulf. Lecture to the Exeter Literary Society. Delivered in the Athenæum. Noticed, *Exeter Flying Post*, Nov. 15 ; *Exeter and Plymouth Gazette*, Nov. 11. (Lecture.)

Nov. 11.—Beówulf. Letter to Editor *Devon Evening Express* correcting mistake in his report of lecture on 9th. (Letter.)

1886 : April.—The Handy Anglo-Saxon Dictionary Trans. of Dr. Groschopp's "Kleines Angelsächisches Wörterbuch." *School Board Chronicle.* (Review.)

June.—The Public School German Grammar. *School Board Chronicle.* (Review.)

Aug.—Outlines of a History of the German Language. By Strong and Meyer. *Journal of Education.* (Review.)

Chief Ancient Philosophies : The Ethics of Aristotle. J. G. Smith. *School Board Chronicle.* (Review.)

1887 : Jan.—An Introduction—Phonological, Morphological, Syntactic — To the Gothic of Ulfilas. By Douse. *Journal of Education.* (Review.)

1887 : June.—THE NEW ENGLISH. By Oliphant. *Journal of Education.* (REVIEW.)

Dec.—PRINCIPLES OF ENGLISH ETYMOLOGY. Skeat. First Series. The Native Element. *Journal of Education.* (REVIEW.)

1888 : Jan. 14—POINTS IN CONNECTION WITH THE TEACHING OF MODERN LANGUAGES IN SCHOOLS. Speech at the Second Meeting of the First General Conference of the Teachers' Guild. Noticed in *Evening Standard,* Jan. 14; *Standard, Globe* and *Evening News,* Jan. 16; *Western Morning News,* Jan. 25 ; *Athenæum,* Jan. 21 ; *Journal of Education,* March. (SPEECH.)

Jan. 16.—COMPARATIVE ADVANTAGES, IN SCHOOLS, OF A SEPARATE CLASSIFICATION FOR EVERY SUB-JECT, AND AN ARRANGEMENT IN FORMS THE STATUS IN WHICH DEPENDS ON ONE OR TWO CHOSEN SUBJECTS. Speech at the Second Meeting of the First General Conference of the Teachers' Guild. Noticed, *Journal of Education,* March ; *Standard,* Jan. 16. (SPEECH.)

March 2.—THE TEACHING OF LANGUAGES. Paper read at Maidstone, probably before the Local Branch of the Teachers' Guild. (This paper gives useful hints on his own methods.) (PAPER.)

March 26.—THE TEACHING OF LANGUAGES. Apparently a Paper read before a meeting of the Teachers' Guild. MS. has no title. (PAPER.)

April.—SERIES OF ARTICLES ON THE TEACHING OF LANGUAGES begun in the *Journal of Education,* which ran through the year. (ARTICLE.)

July.—ELEMENTS OF THE COMPARATIVE GRAMMAR OF THE INDO-EUROPEAN LANGUAGES. Brugman. Vol. I. Introduction and Phonology. Trans. Wright. *Journal of Education.* (REVIEW.)

Nov.—PRINCIPLES OF ENGLISH ETYMOLOGY. Skeat. First Series. The Native Element. *Educational Times.* (REVIEW.)

1888 : Dec.—WILLIAM SHAKESPEARE : A LITERARY BIO-
GRAPHY. Karl Elze. Trans. L. Dora Schmitz. *Journal
of Education.* (REVIEW.)

THE TEACHING OF LANGUAGES IN SCHOOLS. 1 vol.
8vo, 80 pp. London : David Nutt. (At end valuable
bibliographical list of 215 works on educational subjects
arranged chronologically.) (PAMPHLET.)

1889 : Jan.—GRUNDRISS DER ROMANISCHEN PHILOLOGIE.
Gröber. Vol. I. *Journal of Education.* (REVIEW.)

Feb.—THE TEACHING OF LANGUAGES IN SCHOOLS.
Postscript to Articles in *Journal of Education* during 1888.
(POSTSCRIPT.)

March.—THE BACON-SHAKSPERE QUESTION. Stopes.
Journal of Education. (REVIEW.)

April 1.—THE TEACHING OF MODERN LANGUAGES.
Letter answering criticisms of Articles in *Journal of
Education* during 1888. (LETTER.)

April 13.—RECENT ADVANCES IN THE SCIENCE OF
LANGUAGE. Lecture to the Maidstone Branch of the
Teachers' Guild. (LECTURE.)

May.—SCHEME FOR A TEACHING TRIPOS AT THE
UNIVERSITIES. Paper read at the Sheffield Conference
of the Teachers' Guild. Noticed in *The Journal of
Education.* (PAPER.)

—THE PRESENT CLASSICAL RÉGIME. Speech
during a debate at the Sheffield Conference of the
Teachers' Guild. Noticed in the *Journal of Education.*
(SPEECH.)

June.—LECTURES ON PEDAGOGY. Theoretical and
Practical. Compayré. Trans. Payne. *Educational
Times.* (REVIEW.)

July.—GRUNDRISS DER GERMANISCHEN PHILOLOGIE.
Paul. I. Lieferung. *Educational Times.* (REVIEW.)

Aug. 17.—THE¦ INTERNATIONAL EDUCATIONAL
CONGRESS AT PARIS. Report in the *Athenæum.*
(REPORT.)

1889 : Aug. 31.—PUBLIC INSTRUCTION AT THE PARIS EXHI-
BITION. Report on the Exhibition with special reference
to the Educational Section. *Athenæum.* (REPORT.)

Sept.—SECONDARY EDUCATION. *Educational Times.*
Account of the Paris Congress. (REPORT.)

Nov.—EARLY ENGLISH PRONUNCIATION. Part V.
The Existing Phonology of English Dialects compared
with that of West Saxon Speech. Ellis. *Educational
Times.* (REVIEW.)

REPORT ON THE PARIS CONGRESS to the Education
Bureau at Washington. Unfinished at death ; completed
by Mr. Foster Watson and published 1893 in the
Report of the Commissioner of Education for the Year
1889–90. Vol. I. (REPORT.)

1890 : Jan. 1.—THE CRADLE OF THE ARYANS. Rendall.
Journal of Education. (REVIEW.)

Jan.—CLASS TEACHING OF PHONETICS AS A PRE-
PARATION FOR THE PRONUNCIATION OF FOREIGN
LANGUAGES. Pamphlet of 10 pp. 8vo. (Extracted from
the *Educational Times*, Jan. 1890.) Originally read as a
Paper at the College of Preceptors. (PAMPHLET.)

May 1.—AN EDUCATIONAL MUSEUM. Speech at the
Cheltenham Conference of the Teachers' Guild. Noticed
in *Journal of Education.* (SPEECH.)

May 1.—THE TEACHING OF ENGLISH. Speech at the
Cheltenham Conference of the Teachers' Guild. Noticed
in *Journal of Education.* (SPEECH.)

May.—TEACHING OF ALGEBRA HISTORICALLY
CONSIDERED. Paper on the history and methods of
Algebra with critical suggestions as to the way in which
it should be taught. Read at Kensington High School.
(PAPER.)

June 1.—THE HISTORY OF EDUCATIONAL MUSEUMS.
Journal of Education. Reprinted as a Leaflet in
America. (ARTICLE.)

June 1.—PESTALOZZI: HIS LIFE AND WORK. Roger
de Guimps. Trans. Russell. Introduction by Quick.
Educational Times. (REVIEW.)

1890 : June 1.—HARVARD STUDIES IN CLASSICAL PHILO-
LOGY. Vol. I. *Educational Times.* (REVIEW.)

June 1.—A FIRST ARYAN READER. Schrumpf.
Educational Times. (REVIEW.)

Sept. to Aug. 1891.—NOTES ON MODERN PHILO-
LOGY. *Modern Language Monthly.* (The last contribution, marked "To be continued," is dated August
1891. The series of papers was interrupted by death.)
(ARTICLE.)

Nov. 1.—THE AMERICAN JOURNAL OF PHILOLOGY.
Edit. Gildersleeve. *Journal of Education.* (REVIEW.)

Nov. 1.—ESSAYS ON EDUCATIONAL REFORMERS.
Quick. *Journal of Education.* (REVIEW.)

1891 : Feb. 1.—PREHISTORIC ANTIQUITIES OF THE ARYAN
PEOPLES. Trans. by Jevons from the "Sprachvergleichung
und Urgeschichte" of Schrader. *Journal of Education.*
(REVIEW.)

Feb. 1.—DER FRANZÖSISCHE KLASSENUNTERRICHT.
I. Unterstufe, Entwurf eines Lehrplans. Max Walter.
Journal of Education. (REVIEW.)

Feb. 1.—CHRONOLOGICAL OUTLINES OF ENGLISH
LITERATURE. Ryland. *Journal of Education.* (REVIEW.)

May.—LANGUAGE OF THE MEDIÆVAL WRITERS.
Speech after a Lecture on History. Noticed in *Educational Times.* (SPEECH.)

July.—PRINCIPLES OF ENGLISH ETYMOLOGY. Skeat.
Second Series. The Foreign Element. *Journal of
Education.* (REVIEW.)

APPENDIX II

EXTRACTS FROM VARIOUS CRITICISMS OF THE HARNESS ESSAY

According to Widgery the First Quarto of *Hamlet* was an early sketch. "Like most works of analytical criticism, Widgery's essay succeeds in the processes of destruction and fails in those of construction. Nothing can be more convincing than his demonstrations how inadequate to account for differences between the two quartos is the theory that the first is a pirated work, stolen by some dishonest member of the company of the theatre, or taken in shorthand by a spectator of the performance, that it 'is the first conception and comparatively feeble expression of a great mind,' or that it is the surreptitious and mutilated copy of the first." * (*Athenæum.*)

"One cannot look with favour on Widgery's theory (pp. 137–143) that in the Player King we have the 'stealthy purloiner' who furnished the pirate with the material for his bungling work. Widgery's objections to the possibility of a copying of complete portions also will not hold, especially if we assume that the unknown author had the help of a friend in his copying, and that then later on this author out of the combined notes, which were here and there complete enough to reproduce individual portions with proportionate truth, restored Q 1.

"In discussing textual points of interest (p. 146) Widgery

* *I.e.* the authentic "first," supposed (according to this last theory) to be lost.

seems to be less in his element than in the historico-literary investigations, which, in spite of the tendency to failure in general, make the previous portions so interesting.

"Widgery is little successful in drawing any right conclusions from the omissions common to Q 1 and F 1.

"On p. 151 Widgery enumerates some smaller variations, in which Q 2 exhibits a more skilful or more poetic diction than Q 1, and without further ceremony sees also herein a proof that Shakespeare's hand must have improved the original, as if it were not at least as easy to spoil the good as to ennoble the bad. In his endeavours to discredit the theory of copying Widgery has little success." [Tanger in Anglia (trans.).]

"The view Widgery advocates—of Q 1 being a first sketch—is surely the right one." (*Academy.*)

"The question of the true relation between Q 1 and Q 2 is thrust somewhat into the background by Widgery's constantly recurring attempts to establish the traces of the Urhamlet (Original or Fore-Hamlet) in Shakespeare's work." (Tanger in Anglia.)

"Nothing can be less conclusive than Widgery's (constructive) attempts to prove the existence of an earlier *Hamlet* ascribable to Kyd or some previous dramatist. That a *Hamlet* earlier than Shakespeare's held possession of the stage and gave rise to allusions in Nash, Lodge and Decker, seems certain. The attempt to connect it with any known dramatist, or the German play *Fratricide Punished*, or with *Prince Henry of Denmark*, is futile." (*Athenæum.*)

"Widgery 'naturally' gives prominence to the German *Brudermord* (Fratricide), the quagmire which has swallowed up so many men of unsound judgment. This, he says, contains much of the Urhamlet or fore-Shakespeare play, which he sets down to Kyd. The German play lies between Saxo and Belleforest and Shakespeare's First Sketch of *Hamlet*, and 'the German adapter was under no obligations to Shakespeare.'" (*Academy.*)

"The attempt to prove the Urhamlet a work of Kyd is not unsuccessful, but the attempt to show that the *Brudermord* goes back, not to Q 1 but, to Kyd's *Hamlet* as its first source is unsuccessful. The external difficulties are insuperable. (Tanger in Anglia.)

"The fact that in the *Brudermord*, as in Q 1, Hamlet several times addresses the King as 'father' (never in Q 2 and F 1), if it proves anything, makes equally well for a derivation of the *Brudermord* from Q 1.

"The further Widgery goes with his comparison of the *Brudermord* and Q 1 the less convincing do his arguments become.

"The attempts he makes to show the independence of the *Brudermord* from Q 1 are not more successful than his previous ones, the text of the *Brudermord* being so uncertain. Widgery makes the mistake of attaching too little importance to the specific German influence upon the original setting of the *Brudermord*, which was never a translation but from the beginning a free version, whence it happens that h regards insignificant peculiarities in the *Brudermord* as essential differences.

"The acceptable result of the first division of Widgery's essay is the establishment of an Urhamlet—for ought I can say to the contrary also of an Urhamlet by Kyd—but that the former served as a groundwork for the *Brudermord*, that the latter is wholly independent of Shakespeare, appears to me not to be proved by Widgery's arguments." (Tanger in Anglia.)

"The great objection to the date assigned by Widgery for the composition of the first Quarto, *i.e.*, between 1596 and 8, is the omission of *Hamlet* from Meres's list, which has hitherto settled the question. But, as Widgery points out, we must not expect to find in Meres, a Lincolnshire schoolmaster, a full and perfect account of the various authors he has mentioned and their works and dates." (*Examiner.*)

"In the examination of Meres's striking tendency to antithesis Widgery goes to work with as much sagacity as skill, so that he shows how the absence of mention of *Hamlet* has as little significance for our question as the existing statements have importance for the works mentioned." (Tanger in Anglia.)

"The retort to critics who assert that Shakespeare must have been a lawyer's assistant in youth, because of his intimate acquaintance with law terms, is happy and striking." (*Id.*)

"With no small sagacity Widgery discovers in the lines

> 'How some damn'd tyrant &c. . . . . .
>
> .   .   .   .
>
> And cries, Vindicta !—Revenge, Revenge !'

(from the Introduction to *A Warning for Faire Women*) an accordance with *Hamlet*. But the allusion is perhaps quite a general one, not specially referring to *Hamlet*, and the significance of the words 'Vindicta !—Revenge, Revenge !' must not be overrated." (*Id.*)

The critic of the *Academy* makes fun of the passages "As in the quietude of the study &c." (p. 181) and "The warm love-languorous air of Verona &c." (p. 184), which are æsthetically among the finest pieces of writing in the essay and serve to lift it above the dry-as-dust productions of the average uninspired literary antiquary, from whose fossilised temperament one never of course expects anything so living as 'rapture.' The critic of Anglia on the other hand, being the possessor of a German heart in addition to German penetration, says that "Widgery knows how to clothe his discussion in language always lively, witty, graceful, frequently full of verve. The animated æsthetic reflections which conclude the essay form a beautiful piece of poetic diction, affording ready proof of Widgery's intellectual education. They are directed principally against the defender of the vacillation theory and form excellent reading but prove nothing." (Tanger in Anglia.)

This "interesting and instructive essay" (Tanger), "a scholarly piece of work" (*Journal of Education*), gives

"evidence of learning and intellectual accomplishment"
(*Western Times*). " It evinces considerable knowledge of
literature combined with wide scope of reference." (Tanger.)

Singling out Widgery's enthusiastic and unguarded
remark that he is "morally persuaded" about the reasons
for Meres not mentioning *Hamlet*, as if it were not
backed by more substantial proofs, the *Academy* critic
sarcastically observes " Before criticism like this of course
all difficulties disappear." But this critic's wit overreaches
itself and betrays something very like an attempt after the
smartness and crude pungency beloved of the gods of the
gallery in the remark " His is 'an excellent (essay), set
downe with as (little) modestie as cunning.'"

" Some of Widgery's arguments are more clever than
conclusive, and some of his proofs are by no means decisive."
(Tanger in Anglia.)

" One cannot fail to be pleased with the acute way in
which Widgery both props up his own theories and meets
possible objections, especially when one remembers the
doubtful nature of the airy structure." (*Englische Studien.*)

The Excursus on the " Dram of eale" is "able and ingenious." (*Examiner.*)

APPENDIX III

EXTRACTS FROM VARIOUS CRITICISMS OF THE "TEACHING OF LANGUAGES IN SCHOOLS"

WIDGERY'S work on "The Teaching of Languages in Schools" appeared originally in the form of six separate articles in the *Journal of Education* for the year 1888. It attracted a good deal of attention both at home and abroad, was quoted as an authority in Germany and is now, I believe, being translated into Swedish by Mr. Elfstrand of Gelfe.

The work "bears evidence of wonderful research and proves that the author is thoroughly entitled to speak on the subject which he treats. It is a protest against the antiquated methods of imparting knowledge which still prevail in the public schools of this country and of Europe." (Tacoma *Morning Globe.*) "The vast amount of erudite knowledge" it bears witness to is "astounding." (Klinghardt.) "It presupposes, no doubt, what we fear is an exceptional enthusiasm and capacity for his work, and unsparing labour, on the part of the teacher. But its suggestions for conveying the spirit of a new language so that its so-called rules may come as if by nature, as in the case of a native, are not only philosophical but, we are convinced, eminently practicable." (*School Guardian*).

"The sketch of the 'History of Grammar' is as intelligent as it is learned" (Klinghardt in "Englische Studien"), and "should be expanded into an article by itself." (Quick).

"Widgery had a fine gift in bibliography" and "the educational bibliography" at the end of the book "displays rare

Q

learning." (Dr. Harris, Commissioner, Bureau of Education, Washington).

There is "power" in the "pithy style" (Klinghardt), "great freshness in the handling of the subject and much excellent sense." (Quick).

"A work of considerable value, in point of clearness, judgment and sound pedagogical tact it speaks highly for the author's ability and thorough understanding of his subject." (Elfstrand).

"Widgery has a marked inclination for the historical study of language as well as for the historical study of pedagogy. Despite this, he retains a clear unprejudiced regard for the needs of the present, and only very seldom has his fondness for that method led him aside, as when he proposes that English children under thirteen should be taken through a historical course in the English of Queen Anne's time, Shakespeare, Chaucer and fragments of Anglo-Saxon." (Klinghardt).

I shall make but one more quotation. The light of subsequent events invests it with a melancholy interest. An enthusiastic forecast of a great promise, like countless others of similar warmth and hopefulness, it was destined never to be fulfilled. After long and careful study of Widgery's work, I feel convinced that the promise was not overestimated and that the retardation of the progress of educational science caused by Widgery's untimely death has been great indeed.

"Mr. Widgery seems in all his thought and intentions, his ends and aims, especially in his familiarity with the literature of German educational reform, to be so much in the selfsame sphere with that movement, that I anticipate the happiest results from his entry into the continental discussion of reform in the art of teaching and his communication of our views to his English professional colleagues. I have no doubt but that Mr. Widgery will in no distant future be generally acknowledged as standing in the foremost rank of the promoters of a reformed method of language-teaching,

abreast with the most distinguished leaders of this movement who are now busy with practical experiments in the
Northern countries, in France and in Germany.   And I feel
it a most valuable honour that I should have been chosen to
introduce him, as it were, to the readers of this periodical."
(Klinghardt in " Englische Studien ").

APPENDIX IV

EXTRACTS FROM REVIEWS, SPEECHES, LECTURE, PAPERS AND ARTICLES

Note.—*In the following extracts each paragraph is generally complete in itself, but the transition to a new paragraph often marks an omission.*

REVIEWS

I. The New English. Oliphant.

The truism that a man cannot know his own language unless he learns another, has held the field long enough. Suppose we change it by saying that, to learn a foreign language, he must first know a good deal of his own. Surely the quickest way of teaching English children languages like Latin and Greek must be by pointing out to them traces of synthesis in our modern highly analytical English, gradually working back to the earlier stages. Again, in teaching foreign languages, grammars must be written "practically," whereas in English there is enough preliminary knowledge to make possible a living faith that philology is really a science, and for doing this our language, with its long history, its great changes, and strange retention of the old, its wealth of borrowed words, is unique.

II. Principles of English Etymology. The "Native Element." Skeat. *Journal of Education.*

The first reflection which will present itself to a reader of this volume, whether he be a professed philological student or not, is, that the nation to whom the volume appeals must be in a very curious stage of philological knowledge. It seems to be addressed to several different classes of readers, who would naturally, one would think, be kept quite distinct. In the first place, we find numerous exhortations addressed at intervals throughout the volume to some outer barbarians who are apparently assumed to be ignorant of the first principles of philology, and we are left to gather that the number of these is deplorably great. These are dealt with in a half-pathetic, half-humorous way that reminds us of Charles Lamb's advice to an old man on entering upon learning. Then there is much that would seem more properly in place if relegated to a different volume and called a Primer of Etymology. Lastly, there is a class of accurate philological students whom Mr. Skeat's catholic eye has had in view, who will benefit much by his remarks, but who would, we venture to think, have benefited far more had his treatise been addressed solely to them. The work, in fact, bears witness to the chaos in which philological teaching in England is at the present time; and it is a great question whether the scientific teachers of the science of philology would not do better to lead public opinion by assuming, and so tending to create, the existence of a class of serious philological students.

On page 4 Mr. Skeat seems to speak of language as if it were possible for individuals consciously to adopt into language at will elements which suited them from any other language, a view quite repudiated by Paul and modern philologists. On page 21 Mr. Skeat propounds the difficult question, "Is our modern pronunciation a *real improvement?*" The reason why it is pronounced by the author not to be so is because modern spelling, owing to our alteration of the vowel sounds, seems a chaos of contradictions. Surely this is a reason for altering our spelling, and scarcely one for regretting changes of pronunciation which are of the essence of all language. It is very hard to say that modern French is no improvement on Latin as to its pronunciation ; it is the natural outcome of natural laws, and it is as absurd to say, as Mr. Skeat says, that the clipped, affected, and finical pronunciation of the Southerner has done its worst to ruin our pronunciation as it would be to say that our officers or barristers were doing their worst to corrupt the pronunciation of their language by insensibly falling into the pronunciation adopted by their caste.

III. PRINCIPLES OF ENGLISH ETYMOLOGY. The "Native Element." Skeat. *Educational Times.*

"To the advanced student I can only apologise for handling the subject at all, being conscious that he will find some unfortunate slips and imperfections, which I should have avoided if I had been better trained, or indeed trained at all." This is a curious confession for a Cambridge Professor of English to make. Largely through Mr. Skeat's own labours, things are beginning to mend, though the modern student will get little help in being properly trained. At the present moment it is impossible to get any public training in phonetics, the very base of all work on language, the leading subject both in schools and universities. The lack of a strictly scientific method is strikingly shown by the absence of Paul's " Principien der Sprach-geschichte " from the long list of authorities in the preface.

"Modern philology will in future turn more and more upon phonetics," wrote Mr. Skeat more than six years ago. On turning, however, to the statement of Grimm's Law, we find the same old misstatements that have led so many astray, and confused so many generations of school children, filling them with the belief that etymology consists mainly in putting any word you like in a bag, shaking it up with the other letters of the alphabet and taking a few out at haphazard for the " derivation." " Let us provisionally call the sounds denoted by *dh* in Sanskrit, θ in Greek, and *th* in English, by the name of Aspirates ; " which being interpreted is, let us pronounce *father* provisionally as *fat her*.

What is the magic charm of the mnemonic formulæ ASH, SHA, HAS? *Soft* and *hard* are misleading terms as applied to sounds : ASH can only be retained by a hopeless confusion between the aspirates and spirants; in SHA "we should be careful to denote the Teutonic aspirate by TH rather than DH" and then the "meaning" of the symbols has to be explained.

Would it not be far better to give a page of carefully selected cognates to be learnt by heart, and then two or three typical examples of the way in which the primitive Aryan forms are deduced? Nobody has a right to expect changes spreading over two or three thousand years, to be tabulated into a few mnemonic formulæ. In all the ordinary books on historical English Grammar Grimm's Law can be made to contradict itself on the same page: let the teacher avoid these formulæ most carefully. We can compel our pupils to call our juggling a "law," but no sense of law in the changes, which languages undergo, will by this method pass into their minds.

We think it a mistake to attempt to give a "popular" statement of the sound-changes, and then shortly after to correct it. In the long run, the most scientific statement is the shortest.

Unless we hold fast to the inviolability of the sound-changes, scientific etymology becomes impossible. Our theories may at times be rather a matter of faith than certainty, yet we have no other safe guide. In the German *Vater* we see that the *t* has made a complete circle of change; and so it is with the other sounds.

The title of the first grammar written for Englishmen in 1680 runs : "A perfect grammar never extant before, whereby the English may both easily and exactly learn the neatest dialect of the German *Mother-Language*." Is this the prime source of the belief that our language " comes from" German? Mr. Skeat gives two recent examples of this strange and disgraceful jumble, kept alive, we fear, in schools by "deriving" hundreds of words from the German.

IV. Elements of the Comparative Grammar of the Indo-European Languages. Brugman.

When all is said, what is the difference between the old and the new comparative grammar? Formally, it is a difference in the relative weight assigned to one or two large principles. We now say that "phonetic laws are invariable," and, when we are confronted with instances that seem to contradict us, we say, "We stated the law wrongly," or else, "The case before us is not a case coming under the law in question," whereas our teachers used to say, "There are exceptions to the law," and think no more about it. Also, we do not expect to find immediate descendants of primitive words unchanged except by phonetic causes; but, as a rule, we expect to find that our words are the result of countless acts of memory just a little distorted each time, always working on a model, but in at least half the cases on the wrong model.

There are theories in this book that admit of dispute; some which the present writer would be inclined to dispute, if this were the place to do it. But that makes no difference to the learner. Probably no two first-hand authorities on comparative anatomy agree in the affiliation of all the forms of animal life, but Professor Huxley would not say that a pupil had better not read Professor Macalister, because he takes the wrong view of Kennaquhairiensis Crackjavii.

The translator is troubled by "the poverty-stricken state of our language as regards current philological technical terms," and he is afraid that the reader will be scandalised by some of his own equivalents for his author's formulæ. But here he wrongs us; the English digestion has been trained on the strong meat of scientific terminology, and the worst that the comparative philologist can do is lacteally mild in comparison. After "definite coherent heterogeneity," "slurred and broken accent" has no terrors.

V. WILLIAM SHAKESPEARE : A LITERARY BIOGRAPHY.
Karl Elze.

This book embodies the result of many years of devoted labour on Shakespeare. All the scraps picked up by the literary chiffonnier will be found here carefully scraped clean and arranged. In the case of Shakespeare, perhaps, the work was worth doing, but the patient industry of the author is more likely to be admired than imitated.

Such unsafe ground as the Life of Shakespeare requires dainty walking ; the temptation to cross the marches of a biographical romance needs constant checking. For the English edition many small corrections have been made ; one amusing piece of prejudice in the first edition we especially missed. Fishing might suit Cleopatra, but an upright man like Shakespeare could find no pleasure in such a pastime ! Dr. Elze is nearly always objective, and yet he claims a knowledge of foreign languages for Shakespeare because his sons-in-law were linguists ! "The boy Shakespeare" may have done all sorts of odd things that other boys did or did not do. In the absence of some approach to data the fancy had better be curbed, though we are bound to admit that Dr. Elze's method of bringing together every possible scrap of information produces a striking cumulative effect of probability for his views ; not only do we see the other mountain peaks that towered round the highest, the mist lifts, and we can make out something of the country about the base.

The third chapter, headed "London," is admirable, and appeals to a much larger circle than the special student. Could Dr. Elze be transplanted back to the times of Elizabeth he would surprise many a "man about town" by the accuracy and extent of his knowledge. Dr. Elze cannot, however, quite shake off the German ; Shakespeare's keenness in money matters is evidently something of a riddle to him ; the carelessness of Schiller apparently seems to him more consonant with the poetic character than the scrupulous care of Goethe. But it is precisely this streak in Shakespeare which makes him so essentially English : with his feet firm on the earth the poetic frenzy might carry him whither it would.

In the chapter on "The Theatre" Elze, in his most welcome manner, proves the existence of a widespread feeling for the drama among the people, by the side of which the glum puritanism of the city signified little.

Shakespeare's Intellectual Culture hardly needs such weighty proof now, we hope, to anybody save the foolish adherents of the Baconian hypothesis, and they seem hopeless. The chapter on Shakespeare's character and conception of human nature makes an eloquent claim for him as a humanist standing above the quarrels of sects.

VI. Grundriss der Romanischen Philologie. Gröber.

All works of this kind seem open to the Turk's objection to gymnastics, "too much for sport and not enough for earnest." For the beginner they contain far too much ; for the specialist they are not complete enough to give help when some knotty point wants elucidation.

Philology is narrowed in England almost to the meaning of etymology. Since the increased interest taken of recent years by the Germans in the question of method, the exact signification of the word has been a matter of lively discussion. Gröber disagrees with all the others who have tried their hands at it. But his own definitions are not more likely to win acceptance than those of his predecessors. Philology is the "investigation of speech that has grown unintelligible." Are all the modern stages, then, to be left out ? A little lower "The manifestation of the human mind in speech" is much nearer the mark—but then his predecessors say the same.

VII. The Bacon-Shakspere Question. Stopes.

No more melancholy proof of the innate snobbery of a portion of the English race, nor of the great ignorance of Shakespeare's work in his own country, could be desired than the number of heads that have grown addled by brooding over the wind-eggs in the mare's nest of the Bacon-Shakspere controversy. The fundamental argument of the Baconians is the argument from snobbery :—How could a young man from the middle class of a country town show the marvellous learning and knowledge we find in the plays? To which the simple answer is that he had a genius, a gift happily not confined to the "upper classes." Mr. Stopes, finding that "the great Shakespearians consider it beneath their dignity to answer the assertions of the Baconians," brings a new point of view to bear on the question, in preparing "a series of articles on stimulants in the Trade Journal 'Wine, Spirit, and Beer.'" Shakespeare, we find, approved of stimulant in exceeding moderation ; he preferred beer to wine, even for getting drunk on ; but his knowledge on the subject was not deep ; he might have picked it up at any ale-house. My Lord Bacon, however, knew all about it, and was actually connected with the "trade." "The works of Bacon on 'Drinks' would fill a large volume, which might be called 'Wine, Beer, and Cider.'" "The authors of Shakspere's and of Bacon's works drank different liquors, and therefore they did not think alike," argal——. There is a pretty little theory on the other side invented by Herr Reichel in 1887: the plays were written not by Shakspere but by Shakespeare —our old friend the Homer joke again—who also indited the *Novum Organon*, and *him* Bacon plundered shamelessly. Mr. Stopes has paid the Baconians too great a compliment.

VIII. GRUNDRISS DER GERMANISCHEN PHILOLOGIE.
Paul.

Our grammars are full of "exceptions" ; but, strange as it may seem, the days of exceptions are over. Science has annexed the study of language ; parallel to the change that came over chemistry through the labours of Cavendish and Lavoisier at the end of the last century, the time since 1868 has witnessed the rise of philology into an exact science, with fixed principles and a fixed method. This great change has been largely brought about in Germany by a small band, called the "Young Grammarians"; they have had a stormy fight, but their most determined opponents have been compelled to copy their methods. A clear summary of the results won so far has long been a desideratum; the want will be fully satisfied by the work, of which the first part lies before us.

Since the war, an agreeable change has come over the method of writing German books; instead of loading the unfortunate reader with a mass of worthless bibliographical and other details till he almost feels as if he were labelled "Intellectual rubbish shot here" the material is carefully sifted, the best only is presented, with a short characteristic summary, and the work is shared among a group of scholars, each treating his own speciality.

The Grundriss opens with a short article on the meaning of the term philology. The famous definition of philology as "The knowledge of what is known" includes too much, and indeed any attempt to sharply limit the meaning must fail, since a word cannot be recalled to scientific strictness after it has once passed into common use, with a shifting sense due to historic development. According to its derivation, philology means the investigation of literary monuments; in England we have narrowed this further down to the study of the accidence of the language in which the monuments are composed.

We now ascribe the vowels a, e, i, o, u, to the parent language; the primitive condition of affairs is best preserved in Greek, but when once we have a few phonetic equations we can plainly see the beautiful and regular formation of our "irregular verbs."

If, however, the sounds were unchecked in their changes, grandfather and grandchildren might not understand one another; the restraining force is analogy. The mind unconsciously forms categories of sound, of inflexion, of syntax, and these afford a conservative base on which new material is modelled.

These then are the two fundamental factors in the history of language; changes of sound rigorously determined by physical necessities and analogy. Whatever seems to contradict needs a fuller investigation.

IX. EARLY ENGLISH PRONUNCIATION. Ellis.

Students will probably derive great assistance from studying the dialect of their own home ; we all preserve more of our native vowel flavouring than a " correct speaker " would care to acknowledge. A point of capital importance for the teaching of languages cannot fail to be driven home to us through Mr. Ellis's work: the infinite variety and complexity of a language really living, the striking contrast of thorough-going change with the retention of old material, ought to make us ready to throw off the false views of fixity in language which we have unconsciously absorbed from the traditional Latin grammar.

X. THE CRADLE OF THE ARYANS. Rendall.

English is not inferior to Latin and Greek · because it possesses less inflections, but superior. The endings were not lost by a poor language in a state of " phonetic decay " but cast aside as lumber in the endeavour to speak with greater clearness and rapidity. The wonderful grammatical system of Sanskrit grammar is not a proof of its being nearer the primitive type, but the contrary ; the fact that it stands, on the whole, nearest to the Aryan is due, as our author rightly points out, to the conservatism of written records.

Equations on which far-reaching conclusions are based ought to be unimpeachable from the phonetic side. This certainly is not the case with the few words which, in discussions on our primitive home, come up over and over again, like the supers at a provincial theatre. Weakness on this side is regrettable, and obscures the great service rendered to science by Penka's coupling of anthropology with philology. Few have equal knowledge of both subjects, and it looks as if linguists were as ready to accept Penka's results as the general public some time ago took, without a question, Pictet's brilliant fancy pictures.

A curious and subtle error vitiates a large amount of philological work. Lists of words are drawn up on some preconceived theory; the criteria for their selection are then forgotten, while deductions are made from them claiming to prove the theories which set them going. Fick's "Comparative Dictionary" was an admirable work for its time, but it must be used now with the greatest caution; he considered a word as belonging to the primitive stock if it occurred in Sanskrit and *one* of the European dialects. This surely is insufficient. If the Sanskrit *kshurá*, and the Greek *xurón*, show that the primitive Aryan shaved himself, why cannot the Sanskrit *paktár* and the Latin *coctor* prove that he kept a professional cook?

Phonetic changes are conditioned by the physiology of the vocal organs. Parallel changes take place in the most diverse languages, though we can assign no reason why they happen at such different epochs.

Another great difficulty is the lack of criteria for distinguishing primitive cognates from "wander words" handed on from tribe to tribe; these are generally nouns denoting foreign objects, especially animals and plants, both of the first importance for fixing the Aryan cradle.

Penka lays stress on "oyster" as a primitive word; the allied forms are more likely borrowings. Another difficulty of the same kind meets us with the eel, lately promoted to the honour of decisive arbiter of the whole controversy. He does not inhabit the rivers running into the Black Sea, and so Penka rejects South Russia as our home. But the argument is as slippery as the eel; he is claimed as Aryan on the strength of an equation which lacks an Asiatic cognate. But then we have the delightfully convenient argument that, on their long march, etc. across Russia, the future Indians and Persians had ample time to forget the eel and his name. Did the Scandinavians, who had stayed at home all the time, forget him too? They surely should have kept him in tender remembrance. There is not, however, a single word common to Germanic and the classical languages for any specific fish.

A still worse example of the tendency to build elaborate superstructures on an insufficient base is the attempt to couple the linguistic results obtained from a study of the Aryan languages, as Max Müller and Penka have done, with the ultimate problems of the rise of man and of language. To settle the cradle of the Aryans by the primitive home of man is to fix the vague by the vaguer.

If we are to look on Aryan as an actual spoken language we must consider it in full vitality some time between 1500 and 2000 B.C. Further back than this, all is darkness, lit up by the will-o'-the-wisp of archæological finds, which can be made to mean anything or—nothing, according to the needs of the author.

Suppose a shipload of Germans were banished to an island with a cargo limited to Romance books, they would probably come very near to reconstructing primitive Latin, but they would hardly solve any of the fundamental problems of language, nor would they be likely to settle on Latium as the original home. Aryan, after all, is only the grandmother of French.

The hypotheses and guesses of a popular book, summing up a period of scientific research, are so apt to be hardened into "established facts" accompanied by a sort of orthodoxy, making doubly difficult the acceptance of later and more accurate theories, that we have allowed this review to run to an excessive length. Our primitive ancestors lived together at one time somewhere in the east of Europe ; the primitive ancestors of the Indians and Persians somewhere north of the Himalaya. The common centre from which they all spread is yet to seek.

XI. PESTALOZZI: HIS LIFE AND WORK.
Roger de Guimps.

What is the secret of Pestalozzi's influence on education, the deepest since the time of Luther? This above all, that he loved his fellow man. Like that mightier voice, Rousseau, he knew the way into the inmost recesses of the human heart. After the fiery flames of indignation against injustice, comes the tender dew of pity for the outcasts of the world. The influence of Rousseau led to the violent overthrow of external institutions. Pestalozzi, with far deeper insight, saw that the sole chance of raising mankind was from within. He turned to education as the potent weapon for this regeneration. In him the social reformer was doubled by the pedagogue. He based education on conformity to child-nature, and gave it an ethical goal. The psychology may be inaccurate, the ethics may change; but psychology and ethics will remain the two poles on which all real education must turn.

When men are sitting among the ruins of destroyed beliefs, any attempt at positive reconstruction is welcome.

Unless we bear constantly in mind the relation of a man to his times, we shall always be open to the risk of applying remedies that answered in one case to totally different conditions. The exaggerated importance laid on method by Pestalozzi and his followers is probably only another way of stating that the ordinary school of his time had absolutely none.

A bad fault in De Guimps is the ever-present fear that Pestalozzi may be considered unorthodox. We have given up apologising for Burns on the score of respectability; let us cease to trouble ourselves whether Pestalozzi ought to be called a Christian; if ever a man worked in the spirit of Jesus, surely it was he. His pupils, said von Türck, will not talk about religion, but they will be religious. What more can we ask from the school? The first and foremost duty of a biographer is to tell us all the facts he knows about his hero ; you must take a mountain or leave it, says Victor Hugo. If the Bible was never read at Pestalozzi's, as Ramsauer and Pastor Vaudois affirm, such a fact should not be suppressed. The question whether or not the Bible ought to be read is not settled by Pestalozzi's action in the matter : it is only the unwise who value every word in an author of repute.

Education has been greatly retarded in England by the fear, still strongly felt, though its expression is now much more timid than formerly, that the poor, when educated, would grow discontented with their lot in life, that they would crowd into positions so far the exclusive privilege of the middle and higher classes.

As long as our schools prepare directly for examinations which permit a man to obtain a better living " with his coat on" than he can get with it off—as long as society pays more respect to those social parasites, who do no work save to spend the money others have made for them, than it does to an honest and skilful carpenter—so long will the poorer classes strive to " rise." Pestalozzi, however, never thought that primary education and the education of the poor were different things ; he did not dream of raising the people by turning them into scholars. He did not wish his scholars to have something, but to be something. He strove to awake the moral sense, to give a more adequate idea of what man is and ought to be, to set in motion all the forces, physical, intellectual, and moral, that reside in every child, to render it fit in due time to acquire for itself such skill or knowledge as its intellectual capacity or station in life rendered necessary. Pestalozzi strove to discover those first steps in the development of humanity which must be taken alike by pauper and peer.

As we close the book we feel anew the irresistible power possessed by a man who has really seized some side of the truth. Neither war nor poverty, neither neglect nor the bigotry of sects miscalled religious, neither sickness nor the loss of friends, can quench the flame of him who strives after truth in the service of man.

R

XII. Harvard Studies in Classical Philology.

Nearly all the articles are on the minutiæ of classical scholarship; even the discussion on the social and domestic position of women in Aristophanes does not amount to much more than an enumeration of the passages that bear on the subject. Was there not room for one article breathing a larger life than all this intense specialism—not for one article bearing on things of to-day? After the death of Goethe and his contemporaries, who found the gospel according to J. J. Rousseau unsatisfying, and tried to replace it with something still more unsatisfying, the gospel of antique culture, a profound change, due mainly to Ritschl, has come over our classical studies. They have become entirely objective; Latin and Greek are treated scientifically, and the result is the " Museum of Philology " of the present volume.

XIII. Essays on Educational Reformers. Quick.

Sometimes in life it is more important to finish a task quickly in some not wholly inadequate way, than to work and wait for a complete solution that seems to grow more remote the more closely it is pursued.

When we run over the names of the English writers on education, they belong, we find, to the numerous band of distinguished amateurs; the professional teacher is mainly dumb. What should we say to an art of medicine in which the most brilliant suggestions were due to eminent lawyers, divines, and literary men? Ascham, Locke, and Herbert Spencer are finally selected as our three leading writers. How many of them spent a year in the ordinary drudgery of school work? When will the days of our pedagogic disgrace be overpast? Let it once be clearly understood that, for the future, deans and bishops will be chosen from the ranks of those who have devoted the whole of their lives to clerical work, and our headmasters on retiring will have time to enrich the younger teachers with the wealth of their past experience.

The first twenty-six pages are devoted to the Renascence, defined as the re-awakening of a sense of beauty in literature, and lasting over the fifteenth and sixteenth centuries. With this vague term some limitation as to country and time seems essential for a clear understanding of its influence. In Italy the thin thread of continuity with classic antiquity had never been wholly broken. France alone, with its grave defect of conservative instinct, exemplified still more strikingly in the Revolution, made a clean breach with its past. In Spain, Germany, and England the desire to imitate classic antiquity was of no moment beside the outburst of native strength that had been slowly gathering and seeking for an outlet. A deeper knowledge of the Renascence has led us to see that the Revival of Learning was only one among a large number of potent factors in the formation of modern Europe. To Latin and Greek we owe neither our Arabic numeration, oil-painting, paper, printing, gunpowder, the mariner's compass, music, the exploration of new continents, nor the overthrow of the Ptolemaic system. For England, the last to enter upon the Renascence movement, the distinguishing characteristic is that the fields of learning had been surveyed and cleared, and numerous translations, not only of Greek and Latin, but also of Italian, Spanish, and German authors, were to be had at the same time. The common possession of the Bible in the vernacular differentiated England and Germany from the Romance countries of Europe. We see, then, how defective is the passage from the " Life of Casaubon," quoted on page 4, and how important it is to keep the Renascence and the Revival of Learning distinct. Nay, even for the latter, the patient perusal of such pieces of bibliography as the " Répertoire des Ouvrages Pédagogiques du Seizième Siècle " shows clearly that the interest of professional scholars was by no means limited to classic antiquity. Another point peculiar to England is the short intervals between the arrival at our shores of the Renascence, the Reformation, and the counter-Reformation. The delicate task of appreciating exactly the

effects of these three forces has not yet been attempted.
Besides this, we want to know, in spite of their rabid
denunciations of mediævalism, how much of it the Renascence scholars carried unconsciously along with them. Our
official syntax of to-day is drawn straight from the twelfth
century. Even the shortest account of the effects of the
Renascence on education ought to find room for an analysis
of the " De Ratione Studii," published by Erasmus in 1512.
Here we find the clearest statement of the pedagogy of
humanism. Had this passed without adulteration into the
school, we should not now be in so sorry a plight. But
when the scholar desires to act, he must put himself under
the protection of the Church or of some political party. The
price he has to pay is easily divined. Neither the Protestants nor the Jesuits had a special pedagogy of their own ;
they both borrowed from the humanists and added the most
pernicious principle that ever palsied education—not to
develop the whole man, not to train him as a future father,
a good citizen and a seeker after truth, but to increase the
numerical strength of their own party *ad majorem Dei
gloriam—i.e.*, the complete political ascendancy of their own
sect and the destruction of their opponents. The great
success of the Jesuits in details of school method shows how
important method is, but if we put the ultimate test for all
systems of education, " What sort of man does it turn
out ? " our judgment will probably be as severe as Michelet's.

The admirable quotation on p. 96 might with advantage be
read as a sort of pedagogic grace at the beginning of our
educational conferences.

XIV. Prehistoric Antiquities of the Aryan
Peoples. Schrader.

The most effective check on the hardening of opinion into
dogma is a history of its rise and progress.

The chapter on religion is almost exhilarating from the
way in which, by strict application of phonetic equations,

short work is made of the elaborate brain-spinning of comparative mythologists.

Like schoolboys, people are far too apt to accept statements on trust, and too eager to have their intellectual problems "come out" in a neat answer. The avenues for the entrance of new truths must always be kept open.

XV. DER FRANZÖSISCHE KLASSENUNTERRICHT.
Max Walter.

Although in **England the desire for a reform of** language **teaching has in reality got** very little further than a feeling **that the old method** has suffered shipwreck, the Germans, **basing** their proposed changes on a scientific knowledge of **the** nature and laws of language, may be now said to have fully entered into the second stage of progress, where theory passes over into practice.

Pronunciation being the weakest point of **our teaching, the need of phonetics has been most** loudly **proclaimed, till at** times it **seemed as if grammar had dropped out of** the reformer's programme altogether. **The old and the** new method having the **same** ultimate **aims, it is** somewhat **difficult** to bring out the great differences between them ; they **consist entirely in** the order of introduction and relative **amount of the various divisions : pronunciation,** writing and **grammar.**

In the Introduction, the author pleads for the use of **phonetically** transcribed texts for the **very** beginners : all **teachers, as far as** our **knowledge goes, who have been able to test this vexed** question practically, prefer **to postpone** the usual orthography to a later stage.

Since, however, the greatest divergency of opinions meets **us on the threshold, the** question can only be decided by a **set of experiments on a** large **scale,** made under authority **and tested** by a **representative jury of experts.** The proper place for such experiments ought to be the practising schools belonging to training colleges. **but,** as at present there is no effective belief in England in training at all, we must look to our foreign colleagues for light.

Besides the hints given by the author (coloured letters, repetition in chorus, &c.), we have found it useful to ask for the hand to be held up when a given sound occurs in a piece recited by the master, the phonetic symbol for it being pointed out at the same time on a large table containing all the French sounds, those common to English being painted black, and the others red. A preliminary phonetic schooling in the native tongue, before a foreign language is touched, we hold to be indispensable. With the author's attack on the use of exercises in the form of single sentences, we are fully in accord. To ask for a word-for-word translation seems to us as foolish as to demand the payment of an English sum in French money, not in a lump, but coin for coin.

XVI. Chronological Outlines of English Literature. Ryland.

The attempt simply to copy the titles and dates of a hundred books is a fine lesson in modesty and humility. Instead of trying to find mistakes or point out omissions, we shall content ourselves with a pious wish for a second edition. Would it not be possible to recognise pedagogy as a branch of English literature? Mr. Quick disinterred Mulcaster some time ago, and a Frenchman has been found to write a study of him ; but the public still turns a deaf ear to the history of education in England.

XVII. Principles of English Etymology. Second Series. The "Foreign Element." Skeat.

The man of science, it seems, as well as the new poet, has to create his own audience, and hence the slowness of change.

English pedagogy is weak in linking the school subjects into coherent wholes ; the teacher will find this volume very useful in coupling language with history, geography, and commerce. Commerce is the foundation of culture ; a rough map of the world, with the trade routes of the antique and mediæval world, would have thrown light on many obscure points.

Language may be looked on either as an art or a science For school purposes the former is by far the more important, and depends mainly, we are inclined to think, on imitation ; how far science may help the art is a very difficult question. For a practical control over the spoken language of every-day life, comparative philology is almost valueless ; but when we come to the artificial language of literature, with its respect for tradition, it appears to be a necessity ; Milton, for instance, demands a real knowledge of the Latin element in our speech. Ever since Grimm's brilliant discovery, our text-books, especially of the English classics, have been loaded with a mass of inaccurate etymologies ; their peda-gogic value, even if they had been correct, nobody seems to have appreciated. A thorough knowledge of any language must include its history ; is there time in the school-life for this in anything except English ? And who will tell us where the line separating the proper shares of the school and the University ought to be drawn ? Shall we ever possess a Training College where such important pedagogic problems may be worked out ? The rarity with which the literature helps us is another curious difficulty ; the Romance languages are derived from Folk-Latin ; Anglo-French is not the parent of modern French ; our own ancient litera-ture is West-Saxon and not Anglian, and so on.

Is it correct to speak of English as a composite *language ?* The intense striving to make thought clear has led in all modern civilisation to an analytical form of expression, thus cutting us off, linguistically, from the antique world ; in this direction English has advanced furthest, and our freedom from inflexions has enabled us to extend a noble and ready welcome to foreign elements, matched only by the ease and thoroughness with which we assimilate them, and give them a native colour. A composite language and a language with a composite vocabulary may be no more the same than the material and the style of architecture of a building. Until the inevitable German has worked out for us our syntax, phonology, sematology, &c., and shown them to be "composite," we had better keep that epithet for our vocabulary alone. The point is of importance, as this belief is the main hindrance to the recognition of the fact that, as a means of linguistic training, English is not only not inferior to Latin and Greek, but superior to them both ; the great value of classic *literature* is no excuse for an utterly unscientific treatment of the language; perhaps it would be more accurate to say non-scientific, for the arrangement in the Latin Primer is purely empirical, and bad at that.

In a book devoted to the *Principles* of etymology, the method is more important than the results ; the exaggerated love for results is a defect in the English mind.

Again, why should analogy be looked on as an "exception" to the operation of phonetic laws (p. 488)—the only *principle*, by the way, adequately represented in this volume? If the shape of a body is altered by the action of heat, we do not speak of this as an exception to the law of gravity. Surely it is an error in method to speak of the psychic action of the mind as "artificial" while the purely mechanical action of the vocal organs is considered "natural." Unless the mind arranged into new groups the varying forms due to the unchecked action of the phonetic factors, language would speedily fall into chaos. Analogy and phonetic change are independent ; and the former is "false" only if we assume that phonetic change alone has a right to act on language.

A considerable amount of redundance might have been saved, and clearness gained, had a chapter on general phonetics been given, explaining, with diagrams, why and how such a phenomenon as palatalisation, or "fronting," arises. Theoretical phonetics teach us what changes we are to expect ; from the history of a language we learn how far along the line any particular tongue has gone.

XVIII. Chief Ancient Philosophies : The Ethics
of Aristotle. J. G. Smith.

The little book can hardly fail to create in the minds of
the unlearned reader a great respect for the power of thought,
the almost miraculous independence of mind of the great
Greek philosopher ; for even the casual reader can hardly
fail to see that after these thousands of years, with all our
accumulations of knowledge, the men who are capable of
rising to Aristotle's level in keenness and profundity of
speculation are marvellously few. We do not think our
author, who has sat at the feet of modern as well as ancient
philosophers, knows so well as Aristotle does what is conscience, and the quotations from the master are much more
conducive to a clear insight into the subject than the com-
ments of the expositor. Aristotle clearly understood, what
the majority of students of philosophy do not appear to
know to-day, that conscience itself is blind—an impulse to
do not that which is right but that which the subject deems
to be right.

SPEECHES.

I. Points in Connection with the Teaching of
Modern Languages in Schools. Speech at the
Second Meeting of the first General Conference of the
Teachers' Guild.

They must base their teaching on a scientific basis. Latin
had been abandoned because it was not wide enough to meet
the growth of modern thought. Their spiritual life was
larger, broader and deeper than had existed in any previous
age (applause). They could not escape scientific teaching ;
but they must go from the known to the unknown. There
was no language that could stand beside English for beauty
and force, surpassing all languages in richness, compression,
and in simplicity (cheers). Greek alone could dare to stand
by the side of English. They spoke the oldest European

language, and the first epic in Europe was in English. He was decidedly against the grammars that existed, they were fourteen centuries old (laughter).

In future the teacher ought to take his degree in a Modern Language Tripos.

The lower ground for teaching modern languages is the same as that for which Latin was so jealously cultivated in the Middle Ages : they are very useful, as they form the means of communication with the leading civilised nations. The higher reason is to acquire a new soul by thinking oneself into another language, to develop thereby our humanity and save us from insular onesidedness.

The centre of our language teaching is the grammar : it ought to be the reader. Our grammars, too, are based on the model of Latin ones, and these apparently run back without much real variation to the "Ars Grammatica" of Donatus : their one fundamental error, from which spring all our ills, being the assumption of the letter and not the sound as the ultimate element of language. Since fourteen centuries have brought us little improvement, we may now be quite ready to give up our present methods—methods based on tradition, tempered by tips.

On what principles are we to found a new method? First and foremost we must know something of the psychology of the child. The method of Nature is the archetype of all methods—we must pass from the known to the less known, from the easy to the hard, and, we may add, from the interesting to the less interesting. On the first two points we can get some valuable knowledge out of Preyer's admirable book, "Die Seele des Kindes"; from it we learn that the new-born infant lacks the anatomical, physiological, and psychologic means of speech. The child understands much sooner than he can imitate ; he makes all the sounds of the mother tongue before he combines them into words ; he learns greedily what interests him, everything else he forgets in two or three days. This will also be very roughly true for a child of ten beginning a foreign language : we must

give him sounds before letters, we must be content if at
first he simply understands, and, above all, we must give
him things within his childish sphere of interest. We allow
an English child to speak his native tongue for some years
before he writes it ; we ought not to ask a child to turn an
English sentence into written French or German till he has
had twelve months reading at least ; by this means too we
shall be able to avoid the vapid silliness of the usual exercise
books. During the first three months let the child learn
every word first by the ear ; then for the next nine let him
read pleasant stories, working the grammar almost entirely
inductively (he will thus think that languages are "jolly"
and the taste for reading will last him through life) ; then
have translations into the foreign language, chiefly to teach
the syntax.

Phonetics as such is not a school subject, but the language
teacher must be a phonetician. Our phoneticians are not
schoolmasters ; our schoolmasters are not phoneticians.
The study of the sounds must be taught, and that inductively,
first from English ; for sounds of French and German the
action of the lips is very important, and their movements
luckily can be seen by the eye.

After considerable experience I incline to the belief that
comparative philology is of no great direct value in the
practical mastery of a language. When English cognates
are put beside German ones there is a tendency to make
the sounds of both alike, and the great changes in the
meaning are overlooked. Besides, unless boys are practised
in Grimm enough to make them really feel the law, they are
apt to believe that any one word can be juggled into any
other. A knowledge of word-formation within a language
has been found more useful in teaching vocabularies.

Although it may be important for a boy to acquire some
knowledge of foreign languages, it is far more important for
him to know his own. And in this matter we English are
very fortunate, for we possess a tongue that, as Grimm puts
it, surpasses all other living languages in wealth, in common

sense, in compressed sequence : it is a child of the marriage
of the two noblest elements of Western Europe, the Teutonic
and the French. Around English, and around English
alone, can our teaching of language be properly grouped ;
in English, and in English alone, can we make any attempt
at beginning grammar as such ; for in the mother tongue
alone have we enough preliminary knowledge to arrange
into a scientific scheme. For all other languages the
grammar must follow practical needs. A child ought not
to begin another language till it has a firm grip on its
own.

II. COMPARATIVE ADVANTAGES, IN SCHOOLS, OF A
    SEPARATE CLASSIFICATION FOR EVERY SUBJECT,
    AND AN ARRANGEMENT IN FORMS THE STATUS IN
    WHICH DEPENDS ON ONE OR TWO CHOSEN SUB-
    JECTS. Speech at the Second Meeting of the First
    General Conference of the Teachers' Guild.

The class system was preferable on the whole, as it recognised the great diversity of ability and rate of intellectual
progress among children. The skill in solving difficulties
of classification was a personal equation of the headmaster ;
his chief office was to organise. The teaching should be
left more to the assistant masters, and it ought to be possible
for a man to make both a living and a reputation simply as
a teacher. At present he took rank, even in school, below
the scholar and the specialist, and although he stood in
intimate relation to both, his task was different. The chief
weakness of the class system, the failure to bring the child
under the continued personal influence of the same teacher,
might be neutralised to some extent by lively intercourse
among the masters grouped according· to the subjects they
taught. (*Journal of Education,* March 1, 1888.)

We never ought to have in any school a specialist; I have
a great horror of him. Specialists are narrow and cruel.
The class form is, I think, the better plan because it looks

first at the child, and next at the master (applause). (*Standard,* January 16, 1888.)

III. THE PRESENT CLASSICAL RÉGIME. Speech during a Debate at a Conference of the Teachers' Guild.

The present classical régime may be traced back to the *damnosa hereditas* of mediævalism. The study of the mother tongue and modern languages affords a full and liberal education.

IV. AN EDUCATIONAL MUSEUM. Speech at a Conference of the Teachers' Guild.

An Educational Museum would be of little value, unless intimately connected with a Normal School.

V. THE TEACHING OF ENGLISH. Speech at a Conference of the Teachers' Guild.

We must learn English both as an art and as a science. In England, as compared with France, we have neglected our native tongue, and it is high time that that state of things should cease. Search the world through and we shall not find a language comparable to English for the study of Philology.

Teachers cannot hope to come out as a new sort of Bob Acres and ooze literature.

VI. LANGUAGE OF THE MEDIÆVAL WRITERS. Speech after a Lecture on History.

With reference to the remark of the lecturer as to the bad Latinity of the monkish historians, it is not to be assumed that the language of the mediæval writers is incorrect, because it differs from the models of the classic period of Roman history. If a writer expresses himself clearly and picturesquely, his language must be regarded as good, inasmuch as it enables us to gain an insight into the life and thought of the times of which he wrote.

LECTURE.

RECENT ADVANCES IN THE SCIENCE OF LANGUAGE. Extracts from the (unrevised) MS. of a Lecture to the Maidstone Branch of the Teachers' Guild.

Although in Sanskrit we miss the Greek sense for proportion in art, we meet with something higher, a profound respect and veneration for women.

We compel thousands of English children to learn the rudiments of Latin grammar, which they do in the hope of forgetting them afterwards, and yet at our Universities not one per cent. of our students can be spared for the study of the primitive language of India, our greatest possession. Within the short space of a century the study of language has risen from a confused tangle of wild word-guessing into a highly organised science with a distinct method of its own : a science that has thrown light on many obscure points of history, solved many problems in our grammar, improved the texts of our great authors and carried investigations into the growth of man's mind back into the twilight of pre-historic times.

On starting the study of a subject we fancy that everything has been already said and written : when we get deeper we begin to wonder why men have only just made the beginnings.

Each language preserves with great fidelity some of its primitive inheritance : by recovering this in each separate language we arrive gradually at the point from whence each started.

The irregular verbs, we find, are most exquisitely regular.

Voltaire once made a gibe against philology that the consonants counted for little and the vowels for less. His gibe is false on both counts. The belief in philology is a cumulative belief.

Grimm's discovery of the consonant changes into Teutonic was an act of divination rather than of strict inductive proof:

with imperfect materials and through the tangle of a network of crossing effects he felt the presence of a law. Although his statement has now an historical rather than a scientific value, the wonder of it is none the less. As scholars pressed along the road he had pointed out they gradually collected a number of "exceptions." Now science knows nothing of "exceptions." If a law is once broken, it ceases to be a law : not only does the "exception" not prove the rule, it shatters the rule utterly. Of course if we make a schematic arrangement for so-called "practical use" we shall have exceptions enough : our scheme and not the nature of things is at fault.

The statement of Grimm's and Verner's laws in Skeat's "Principles of English Etymology" is incorrect, as it confuses the letter with the sound : the spoken and not the written sentence is the unit. A strict phonetic statement is this :—

Stop unvoiced.	Open unvoiced.	Open voiced.	
p	f	ƀ ´—	Common
t	þ	ð ´—	to all the
k	χ	ʒ ´—	Teutonic
s	s	z ´—	dialects.

Stop voiced.

b
d
g   } Variously in the various dialects.
r

To the domain of law in the physical world we have grown accustomed since the sublime and accurate imagination of Newton knit the falling stone with the sweep of the moon in her orbit and gathered the universe into one family. In our age another as great, with a mass of knowledge such as never before stood at the service of any single man, saw with clear vision the vanished forms of ages long past and linked into one chain the varied life of our globe ; under his hands continuity became supreme and the saying that the present is the flower of the past and the seed-time of the future passed from a metaphor into a simple statement of fact. Like a subtle leaven his thoughts have entered into all the intellectual life of our times, bringing light into our science as well, for now we know that the changes of language are gradual, incessant, unbroken, subject to law. The words of the poet chanting to his god in the dim dawn of history, the words of Sappho in her impassioned songs, of Demosthenes as his rolling periods stirred the Athenians to save their liberties, of Shakespeare mirroring the whole world with his myriad mind, these all obey law : law reigns supreme : the sky is her realm, the sea her domain and the earth her habitation and the soul of man is subject unto her.

PAPERS.

I. SCHEME FOR A TEACHING TRIPOS AT THE UNIVERSI-
TIES. Paper read at a Conference of the Teachers'
Guild.

Exhibiting a series of diagrams illustrating the working of existing triposes, which showed the immense preponderance of the classics over all other subjects, although he was afraid to speak of the classics as the upas tree, he asked whether the subjects could not be shared out in a wiser way. Our neglect of English—not only our native tongue, but the best language which the world had yet seen — was a national disgrace. He feared, however, that where the scholarships were there would the teachers be gathered together. He argued that, as a nation compelled every one to go to school, it was bound logically to see that teachers were competent, and that the Universities especially ought to take the greatest possible care for their proper education. He proposed three degrees of Bachelor, Master, and Doctor of Teaching.

(Notice in the   ?)
(This paper cannot be found. The following extracts are

from a MS., apparently bearing on the subject, endorsed "Teacher.") (Mere fragment. Quite unrevised.)

The chief idea of elocution of many University men is to put their hands in their pockets and address a spot on the floor about three feet from the platform.

There is as much bad teaching in England as there is poor preaching.

Teacher must continue to work at his own perfection.

Avoid prejudice that depth of knowledge hinders power to teach : the two stand apart.

Necessity of training of teacher runs parallel with scientific development of education and instruction : absence of care with imperfection of method. Child now worked from inside not from the outside : how can we work from the inside unless we know the inside?

University teacher works through the plentitude of his knowledge, school teacher through the weight of his personality, elementary teacher through the perfection of his method.

The answer in Germany to the collapse of the old régime caused by the French Revolution was a reformation of the schools. Not nobles—citizens, but educated—uneducated.

At one end theology rids us of men who have spent their time on preparing for a bishopric instead of on psychology : at the other the incapables drop down into curates, who inflict twaddle on an unresisting audience.

For the beginning of education is scholarships, and the end of education is scholarships.

" Then your scholarships produce scholars ? "

" Oh no, fellows ! "

" I don't understand."

" We have had scholars and lo ! they are bishops."

The great work of our schools is to heave the mass of mediocrity one stage higher in the scale of culture.

The teacher's honour ought not to consist in the rank of his class nor the honours obtained in it but in the psycho-

S

logic activity demanded from him, and that will often be greatest in the lower classes.

Is it necessary to remind those who deal with children of the delight of surpassing expectation? Gross materialism to lay more weight on subject than on teacher.

It is the first duty of a University to be universal—to afford a refuge for those studies which do not yet " pay " in the outer world.

Like the children under his charge the teacher must set his face towards the future and not the past.

What is the chief duty of a University?—to send out so many "hall-marked" men every year?—to give an intensely specialised education so that a large number of men after their degree sell their books second-hand?—or is it to inculcate a love of truth for its own sake regardless of consequences whither the truth leads : to inculcate the taste for independent investigation?

II. THE TEACHING OF LANGUAGES. Apparently a Paper read at Maidstone before the Local Branch of the Teachers' Guild.

Our Latin Grammar is based on analyses of language made in the first and twelfth centuries.

Language like music or art is a manifestation of the mind, expressed by means of the nerves and muscles : like a billiard ball rebounding from the cushion, an impression carried inwards by the nerves naturally rebounds with an expressive cry : meaning is coupled with this cry by the bystanders and language gradually arises : the whole process of learning a foreign language consists in attaching meaning to sounds at first meaningless.

The two opposing factors incessantly at work in language are the regular changes of sound and analogy : since sounds are reproduced entirely by memory and subject to all the varying influence of climate and social surrounding they are obviously liable to incessant changes, and yet though these changes spread over thousands of years they take place with perfect regularity. This tendency if unchecked would soon make a language unintelligible : analogy is the opposing force. Quite unconsciously the mind groups the words stored up in it either according to meaning or grammatical forms, and new words must accommodate themselves to the old framework.

Teachers should possess a knowledge of their subject far in advance of what they may have to teach. By this means alone can they give their teaching that clearness and proportion necessary to lead a child aright : how can they tell which road to choose unless they know whither all the roads lead? Another virtue higher than these he cannot possess unless he has gone far and deep in his own work—I mean simplicity. The more complete a science becomes the more simple are the statements of its laws.

Are classical men more alive than other Englishmen to the inner force of our words? Language means "tongue-action:" how many teachers know the exact amount of tongue-action required to change the vowel of *pit* into *pet*, or *pet* into *pat*? Of the four elements of language, hearing, speaking, reading and writing, our examinations test only the last and we have the curious fact that the highest honours in our classical language tripos can be won by a deaf and dumb man !

Five languages in a modern school is perhaps too much of a good thing. We are endeavouring to face the twentieth century by piling the nineteenth on the top of the sixteenth, an attempt in which we shall certainly fail.

Silently and unnoticed a complete change has come over our attitude to antiquity : it has changed from the subjective to the objective. Instead of being mainly a source of daily thought, the delight and refuge of our leisure hours, it has become an object of scientific investigation, pursued in the same spirit and with the same weapons of research as botany or histology. We can get as much humane culture out of the one as the other. The attempt to foist philology into school work has, I am inclined to believe, been a failure owing to this confusion of aim : a confusion of æsthetics and science.

Let us be on our guard against similes : we must not compare language to the leaves of the forest or to a living organism, simply because speech has no existence outside of our minds. Still less must we allow terms proper to morals, such as " corruption," " decay," to influence us in ascribing, so to speak, a touch of original sin to language. When the classical scholar looks on the serried series of paradigms in his grammar and then learns that in English the rules, when phonetically expressed, for forming the plural can be stated in three lines, he feels inclined to cry " Why what a falling off is here ; " but simplicity is not poverty and when we are agreed to call an 81-ton gun a decayed or corrupted form of the flint lock we shall be right in using the same terms for modern English.

Language is not a ready made product which can be handed from man to man but spiritual activity acting through the organs of speech : it is not an ἔργον but an ἐνέργεια.

Language consists primarily of spoken sounds and not of written letters. In language the sentence is the unit. If these theorems are true they must of necessity revolutionise our teaching, for we change at once from the deductive method of the Latin Grammar to the inductive method of modern science. The reflecting self-conscious method which consists in piecing together a mosaic according to set rules will never lead to the spontaneous production of free speech : under the most favourable circumstances and with the best heads it can never come nearer to real life than a well made wax flower to its original : we may at the first glance be deceived but closer scrutiny cannot fail to detect the imitation.

The proof of the unconscious activity of the brain is one of the fairest triumphs of modern psychology : the neglect of this faculty of the soul is I think the chief source of the so-called stupidity of children.

When the small boy of ten does his Latin exercise by putting the Latin down without any attention to the inflexion his mind is acting with perfect consistency : his English doesn't make him attend to the tails of his words. Again we make him learn the exceptions to the gender rules before he has any sense of the rules : after he has met with fifty feminines ending in—*a*, say, he is fit to withstand the disturbance of an exception.

The sentence is the unit : words by themselves have no more meaning than a single bone : we do not teach anatomy by giving the student a disjointed skeleton in a heap.

The prime object of language is to convey meaning : hence our arrangement (of words in a vocabulary) must be neither alphabetical, grammatical, nor etymological. It must be psychologic. We want some modern philosopher to arrange our 3000 words in their proper groups and then to fill up the same pigeon-holes, so to speak, with the words of the new language. If we had at the same time a common phonetic notation I am certain you could soon learn the leading languages of Europe.

Had I a free hand to legislate for the teaching of languages, I should make it both practical and scientific in English and carry it back to our origins by reading the earlier authors in connection with the history. In French and German I would have it practical only, putting the power to speak with a passable pronunciation in the first place : I would read almost entirely modern prose and hope that the children would take to the masterpieces of literature for themselves in after life. For Latin and Greek I would confine the demands rigidly to the capacity of reading with some fluency. The arrogance of the Grammar paper should be abated and "prose composition" done away with altogether. Theoretical and too much in the air you will say : full of untried theories you will object with perfect justice. Things have an awkward knack of working out quite differently to what the starter wishes. I have ventured to bring these theories before you because I feel so strongly that the respect and esteem for the teacher will mount the higher the more eager the public finds him to teach with scientific method, and this method can only be obtained on the basis of a large induction obtained from practical experience.

III. THE TEACHING OF LANGUAGES. Paper read before a Meeting of the Teachers' Guild.

The spiritual activity of man follows not only the laws of logic but those of moral law, of æsthetic law and sometimes neither: logic gives the laws of *true* thought but not of thought. It was an error therefore to suppose that the categories of logic covered those of language, an error unfortunately engrained in our grammar books and the cause of all that hair-splitting which makes the analysis of sentences such a troubled delight. A part of language has no reason, or rather it had a reason once which has now disappeared: in the same way Darwinism has taught us to discover on the body curious marks and relics of organs whose use has now ceased.

When the upholders of the theory that the laws of sound work without exceptions were confronted with an example apparently contradicting their statement they at once replied "analogy": the word has been attracted out of its proper sphere and arranged in another group.

The study of comparative syntax is still in its infancy, but the recognition of the truth that the sentence is the unit and that in consequence the accidence is derived from the syntax will have important results on our teaching. We shall give up the attempt to make a painful mosaic by means of rules and paradigms learnt by heart. We shall give sentences and deduce all the rest.

Let us clearly fix in our mind that speech is an outward manifestation of a mental process caused chiefly by the action on the speaker of his fellow men: that language is in a constant and incessant state of gradual change unnoticed by the speaker and that the two chief opposing forces are regular changes of sound and analogy.

IV. ALGEBRA. Paper on the History and Methods of Algebra with Critical Suggestions as to the Way in which It should be Taught.

"Is there any connection between Arithmetic and Algebra, Smith?"

"No, sir!"

"Indeed! May I ask why?"

"Please, sir, we don't do them in the same class."

This little conversation shows, I think, very clearly a common error of taking each subject by itself: the child doesn't know how it arose, why or how its study is carried on, nor its use.

Three years ago Mr. Hudson gave a remarkable lecture on the teaching of Algebra to our Guild. At our recent sectional meeting, I happened to tell him that it was a good deal quoted in Germany, when he remarked :

"I find I am altering my whole way of teaching Algebra. I used to start with a scientific plan as I did at Cambridge, but the younger students seem incapable of taking it in."

"Precisely : the recipient is as important as the subject. You are changing—I suppose I mustn't say rising—from a professor to a teacher."

He laughed and hurried off to catch a train.

Not only is it important to have good seeds, the soil and the time of sowing must be taken equally into account. The total neglect of the condition of the child's mind as compared with the subject seems to me a fair and fatal criticism for nearly all our text books.

What method are we to put in its place? Well, I think our first duty is to win the child for the subject and to do this we must make it interesting : we must show him that sums in Arithmetic which he thought very hard are only very special and easy cases of sums in Algebra. For all subjects I think we ought to have two books : the first easy, popular, discursive, historical, starting as far as possible with a knowledge of what is already in the child's mind, and the second strictly scientific with all the parts elementary as well as advanced taking up their proportionate space in the treatment, or, as De Morgan more neatly puts it, "to draw upon the surface of the subject a proper mean between the line of closest connection and the line of easiest deduction." Although the mind of the child follows in its main outlines the mind of the human race, the application of the historical method requires much tact.

ARTICLES.

I. THE HISTORY OF EDUCATIONAL MUSEUMS.

The English seem to have a faculty for discovering some new mine of intellectual wealth, and allowing others to exploit it. We brought Sanskrit to Europe, and left Germany to create modern philology.

All movements of durable value spring from the immediate needs of everyday life.

Paulsen says somewhere that the training of the teacher needs protection against that of the scholar and of the man of science. For the teacher the centre of interest and activity is the child, and the various scientific subjects must be co-ordinated to him for their origin ; for the man of science the standpoint is quite distinct : he is interested with the development and organic coherency of his subject.

(The article traces the history of educational museums from the first exhibition of educational apparatus at the Mansion House, nearly forty years ago, the Society of Arts' Exhibition in 1854, to the sectional display in the great Exhibition of 1862, notes the numerous foreign museums, describes the Musée Pédagogique in France, the *Revue Pédagogique* and the organic law of October 1886, and concludes—)

Is it not time to recognise that education is one and indivisible? Our educational nomenclature is not characterised by accuracy; can we have such a thing as an Educational Museum? Will the growth of a pedagogic sense in the country give us at last a Teachers' Museum?

II. NOTES ON MODERN PHILOLOGY.

During the last twenty years philology has made many brilliant and rapid advances; although the common property of scholars, the main results have not yet found their way into the ordinary school books. We propose to lay before our readers a few chapters which, we hope, they may find useful in the higher English classes. Most of the matter has been worked over by a set of boys preparing for the London Matriculation.

(This opening paragraph gives a fair idea of the scope of the article. The following are heads of sections :—Grimm's Law. Change from Aryan to Primitive Germanic. Verner's Law. The Vowels. Verbs. The *ei*-group. The *eu*-rank. The *en*-rank. The *el*-group.)

Although we all of us at school used to end up the list of vowels with the tag "and sometimes *w* and *y*," our masters probably knew as little as we did what the phrase meant. In reality there is no hard and fast line between vowels and consonants, and a certain number of sounds, that I have ventured to call "medians," lie on the border line between the two. In the presence of well-marked vowels they act as consonants; but when the surrounding sounds are strongly consonantal, they perform the function of vowels or "syllable carriers." The two most marked medians are *i* and *u*; for them in their consonantal value the Latin alphabet has the letters *y* and *w*.

INDEX

" W<small>ANDER</small> words," 254.

Widgery, William, 3, 15, 31.

Widgery, William Henry, as colleague, 195 ; friend, 200 ; lecturer, 175 ; man, 203; philologist, 182, 183; philosopher, 181 ; teacher, 165 ; thinker, 181 ; writer, 177.

———, ——— ———, his *Character* &c. :—breadth of mind, 194 ; communicative faculty, 172 ; conscientiousness, 220 ; energy, 166 ; enthusiasm, 165 ; expositive power, 170 ; humour, 185 seq.; interesting and inspiring power, 169 ; intolerance, 198, 199 ; moral influence, 173 ; Nature, love of, 7, 12, 14, 43, 188-191, 225 ; nobleness, 221 ; observation, readiness to allow, 48, 58 ; organising faculty, 154 ; patience, 171 ; pedagogy, position in history of, 153 ; personal influence, 172 ; poetical taste, 191, 192 ; public spirit, 224 ; rectitude, 205 ; religion, 211 ; simplicity, 209 ; sympathy, 195, 202, 214 ; system, summary of, 146 ; tact, 197 ; truth, love of, 219, 220 ; unselfishness, 207 ; wit and humour, 185-188.

———, ——— ———, his *Life*, events &c. of :— Art for Schools Association, member of Council of, 26 ; Berlin, Educational Congress in, attends, 18 ; Berlin, matriculates in, and attends lectures on pedagogy and philology, 18 ; Brewers' School, 15 ; Charity Organisation Society, Stepney Committee of, 15 ; Continent, visit to, 17 ; Dover College, 13 ; Goethe and Shakespeare Societies, Hon. Secretary of, 26 ; Harness Prize. See *Hamlet;* Hele's School, 4 ; M.A., 15 ; Memorial Library at Teachers' Guild, 29 ; Morley, Professor, his Literature classes, 15 ; Paris Exhibition, Educational Section of, reports on, 25 ; Pietermaritzburg, Girls' Collegiate School at, London representative of, 26 ; School, Exeter Grammar, 5 ; Senior Optime, 10 ; Teachers' Guild, Hon. Librarian of, 24 ; Tour through Devonshire and Cornwall, 14, 205 ; Tripos, 9, 10 ; Unitarian ministry, 13 ; University College School, 16, 24.

Wilson, Bishop, his "Maxims," 11.

Words, grouping of, according to psychological categories, 83 ; order of, in sentence, 119 ; single, meaningless, 134, 277.

Printed by B<small>ALLANTYNE</small>, H<small>ANSON</small> & C<small>O</small>.
London & Edinburgh